RUNAWAY ROGUE

DAMSELS IN DISGUISE

LILLE MOORE

WILDFLOWER PRESS

www.lillemore.com

CONTENTS

To Sarah MacLean and Jen Prokop, for the comfort, joy, and endless inspiration.

ALSO BY LILLE MOORE

Keeping the Countess
Stirring Up Scandal

Content Guidance

This novel contains gun violence, physical violence, physical injuries, and illness. It also includes recounting of off-page opiate use, human and sex trafficking, imprisonment, and sex work.

If you suspect the exploitation of vulnerable people for their bodies and labor is taking place somewhere close to you, you can find local contact numbers for support or file a report at a21.org

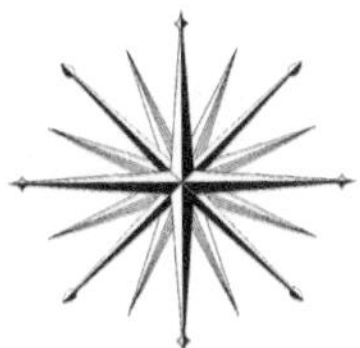

CHAPTER ONE

The worst morning of Ian Holt's life was shrouded in flowers.

Blooms covered every inch of the Mayfair home where he'd spent his childhood. It was a veritable sea of white and pink petals and Ian could not—and would not—fathom how much it all cost.

He paced the last bastion of free space in the drawing room like a caged tiger until an enormous arrangement of orange blossoms and birds of paradise arrived and forced him to halt.

He gave the thing a halfhearted shove, to prove he had influence over something in his life.

"Have you resorted to smashing things?" Henry Eden strode across the room and extended his hand to offer a pacifying handshake.

Ian accepted it with a huff. "I recall from our Harrow days that we both became rather good at smashing things."

"As your legal counsel, I'd advise neither of us confirm or deny that statement."

Despite his sour mood, Ian fought off a smile. Their public school prefects had tried to make cowering servants out of them. He and Henry had endured daily humiliations of being pelted with eggs, and nightly beatings, until they'd learned how to throw a punch. Not getting caught was Ian's first lesson in self-preservation.

"I'm not condoning violence, but one thing that could do with a clearing out is that gaggle of reporters outside," Henry remarked.

"They're still there?" Ian ground his teeth. He'd sent some of his men to spook them off hours ago. New vultures must have arrived, eager for a scoop on the biggest society wedding of the season. They were like vermin, nearly impossible to shake without force, which Ian would have enjoyed using immensely if he could have evaded the consequences.

He swatted a wreath of roses instead.

"I don't think destroying the drawing room is going to dispatch them," Henry said. "Or make your brother arrive any sooner."

"Are you sure about that?"

Henry was at a loss for words. Ian couldn't blame him. Few people would have anything courteous to say when a man went missing on the morning of his wedding.

"The groom is always late," Henry finally managed. "Jared is no different."

Ian refrained from asking how many of those grooms never returned home the night before their weddings. He'd sent his most trusted man to search for Jared discreetly, but so far there was no trace of his brother at any of his usual haunts.

"And what about the brides? Do they struggle with punctuality?" Ian deliberately did not turn an eye upstairs, where Jared's intended was finishing her bridal preparations. If he allowed himself the indulgence of turning his thoughts in Diana's direction, he'd lose what little control he was hanging on to.

Henry carefully moved a swan-shaped cascade of lilies out of Ian's striking distance. "This has to be difficult for you. If it were me, I'd hate—"

Ian's glare promised a violent follow-up if Henry violated their long-standing, unspoken agreement never to utter Diana's name in his presence.

"I'd hate being shut out of my family's business," Henry amended.

"On the contrary. My new position as lead clerk in the Bombay office will be most rewarding. I'm looking forward to it."

Both of them knew it was a lie. Neither acknowledged it.

After the wedding, Ian would depart London. But he was leaving the newly aligned family business far behind.

Jared's marriage to Diana Rives would conclude a merger their fathers had dreamed and schemed about for years. Uniting Holt & Company's trading venture with the Rives Shipping empire would grant them many competitive advantages and the lion's share of the market. Ian had successfully manipulated the business papers to report it that way. So they would avoid digging around and uncovering the significant debt Holt & Company had acquired in the years Jared had assumed control of the business.

His brother would have run the company into the ground after their father's death, had it not been for Ian's quiet interference. Practically, it was a matter of his survival. Their father had named Jared as his sole heir, leaving Ian financially dependent on the small salary the company paid him to officially—and unofficially—arrange things.

Ian detested the role. But it was necessary, to keep the promises he'd made to his father.

"You don't have to go through with it," Henry said in a low voice. "I can't believe your father would want you to make this dangerous gamble."

"I never should have told you. The less you know, the better."

Henry regarded Ian's clenched fists—and the grazes on his right knuckles—for a length of time. "Is Jared still in the dark about it all? Or did you tell him last night, and he reacted...badly?"

"Getting physical with the groom would have been poor form the night before his wedding."

Thankfully, an attempted cargo theft at the docks had required Ian's immediate attention, and he was happy to depart Sunderland's Club after the first round of drinks. He rarely handled enforcement himself these days; his men were exceedingly well-trained and needed little oversight. But last night, he'd welcomed the chance to demonstrate what happened to the jackals who had the audacity to come after Holt & Company.

And the Devil of the Docklands, as Ian was known there.

Afterward, when the heat in his blood had cooled, he'd felt hollow. And the emptiness only exacerbated his conflicted emotions about his brother's impending marriage.

Henry's mouth quirked around another probing question, but a sharp knock and muffled shouts from outside prompted them to hurdle over the flowers and dash into the foyer.

The door flung open.

A footman staggered inside with Jared's unconscious body. His brother's coat and waistcoat were missing, as was his tie, and his shirt was half open. A sickeningly sweet scent, peppered with whiskey, wafted off him.

This sight was further complicated by the other man who stood propping up Jared's slumped body.

"Don't worry, he isn't dead," Leo Ashton, the Duke of Sunderland, quipped. "But he's well and truly sozzled. Even a bucket of water wouldn't revive him."

Ian clapped his gaping jaw shut, and Henry had the sense to mutter something that ended in "Your Grace," as they relieved the duke of Jared's weight.

Sunderland's glance darted between Jared and Ian, as was often the case when people found out they were brothers and searched for some physical similarity. The duke wouldn't find much evidence of it. Jared's fair skin and hair were even more washed out with his pallor. In comparison, Ian must have appeared like a dark-haired, dark-eyed fiend.

With the help of the footmen—and the duke himself—they transported Jared upstairs. Mrs. Turner, the housekeeper, gave a small squawk before she harangued a footman to send for a doctor and took command of settling the patient into his bedroom. She tossed a glare at Ian, Henry, and the duke before slamming the door.

In the sudden quiet of the corridor, the three men carefully evaluated each other.

Ian finally said, "Thank you for your...help with my brother, Lord Sunderland. I would be most grateful for your discretion about all of this."

"Where did you find him?" Henry asked.

When the duke replied with an infamous address in Soho, Ian and Henry exchanged a grave look.

"That wasn't where his friends said they were taking him," Ian said tightly.

"No," Sunderland confirmed. "He departed after them in a separate carriage."

"How keen of you to make note of it."

"They were at my club. Everything that happens at my business is my business."

"And to protect Sunderland's reputation, you wouldn't want people to think he left your establishment in the state he's in now," Ian said.

"Precisely. When your man turned up this morning inquiring about your brother's whereabouts, I thought it best to go myself."

"Was there anything else...of note, where you found him?" Ian kept his expression intentionally blank.

"Not that I recall." Sunderland assessed Ian with a chilling air. "My discretion has a price, Holt. It would be in both our interests to talk about it soon."

As the duke barreled down the stairs, Henry murmured, "Should I be worried about that?"

"No more than usual."

"Right, then. Back to our present debacle." Henry clasped his hands together. "Someone must give Miss Rives the disappointing news she won't be getting married today."

"Why?" Ian snapped. "Jared's drunk; he'll revive. When he does, things will proceed."

"Kind of you to consider Miss Rives's feelings. Don't you think she should decide for herself how she wants to handle this?"

If Diana knew the true state Jared was in, she might call off the entire thing, and that brought a host of uncertainties that made Ian's head throb. Their engagement had tormented him for eight years. The wedding had to happen today. So he could move on with his life.

He swallowed the lump that rose in his throat and said, "I'll tell her."

A maid greeted Ian's knock with a stricken expression.

She ducked her head as he walked into the room, and directed her agitation at a vase of flowers that rested on the floor at the edge of the room, as though someone had placed them in a sort of quarantine.

"Good morning, Mr. Holt." Amelia Hunter's soft voice was a contrast to her statuesque height. Diana's friend and bridesmaid wore a subdued frock the color of milky tea. Ian would have sworn it was the same shade as the beige damask wallpaper.

"Mind the flowers," she cautioned.

"What's wrong with them?" Ian asked.

"They're nefarious."

The voice that haunted his dreams and nightmares directed his attention to the window.

Diana sat on a small stool at a dressing table. A stray beam of watery sunlight gilded her from the crown of her chestnut hair to the hem of her multi-tiered white silk gown.

Her hair appeared darker pinned up in its elaborate coiffure. When they'd run along the shore together as children, it used to tumble down her back, glittering gold and copper. Like pennies in a fountain.

Ian silently pleaded to a pantheon of divinities that she would remain seated. The moment she stood and he took in the full depth of her in her wedding costume, she'd steal his last remaining breath.

Then again, she could wear a sackcloth, and she'd stun the hell out of him.

"Nefarious...flowers," Ian intoned. His tongue dragged as if it were moored to the bottom of his mouth with treacle.

The maid wrung her hands. "White oleander with yellow roses!"

"You think someone tried to poison Miss Rives?"

"Only if they expected me to eat them." In the mirror, Diana raised an elegant eyebrow, which Ian knew rationally was not a gesture of seduction.

His body didn't understand the difference. A familiar tightness gathered south of his waist, and heat rose along his neck.

"In the language of flowers, this arrangement relays a message to beware of betrayal," Miss Hunter offered rationally. "The card was addressed to Diana, but there was no signature."

"It must be from some seedy journalist," Diana said. "They love to manufacture a scandal."

Ian swallowed a growl.

"We'll get rid of them." Miss Hunter nodded to the maid to retrieve the vase. "Be back in a moment."

When the door had closed behind them, and Diana turned to him, a small frisson hit the room.

Neither of them acted surprised. It often happened in the rare circumstances they found themselves alone together. And being alone with Diana was something of a terror, because unlike the rest of their mutual acquaintances, Ian knew the danger she could render.

She radiated with a restrained feminine power, but when he regarded her sitting there alone, a slight pain bloomed beneath his ribs. She'd no sisters, no aunts or female cousins to help with her preparations for the day that would transform her life. Even her dearest childhood friend had been lost to a watery grave a week after the announcement of Diana's engagement to Jared.

As she rose from the stool, Ian couldn't resist staring at the way the silk folds of her dress hugged the curves of her body. The journalists they despised would pay a fortune to see it; she was the most drawn woman in London. She'd spent the last year in mourning for her father, but the scandal sheets couldn't resist sketching her on the few occasions she'd ventured out in society. They never quite captured the color of her eyes—green like a Chinese jade statue—nor could they depict the precise way her bow-shaped mouth dipped with her true smile.

His eyes clapped on the fortune of emeralds and diamonds resting on her collarbone and he was grateful for the sharp and necessary reminder of what was at stake if the wedding didn't take place.

"Now that the threatening petals are gone, are you going to tell me why you're here?" she asked.

"Jared is ill," he said bluntly. "He overindulged last evening."

"Given it was his stag party, I expected him to."

"As did I. But I've never seen him so foxed."

"That explains why it took so long to find him." In a softer voice, she added, "You don't have to hedge. I know he didn't come home last night."

Ian made specific plans to hunt down and fire every one of his brother's traitorous, gossiping servants before the day was through. "Jared wasn't where his friends said they were going."

"You didn't join them?" She seemed surprised he'd refrained from carousing with his brother.

He couldn't decide if this flattered or insulted him. "No. I left early to attend to business."

"Do you think he was...interfered with?"

She brushed her fingers against the necklace in a casual motion that agitated him. If she had an inkling about what they truly were, she wouldn't handle them with such little care.

His father's will had included an eccentric instruction to gift the necklace to "his son's intended" to wear on their wedding day. Diana wore it now out of respect for him, and the deathbed promise she'd made him to wed Jared. If she had disliked the look of the thing, she could have bought a hundred other jeweled collars without putting a dent in her fortune.

It made Ian feel slightly guilty about his plans to steal it from her.

"We should come up with a plan. The guests will arrive in less than an hour," Ian said. "Perhaps we'll ask people to attend the breakfast first, until Jared recovers, and then do the ceremony?"

"You didn't answer my question." A small furrow surfaced between her lovely brows. Most of Diana's admirers would have interpreted it as an adorable look of puzzlement, but Ian knew her face too well.

She was angry with him.

The trouble was, he liked her angry. She behaved unpleasantly when she was infuriated, and it was one of the few honest things he knew about her. It made him want to forget about all the lies between them.

"Was Jared interfered with?" Diana repeated.

The edge in her voice could have been the result of her frustration with him for withholding his answer. Or she was truly worried about her fiancé.

He hoped it was the former. "I don't know."

Her nod assuaged him.

Briefly.

"We must find out what happened."

As she gathered her skirts and crossed the room, Ian was so distracted by the hypnotizing sway of her bustle that he was slow to process her words.

He scrambled to block her path. "You don't need to do anything. I'll take care of it." Like he always did.

"Don't be daft. We both know it will be hours before Jared wakes, and I can't sit here." She deftly dodged around his larger frame and headed toward the back of the room, where a small shade concealed the dumbwaiter.

Horror washed over him, along with a chilling sense of déjà vu. "Don't try it."

"That's what you said last time I dared you to beat me down to the kitchen." She lifted up the shade with a devious grin. "How old were we?"

He'd been twelve; she ten. "It was a foolish idea then. It's a mad one now. The draw rope will snap and—" He couldn't threaten that she'd plummet to her death out loud because his superstitious constitution would not allow him to speak the words he dreaded coming true.

"Nonsense. Do you know how much a silver service weighs?"

With characteristic grace, she tucked herself into the dumbwaiter.

And then, in a diabolically sweet voice, she asked, "Are you coming after me or not?"

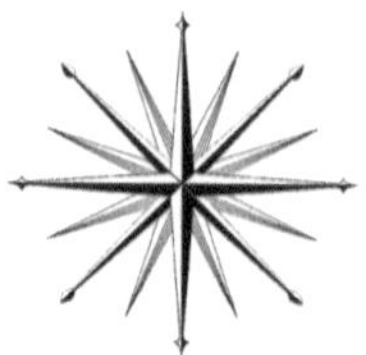

Chapter Two

As the dumbwaiter lurched downward, Diana prayed Amelia hadn't caused too much commotion in the kitchen, and that her friend had enough coin to bribe the footman to keep his mouth shut.

The man was taking his bloody time pulling down the dumbwaiter. At this rate, Ian would beat her downstairs, and she'd have to improvise something to distract him from overthinking what they were doing. Her thoughts ran in a scintillating direction before she corralled them back to focus on her escape.

She thumbed the black-edged envelope tucked into a hidden pocket in her skirt. The letter's arrival with the menacing bouquet conveyed a simple message, with a complicated outcome. Its sender demanded that Diana make a choice. And left no time for debate.

By the end of the day, she would have to sacrifice something.

The fortune she'd inherited.

The mission she believed was her life's purpose.

Or the only man she might ever love.

Chaos greeted Ian in the kitchen.

The entire staff had abandoned their posts to gawk at the ominous flower arrangement.

"I won't have it here!" the cook wailed.

"'Course not, it's poisonous!"

"And a bad omen."

"We should burn it!"

"No, that's worse. We must bury it."

Despite their overall fear of the thing, they all stood in a close clump around it. Blockading Ian's route to the dumbwaiter.

Diana had wanted the wedding ceremony at home, rather than in a church, to avoid the rabble-rousing press. Ian had taken it upon himself to secure the special license for them because holding the wedding at the house was ideal for his own plans to lift the necklace.

He hadn't calculated that if anything went amiss, there would be no retreat from the entire *beau monde*.

Mrs. Turner bustled into the kitchen and ordered the servants back to their work. Her mouth pursed as she regarded the special dishes for the wedding breakfast. Silver trays held cold meats and roasted fowl with aspic jelly. Glass bowls glittered with trifle and custard creams and surrounded the five-tiered plum cake frosted in snowy white royal icing.

When she spotted Ian, Turner gestured for him to follow her toward the hallway that housed the dumbwaiters. He placed himself in front of it, hoping that in the event Diana suddenly leaped out of the thing, his height would block Turner's view.

"Your brother remains unconscious," the housekeeper said in a hushed tone.

Her stance remained stiff. The woman had overtly resented Ian for years. When his father had returned from Italy one summer with a new wife—and a son he claimed as his own—Turner had glared at Ian with the rancor good society demanded anyone bestow on a bastard.

Over the years, it became harder to deny that Ian wasn't John Holt's natural son. They both possessed a cleft in their chin, and Ian grew into the same tall height and rangy build as his father. But Turner never warmed to him; her favor rested with Jared.

"The doctor believes his condition isn't from drink alone," Turner went on. "He says Mr. Holt's been at the *opium.*"

And not for the first time. "Did the doctor say when Jared will revive?"

"He believes it will be hours. And Mr. Holt will be very ill when he comes out of it, possibly for days." She pressed a handkerchief to her lips. "They will have to cancel the wedding."

"Postpone it," Ian corrected. "The scandal sheets already have something to write about. We must avoid trying to make it worse by suggesting the wedding won't happen. Miss Rives's reputation would suffer."

And Jared's debtors would become uneasy at the prospect he wasn't getting his windfall. They were the most probable suspects responsible for his brother's condition.

Ian needed to investigate the place Sunderland had found Jared. He didn't want to entertain the thought that his father's old adversaries had targeted his brother. It complicated things unnecessarily.

And made it even more dangerous for Diana to go sniffing about where Jared had spent the night.

Turner tipped her chin. "All the same, I must tell Miss Rives."

"Please wait." Ian held up a hand. "Diana has asked for some time alone with her thoughts."

"I don't think she should be. Sir."

"We should honor her request, given the circumstances."

Ian's voice carried enough edge to make Turner pale.

"Someone must deal with the guests, who will arrive any minute," he added. "I must entrust you to manage things while I attend to something that could help with Jared's care."

When the housekeeper was safely out of earshot, Ian cautiously lifted the door to the dumbwaiter.

Diana's exquisite face poked out of the darkness.

Her thunderous expression made it marginally less beautiful.

She opened her mouth to rail at him, but he clamped a hand over it, swiftly lifted her out of the dumbwaiter, and pulled them both into the nearby pantry.

"The entire household, minus your fiancé, is here in the kitchen," he warned before he removed his hand.

"Then there's no need to linger," she retorted. "Show me the route out."

He paused. "The doctor believes Jared consumed an illicit substance, which explains why we could not wake him."

Diana's face remained impassive while she waited for him to elaborate. He had a stray thought that this was how others reacted to him when he signaled nothing, gave away nothing, and he wondered if they were as infuriated by his patience as he was by hers.

There were a hundred reasons she'd keep a rein on her composure, particularly around Ian. But most women—even those who had little regard for their betrothed—would show more than a hint of emotion at learning their intended was in such ill health.

The logical explanation was that Diana knew something about what had happened to Jared.

Ian immediately detested the thought, and himself for thinking it, while also knowing he was likely right.

"Whatever Jared...took...the doctor believes he will recover from it?" Diana asked calmly.

"If it is opium, then he should wake within a day."

"But if it is something else, he might be permanently affected. We must find out what happened."

"That would not be wise. You are not inconspicuous." Dressed in a dream of a wedding gown. With a fortune of emeralds—his future—wound around her throat.

"No one here will notice my absence. You know every escape route to this house," she countered. "And I don't care who sees me. Once word breaks about Jared—and it will get out—no one would blame me for needing to escape for a bit of air."

"That will be difficult to explain since everyone believes you have taken to your bed with abject fatigue from disappointment."

A smile spread across her face, lighting it up like fireworks.

The small burst of delight it roused in him was all too brief. He'd revealed too much by admitting he'd invented a believable excuse to buy them time, and now she knew how easily she could entice him into doing what she wanted.

If they proceeded, they'd be poking around in something more dangerous than his brother's riotous habits and gambling debts. They'd confront secrets Ian had fought to protect.

But if they didn't resolve their investigation quickly, he'd lose his one chance to take the emeralds.

"Sunderland gave me an address," he conceded. "I expect what I'll find there would make you uncomfortable." An understatement, but he was a cold man, not a cruel one.

"I'm a woman." Diana lifted a shoulder. "My entire life revolves around navigating discomfort."

There was no safe response to acknowledge it, and he was both envious of and irked by her clever retort. He'd forgotten how adept she was at twisting him into a corner with innocent-sounding verbal traps.

He reached for a similar weapon to disarm her. "Forgive me. I've been so single-minded about finding out what happened, I've overlooked the fact that you must be so worried about Jared."

The sharp breath she drew made him discover new ways to detest his existence.

But he wouldn't apologize for what he needed to do to keep her safe.

"As troubling as the circumstances are, I shall not let it overwhelm me," she said carefully.

"Leave this to me." He attempted to gentle his tone. "I'll fix it. For both of you."

"What if it can't be solved easily? What if something happens to you there, on your own?"

Her voice took on a husky, almost breathless tone, and Ian became acutely aware of how close they were standing next to each other. In the dark. Where forbidden, hushed things happened.

The scent of her perfume made him think of violets that grew in the small garden of the house he and his mother had shared in Florence, and a sense of longing that was both distant and familiar assaulted him.

"It's not wise for you to go," he repeated. He wouldn't insult her by stating it would be too dangerous. She'd once saved both their lives without even losing a hairpin.

"No, it isn't wise. But we're going to do it." Diana lifted her chin. "Neither of us can let it go."

The emeralds bobbed with her uneven breaths. Ian had to glance away quickly to bury his ambivalence about his own plans to lift them.

Something clattered outside the hallway, and footsteps sounded.

"A servant will find us if we don't move quickly," Diana whispered. "How do we get out of here?"

It was tempting to let someone catch them; that way, Ian could force her back upstairs. But she'd likely try the dumbwaiter again, and the thought sent a shudder through him. If he helped her out of the house, he could see her safely home before retracing Jared's trail.

He huffed his discontent while he moved a stack of boxes aside and found the lever hidden among the shelves. It sprung a partition in the wall, and he reached inside and fumbled around for the book of matches and candle resting on the small inlet.

Diana's mouth parted. "Where does it lead?"

"To the mews. It's just a few feet from here."

"Then I won't need to take your hand."

He paused. "No, it's a short distance."

"Lead on, Captain."

The dim light of the candle wouldn't reach far, so she kept close to him. Her silk skirts swished; her sweet scent engulfed the narrow space, and Ian congratulated himself on his ability to act as if what they were doing was as simple as an amble across the park.

Mercifully, they surfaced a few minutes later into the back of the stables. He held up a hand to caution Diana back in the shadows until he could determine the stalls were vacant.

They crept along to the door. When he peered out at the yard, Miss Hunter was waiting.

Ian swallowed a smart remark about her uncanny timing.

"No one else is about." She waved them out. "I told Mrs. Turner I was taking Diana back to Hunter House until we know more about Mr. Holt's condition."

Ian looked intently at Diana. "Tell me you're going to do exactly that."

"Certainly." She nodded. "I'll return to Miss Hunter's house. As soon as you and I find out what happened to Jared. Amy, may we take your coach?"

"Of course, it's the fastest." Miss Hunter's father designed and manufactured the most exclusive carriages in Europe. "And it's the closest one to the entrance."

"No."

Ian delivered the single word with all the intimidation he could muster, without losing the appearance of calm.

Diana's eyes widened theatrically at his objection.

He desperately wanted to call her out for over-performing. From the moment she hopped into the dumbwaiter, he knew she wasn't improvising.

She was a woman who could adapt quickly to a situation and formulate her advantage.

And just as successfully, design and execute something more deliberate. Something that might take months—or years—to plan.

Like sabotaging her own wedding.

Diana ducked around him to head toward the carriage.

He caught her arm in a firm grip. He expected her to protest with a wriggle that might have progressed to a delicious tussle.

But she paused and stared at him calmly as he held her.

He was so stunned that he could only spit out one word.

"Why?"

The question was dangerously close to acknowledging everything they never spoke about. Her serene countenance made it impossible to detect if she'd expected it.

If she successfully manipulated an escape from a marriage no one suspected she truly wanted, there was no scenario where she would choose Ian instead.

He'd never let her. To do so would sign her death warrant.

"I'm going to have to make a choice about my future," she murmured. "And I need to know what happened. Not your filtered version of it."

Slowly, he released her arm. She acknowledged the surrender with a gracious tilt of her head before she darted inside the carriage.

Ian took several more breaths of the chilly autumn air while he tried and failed to find an excuse to keep her locked inside the house.

He leashed his anger and suspicion and climbed into the carriage.

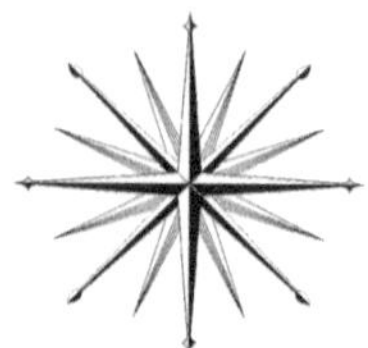

Chapter Three

Diana couldn't endure Ian's protracted silence on the walk home.

Evening fog clouded the pristine streets of Mayfair, making everything appear as ominous and insubstantial as what had transpired at his father's bedside moments before they left the house.

Her mind was still reeling with it. She impatiently waited for Ian to say something first, so she wouldn't have to. But he wasn't cooperating.

When they approached her street, she finally blurted, "You stopped writing to me."

His weekly letters had ceased four months before. She'd kept writing hers. She'd pretended his silence hadn't impacted her a wit, while she racked her brain for what she could have done or said to offend him so greatly that after years of friendship, he'd given her the cut.

If he'd written her back, she could have confessed she was worried about her own father's health. Or how, halfway into her debut season, everything about society exhausted her.

And she was anxious for his opinion about the mysterious missives she'd received from someone who only identified themselves as "Widow."

Then again, if she told him about the letters, she feared he'd discourage her from giving them any credence, and that would put her in a quandary. She very much wanted to believe Widow represented a clandestine organization dedicated to saving women's lives. And they'd chosen Diana to join them.

But mostly, if Ian had written her, she would have said that after the way he'd held her when they'd danced at her coming-out ball, she missed him more than she'd ever had in the fifteen years they'd known each other.

He kept walking, as if movement could conceal him from her interrogation.

"You stopped writing," Diana repeated in a distinctly louder voice. "Don't pretend you didn't receive my letters."

"I wouldn't do that."

When he refused to look at her, or slow his pace, she halted abruptly on the footpath. "I came to London to find out for myself if you were still alive."

The acid in her tone finally stopped him in his tracks. "I've been busy. As you saw, Father can't do much these days."

Mr. Holt's illness was the excuse Diana had offered to call at the house. She never thought Ian's father would ask her for a private moment with him. And only her dreams could have conjured the message he delivered from her mother.

Promise me, lass… Promise you'll honor our wishes. Marry my son.

Ian had overheard everything. And had said nothing to Diana about it.

He must have been too overwhelmed with his father's condition to think about anything else.

"I know he's had a bad go of it, but I thought your father was in good form tonight," she said optimistically.

"Today was a good day. An exception. The doctor says his heart will never recover. He has weeks, maybe a few months left."

Ian kept his voice low, but she still heard the pain he tried to cover. She clutched her coat in her hands to avoid reaching for him.

"You shouldn't have to face this alone," she said. "Why is Jared persisting with his Grand Tour? It's been two years."

"Now he finally has something to entice him home."

The rancorous insinuation cut like a knife.

Ian believed his father wanted Diana to marry *his brother*.

And that she'd agreed to it.

As rain misted around them, she searched for the words to contradict his false assumption. She was livid that she had to. Grief must have scrambled his mind if he imagined she would ever promise herself to Jared.

How could he think she'd do something so unimaginably cruel to him? Or to herself?

The only acceptable option to preserve her pride was to whirl gallantly past him and march ahead on the footpath.

A shadow darted out of the side lane and blockaded her progress.

"Evenin', luv," drawled a man in a rumpled coat. The scarf tied around his mouth muffled his voice.

Ian rumbled from behind her, "We've no coin for you."

"Now that's a shame, innit?" The man drew a pistol from his pocket and whistled.

Three more toughs brandishing knives quickly surrounded them.

Diana's lungs fought for air. Breathlessness was never something she'd had to account for in all her years of training with her fencing instructor. It irritated her beyond measure.

Ian swiveled so his back brushed against hers. His protective stance momentarily soothed her galloping heart, until the assailant whistled again and cocked the gun's trigger.

"Hands up, where I can see 'em, mate."

Out of the corner of her eye, Diana saw Ian slowly comply as he mumbled an Italian curse.

"Find it 'ard to believe you're the only toff walkin' about these streets wiv no coin," said their assailant. "So I'm gonna do a wee inspection. You get defensive, you'll get personal wiv me pistol, and me men will get personal wiv your lady, 'ere."

The thieves guffawed, but Ian's feral rasp silenced them. Diana could only imagine the glower he was giving them. She appreciated that he'd captured the attention of the thugs, so none of them would notice her slipping her hand into the hidden pocket of her skirt.

The leader stalked toward them and eyed Diana. "Ain't you a pretty dove. Reckon I'd like to keep you in a cage."

Diana could feel Ian's back muscles tense; he was primed to spring at the man.

"Easy," she murmured.

The brute chortled, thinking she spoke to him. She seized on the distraction and beamed her brightest society smile at the lowlife.

The man halted and blinked.

The rest of his crew were equally stunned when she shouted for Ian to move before she hurled her throwing knife at the assailant's throat.

Ian shifted so quickly, he blended in with the misty night and the fog curling around them. He knocked out the next man with a blow that solicited an audible crunching of bones. Diana shook off the sound with a shudder.

One of the goons recovered his wits and barreled toward them.

She drew a breath. Reached again for her pocket. And let her steel fly.

The man met the end of her second dagger and collapsed to the ground.

After that, she lost sense of how time unfolded. There was an ensuing scuffle, and more rain swirled around them. Ian seized the pistol the first thief had dropped. Shots reverberated.

Diana didn't surrender her attention from the felled bodies until Ian's harrowed face bent toward her.

"Are you hurt?"

A flush burnished the fine planes of his handsome face. Somewhere in the altercation, he'd lost his hat, and his black hair tumbled over his forehead. These days, he always dressed in shades of black and gray. The starched collar of his shirt was his lone splash of brightness. A spot of blood now marred it.

"Diana?"

Slowly, she shook her head. Her gaze returned to the bodies on the footpath.

Ian stole across and examined each of the men before confirming, "They're all down."

"Down or..." She couldn't bring herself to say *dead*.

"Doesn't matter." He retrieved her knives and wrapped them in a handkerchief. With his free hand, he clasped hers and towed her down the street. "Come quickly. There could be others following."

They broke into a run. Ian directed them through the back lanes to the service gate of her father's London house. The familiar sight of the little stone bench where the servants sat to smoke made Diana's knees buckle. She fell upon it, dragging Ian with her.

"I think I might have killed those men," she whispered.

"They had it coming. Don't worry about the scene. I'll sort everything out."

She tightened her arms around him. "Don't go alone."

"I won't," he murmured against her hair in a soothing voice. "We're both safe for the moment. Thanks to you. Have no remorse for defending yourself. It was…brilliant."

His hand stole under her chin and tipped her face toward him. "*You* are brilliant. And beautiful."

The awed expression he wore made warmth bloom in her chest and quieted the riot in her stomach. If he kept looking at her that way, she was going to kiss him. She wouldn't be able to stop herself.

"You were quite remarkable too," she said, leaning closer. "Where did you learn to shoot like that?"

The transformation in his countenance was like a cloud blocking the sun.

"It's all part of the job."

"What job?"

He slowly released her and stood up from the bench. The sudden absence of his warm embrace made her fight off a shiver.

"What job?" she repeated. "What does that mean?"

"My legacy. I made a promise to my father too. When he first fell ill."

When he'd stopped writing to her.

Ian threw a hand at the street. "What happened back there wasn't an opportunistic crime. Those men came here because of that promise. They came for me."

Diana staggered to her feet. "Then we'll go to the police—"

"They won't get in the middle of this."

She refused to accept the defeat in his voice. He was starting to frighten her, more than the toughs. "Tell me what this is all about, and we'll find a solution. Your father—"

"This isn't something he'd want you involved in."

The arrogant dismissal stoked her temper. If he thought she would give up that easily, he knew nothing about her. "If that were the case, he wouldn't have asked me for *my* promise."

Ian carefully removed her knives from his pocket and wiped them clean with his handkerchief. As he handed them to her, he avoided brushing his fingers against hers.

"You're mistaken," he said in a soft voice. "The promise Father asked of you was to marry Jared. For your protection. From the promise he asked of me."

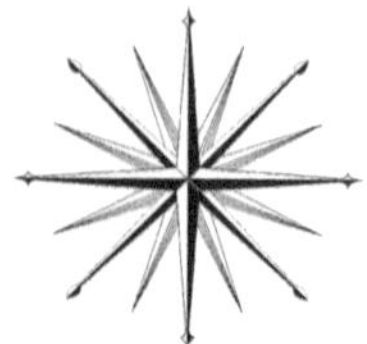

Chapter Four

In the carriage, Diana waited an interminable length of time for Ian to capitulate to her plan.

She hadn't calculated on him hesitating, and she chided herself for it. One of the few things she'd been able to rely on in her life was his wariness of surprises.

Her hands itched to release the nervous energy that had been building in her muscles since he'd led her through the tunnel. She reached for the throwing knife sheathed in the pocket of the cloak Amelia had placed in the coach. Its twin was strapped to the satin blue garter around her thigh.

The message she'd received with the dubious flowers had warned Diana to be cautious. The flagrant reminder made her bristle; she'd no need for it. She'd spent the last eight years carefully concealing the White Stags and their work to protect the women they served.

She forced herself to push her troubling thoughts aside to focus on the journey ahead. Ian hadn't mentioned the address, but she knew where they were going. And where their trail would ultimately end.

But she didn't know the route that would lead them there. For that, she'd have to depend on Ian.

The possibility terrified her.

And thrilled her.

The coach traversed Mayfair at the promised fast clip. Ian should have been relieved that Diana didn't pepper him with questions about Jared that he didn't want to answer. But her sudden reticence made him nervous.

She must have known he wouldn't let her get far without asking questions of his own. Like whether she was truly concerned about Jared's welfare, as she claimed, or if she was using the search as her excuse to escape.

Her serene expression gave no hint of the truth as she peered out the window, with the most dangerous set of gems in the world curled around her neck.

For twenty years, they'd occupied a safe deposit box in Westminster Bank. When Ian's father first fell ill, and he'd told Ian about his legacy, he'd promised Ian the necklace. But after his father's death, the ownership of the box had transferred to Jared, and his brother had refused to surrender it. Ian feared Jared would foolishly try to sell the emeralds. Until he learned his father had left Diana the key.

Ian had contrived a hundred different ways of breaking into the bank itself and blackmailing one of the bank's employees to get him access to the vault, so he could make off with the necklace. There was no scenario where he'd escape.

So he'd waited for the day of the wedding, knowing he'd eventually find an opportunity to swipe the gems with little fanfare or notice.

Now, that plan was in danger of being irretrievably compromised.

He cleared his throat and reached for the lace scarf on the seat next to her. "You should put this on." He gestured to her throat.

She darted a look at the necklace, and the corner of her mouth tipped up. "There are so many stories about these emeralds. Are any of them true?"

"What did Jared tell you?" He had no intention of revealing what she didn't already know.

When she flapped a dismissive hand, he issued a long exhale. "The two of you never spoke about it?"

"We've never had a conversation that didn't involve at least half a dozen other people, and you know it. You were often one of them."

She said it breezily, as though she'd asked a gentleman to walk across a ballroom and fetch her a glass of lemonade. He admired she'd mastered the art of detachment without sounding frigid.

Ian leaned forward and braced his arms over his knees. "Tell me what you've heard."

While he was only a few inches closer to her than before, the incremental invasion of her space made her lean as far back as the plush leather seat would allow. It stoked his confidence.

"It was part of a pirate's treasure," she ventured.

"Possibly." He'd spread that rumor himself, to raise the perceived value of the gems. "Couldn't say if it's true or not."

"Then the bit about the curse is also factitious."

"Probably."

"Did your father stake half of his business so he could give it to your mother as a wedding gift?"

A creative interpretation of the truth. His mother had possessed the necklace years before his father returned to Italy and discovered that he'd fathered a child with his mother. "That is a great exaggeration of what happened."

"The one I'm most curious about is that the necklace can never be bought or sold, it must be won."

When he didn't reply, her lips curved. "I didn't realize your father was such a talented card sharp."

Another false assumption. His father had possessed little talent for cards. But his mother's prowess had bordered on genius.

Jared was the heir to everything their father had built, but the emeralds were Ian's legacy. His father had won them in a competition so furtive and treacherous, the few who knew about it rarely dared to breathe its name. No one in London understood the danger of Ian's inheritance. And Diana couldn't comprehend what he was prepared to do to possess it.

"Is the other thing true?" she asked.

The forced lightness in her tone made him immediately suspicious. "Are we still talking about the necklace?"

"India. You're not really moving to Bombay."

"Did you honestly think I'd stay after the wedding?"

Her breath caught in an audible rasp.

The sound made his chest burn. He was behaving spitefully, but he couldn't help himself. He was desperate for some sign that his absence would affect her half as much as hers impacted him.

The carriage came to a halt, and Diana impatiently moved toward the door. She'd fled the house with no gloves, only a dark cloak and the shawl Miss Hunter had left for her in the coach. Both would do little to conceal her wedding costume.

Ian blocked her exit by gripping the door handle.

"You don't have to act like a mastiff." She sighed. "I know where we are."

This did not alleviate his unease. "It would be wiser for you to remain in the carriage. They may not respond candidly to questions with you there."

She gave a low laugh and shoved aside his arm.

"Wait."

He clasped her shoulders with enough force to stop her momentum.

The scorching glare she threw him would have shredded another man's dignity, but Ian couldn't let her out onto the streets of Soho so exposed. He pulled the dark cloak roughly over her shoulders and fastened the clasp. Her low grumble made him apply more caution as he wound the lace shawl around her throat until it obscured the necklace.

When he tied it closed, his gloves brushed her neck.

She trembled faintly, before she caught herself.

Small as her reaction was, his touch affected her; it was as fortifying as a good night's sleep.

"I have never been here before, but I have a fair idea of what and who we will find," he said cautiously. "They are unlikely to be forthcoming with information. And I don't need to remind you that every minute we delay could impact Jared's recovery."

"Then we must be swift about it," she insisted.

"Leave the questioning to me. If they resist, I'll have to resort to ungentlemanly tactics. There's an excellent chance that my behavior will disappoint you."

She evaluated this for a moment before concluding, "Only if you don't succeed."

He alighted from the coach first so he could hand her out, which she managed smoothly considering the morass of her skirts. Without a word, she threaded her arm through his so he could lead her across the cobblestoned lane to a faded green door.

The burly doorman allowed them in without a protracted negotiation and nodded to a set of ungodly steep stairs, which opened into an elegant receiving room.

Ian didn't make a habit of visiting Soho brothels, and he was relieved to find themselves in one of the more discerning establishments, judging from the sumptuous parlor furnishings. A generous fire burned away in the small grate to accommodate the sparse wardrobes of the working women. The one who greeted them wore little more than a negligee.

He didn't know where to point his eyes. Staring at the floor wasn't an option; there was no telling who might walk through the door, and while Diana could handle herself against many threats, rich punters behaved badly when their blood was high with lust. And if he looked at Diana, he'd risk betraying the inappropriate thoughts their surroundings roused in him.

A woman wearing a more modest silk dress with a plunging neckline approached them. "What can we do for you, my dears?"

"You're the proprietress?" Ian asked.

"I am. Don't tell me you're the tax man, come ta collect," she teased.

"My brother was here last evening. You may recall him as the man who could not remove himself this morning."

The madam gave a short, throaty laugh. "That was *your* brover?"

"It's true, although they don't resemble each other at all. Different mothers," Diana offered from behind her cloak.

This did not appease the proprietress. She retreated to the fireplace and laid a casual hand on the iron poker.

"We're not here to stir up trouble," Ian said evenly.

"And we're not with the police," Diana added. "They're the last people we want involved with this."

Ian nodded. "My brother is ill, and we are trying to trace his movements so we may understand what would help him. We'd like to speak to whoever was with him last night."

"How do I know you won't send the bobbies chasing after us?" the proprietress asked.

"Because the scandal would be too costly for my family."

The madam was unmoved by this.

"We will, of course, compensate you and your staff for their time away from their duties," Diana offered.

Ian clenched his teeth. It set a terrible precedent to offer payment so quickly. He could be exceedingly convincing without resorting to such expenses.

Begrudgingly, he reached into his pocket and withdrew a shilling.

The proprietress lifted it from him with the ease of a veteran pickpocket. "The gentleman was wiv Patrice last night. This way."

The madam led them down a dim hallway and rapped on the door at the end. "Patrice, you've got special visitors."

A long-lashed man, clothed in a half-buttoned shirt and form-fitting trousers, answered the door. His eyes traversed the length of Ian's body, and then widened when he took in Diana, standing behind him.

Ian had known for years that Jared had shared his bed with men and women alike. Both he and his brother had gone to great lengths to keep it secret, to protect the reputation of the family, and Holt & Company.

But if it was a surprise to Diana, she barely registered it. The lack of emotion she displayed was almost unnatural.

"These two just want to talk." The proprietress drawled out the last word like an indictment. "They're payin', so treat 'em sweet, like you do."

Patrice coquettishly bobbed his head between his two visitors before his attention fixed on Diana. No one who traded in sensuality could ignore beauty like hers. The fool didn't even attempt to conceal the lust from his stare as he ogled her.

Ian stepped between them to obstruct Patrice's view of her. The bolt of heat that rose on the back of his neck appalled him.

"You must tell us about your evening with Mr. Holt," Ian said. "He still hasn't woken from the stupor you found him in this morning."

"I know nothing about it."

"Now that can't be right," Ian countered in a low voice. "You were the last person to see him before he became ill."

Patrice leaned around Ian to catch Diana's eye. "I didn't do anything."

Ian defensively tilted his body, but Patrice ducked around him to gawk at Diana's white ruffled silk. "That looks a hell of a lot like a wedding gown."

"Jared is the groom." Diana flashed a demure smile. "We must find out what happened so we can help him heal as quickly as possible. Will you help us?"

Patrice gave a slow nod.

"Do you recall when Jared arrived last night?" she asked.

Patrice shook his head. "Not exactly. It was late, gone after midnight."

Diana's honeyed approach had thawed some of Patrice's reserve, but Ian refused to surrender control of the investigation. "What was his condition when he arrived?" he asked.

"Shattered," Patrice replied. "His eyes were all black. Had the same blank look as the coves who visit the Angel's Lounge." An infamous opium den near Covent Garden.

"Did he eat or drink anything here?" Diana inquired.

"Nothing."

"So you knew he was well off his head." Ian's voice carried a threatening edge.

Patrice glanced at Diana, but Ian sidled between them and pointed to his cheek. "Eyes here. What happened next?"

"I—I started to remove Jared's clothes. Could barely understand a thing he said," Patrice recounted. "Then he got all tetchy, insisted on having his lady join us."

"And did she?"

As steady as Diana's voice sounded, Ian didn't miss the blush rising on her cheeks. When he took a protective step closer to her, and her flush deepened, prickling heat resurfaced along his skin.

"Did she join you?" Diana prompted.

Patrice glanced nervously between them. "I—I ducked down the hall to check if Ambrosia was free, but by the time I'd brought her back here, Jared was asleep. I couldn't wake him. Thought it was the drink, catching up with him."

"Unfortunately for Jared, it wasn't just drink." Ian loomed over Patrice to force him to retreat to the wall. "Who would have wanted to harm my brother?"

"I don't know," Patrice bleated.

Ian wished Diana had stayed in the carriage. They were running short on time, but he was reluctant to get rough with the man. He resorted to force only to defend himself and his people. And Patrice was clearly weaker. It wouldn't be a fair fight; even threatening the wretch was distasteful.

"I swear I know nothing," Patrice whispered. "If I did, I'd tell you."

"Give me a name." Ian kept his voice low. "And then I won't have to worry it was you."

"If I could, I would! Jared was half out of his head the moment he walked in the door. And even if he hadn't been, we don't do a lot of talking here!"

"Of course you don't." Diana popped up between them. She extended her hand to offer Patrice a shilling, which he nabbed quickly.

"If you remember anything else, Patrice, you'll contact Mr. Holt, won't you?"

An amorous moan sounded from the next room, and a fever broke out across Ian's forehead. His control was in grievous jeopardy of fraying if they stayed one moment longer. He wrapped his fingers around Diana's elbow and urged her down the hallway, into the parlor, where the madam waited for them.

Before he could herd her downstairs, the proprietress placed a hand on Diana's arm.

"Hold one minute, pet," she drawled.

"We're pressed for time," Ian clipped.

"Indeed, you're a busy man." The madam leaned a protective arm around Diana. "Don't let us keep you wiv our talk of female matters."

The woman must have thought him deranged if she expected he would let Diana out of his sight in a bordello bordering St. Giles.

When he didn't retreat, Diana murmured, "Go on. You can watch me from the doorway. I'll be along in two shakes."

The situation was too contrived not to be suspect.

He stomped his protest down the steps, walking sideways to keep Diana in view.

And the thousands of pounds in gems she wore cradled at her throat.

Her *tête-à-tête* with the madam was thankfully brief, and Ian found himself able to breathe more easily when they finally darted out into the fading light of the afternoon. The wind gusted and dampness clung to the air as he directed Diana to the carriage. "It's going to rain. We must leave."

"Aren't you going to ask me what she said?"

"You can tell me in the coach."

"I'm not ready to go," she said softly.

Her placid dissent infuriated him. He resented her ability to maintain such control, while his emotions were, uncharacteristically, running rampant.

Through gritted teeth, he asked, "Why did the proprietress want to speak with *you* alone?"

"Careful, Ian. Your envy is showing."

"No, only my misanthropy."

"You should have that looked at." Her lips curled into a half-smile.

He refused to indulge her by returning it.

"The proprietress believes Jared made a stop before the brothel last night," she conceded.

"How forthcoming of her to tell you. Let's discuss this development *in the coach*."

"Patrice said Jared asked for *his* lady. Not *a* lady. Someone he visited regularly."

Jared's current mistress was the latest in a long line of his brother's companions, dating back far longer than his engagement to Diana. Ian had met none of Jared's paramours, but he directed one of his men to monitor things, to ensure Jared didn't mistreat them.

He didn't regret keeping Jared's affair from Diana. He suspected she'd known and turned a blind eye to it, as many women of her position in society did.

"The proprietress told you exactly where to find this woman," Ian surmised. "She's protective of the girls who work for her, so she wouldn't tell me."

"There you go. Doesn't that feel gratifying to have worked it out yourself?"

Diana's smile had never struck Ian as something dangerous before.

It did now. "What convinced her to tell you?"

"I promised no harm would come to the woman."

Ian scoffed. "How much did you pay her?"

"Half a crown."

Which she'd lifted from his coin purse.

"Fortunately, the good Polly Wren lives a short walk away," Diana said. "Off Shelton Street."

"Shelton Street is in the heart of St. Giles, surrounded by rookeries."

"Oh, so you've been there?"

"No," he said, a little too forcefully, to cover his annoyance that she was coercing so much out of him.

"We must consider that Jared's...lady could have drugged him."

Ian shook his head. His brother's mistress was a probable suspect, and until he ruled her out, he wanted Diana nowhere near her. "Paying a visit to St. Giles is the height of foolishness."

"Neither of us is helpless, Ian." She raised her chin in a modest display of defiance. She'd venture into the cutthroat neighborhood, with or without him.

It left him feeling hollow, and a little awed at what she was willing to risk.

"Why are you pursuing this?" he rasped.

"You're satisfied by what we found at the brothel?"

Most women in her station would be terrified to say the word brothel out loud to anyone. Never mind visit one to investigate the drugging of her fiancé. Now, she wanted to venture into the dodgiest corner of London, to confront her intended's lover.

He almost laughed at her fearlessness.

"We don't know what we don't know," he insisted. "Which is why we can't chase down shadows. It's unsafe—and I'm talking about care to your person. Not your reputation, which becomes more and more precarious the longer we stay at this. To continue on is not only asinine; it's an enormous waste of time."

"But we are certain that someone hurt Jared. Until we know what rendered him in that state, we won't know what will wake him from it. Or if he'll ever wake."

Ian hadn't seriously entertained the idea that Jared *wouldn't* recover. He was surprised at the twinge of guilt that surfaced when he thought he might not.

His relationship with his brother had been as strained as a tightrope from the moment they'd met. Little had changed over the last twenty-five years, but that didn't mean Ian wished his brother dead.

He hoped to hell Diana didn't either. Wanting Jared to depart the earth would imply she had deeper feelings for his brother than he'd dared to consider.

"No matter what happens to Jared, this series of events leaves too much unanswered," Diana continued. "There are things that are forgivable and other things that are indefensible."

She met Ian's eyes. "If you were me, you'd want to know."

Christ, she knew exactly where to aim her arrows.

Ian's mother had concealed his existence from his father for the earliest part of his life. As an adult, he understood her reasons had been noble and justified; at the time, she wasn't free to marry. But as a boy, learning he had a father and a brother had changed everything.

Diana knew this better than anyone else in his life.

And he knew, better than anyone else in her life, the havoc she could wreak when she discovered a justifiable motivation.

"Tell me honestly," he said. "What will you do when we find out the truth of what happened?"

Her eyes drifted toward the darkening sky above them before returning to him. "I honestly don't know."

Over the years, he'd learned to detect lies by the tenor of a person's voice, the small facial tics, evasive eyes, and rigid, distancing postures. None of them were present as Diana confessed her uncertainty.

The very fact she did made him want to believe her.

With a sigh, he reached into the carriage and retrieved an umbrella from beneath the bench. "This is not wise."

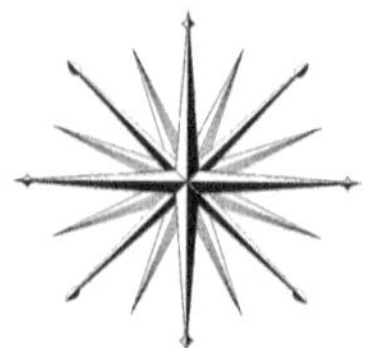

CHAPTER FIVE

As Diana threaded her arm through Ian's, she slipped her other hand into the hidden pocket of her cloak and traced the outline of the envelope that the bordello proprietress had slipped inside.

One unexpected note from Widow was surprising. A second missive from her handler, arriving hours after the first, was wildly out of protocol. It validated the trail of evidence Diana had compiled for months and the fear that had gnawed at her for weeks: there were tears in the fabric of her organization. And the repercussions on their mission could be deadly.

With Ian watching like a hawk, the bordello proprietress couldn't reveal much when she passed the note to Diana. They'd never worked together before and had no established signals. White Stag operatives rarely met outside their own crews. It ensured they protected themselves as well as the women they served.

The madam had looked at her plainly, with the respect Diana had only seen men give to other men. She was unaccustomed to it, and found it unexpectedly, pleasantly, satisfying.

From an early age, Diana had learned the value of her beauty was second only to the staggering fortune she'd inherit. Her mother had reminded her about it with every scrape and bruise she'd collected running along the rocky shore of their Bristol estate. When she was six, she'd knocked out her front tooth trying to escape down the chestnut tree outside her bedroom window. Her mother's caustic warning still rang in her ears.

Get on your knees and pray that the new one comes in as straight as the old one. I will not allow you to waste your beauty. You have a handful of years before it fades, so make hay with it while you can. Before you can blink, it will have slipped through your hands. Just like your fortune will when you marry.

Diana's first act of true rebellion was to doubt there was any truth to what her mother declared. She never considered her features to be any lovelier than those of the women of her acquaintance. As she grew older, she distrusted anyone who remarked on her physical attractiveness; if they did, she assumed they were liars.

Ian had called her beautiful once, on the night they'd saved each other.

Then he'd reminded her of the promise she'd made his father. And insisted that he wasn't the son she was meant to marry.

Before she left London, Diana needed to find out why Ian believed it.

She never had.

The rain held off as they traversed the narrow lanes of Soho and turned past Seven Dials Market.

Ian walked them through the crowded streets with the warm weight of Diana's hand on his arm. It had been years since he'd permitted himself such an indulgence, and the urge to draw her closer was profound. He contemplated what she'd do if he made such an overture, and realized he couldn't predict how she'd react.

There was only one instance when he'd come close to acting on the spark that simmered between them. That brutal night eight years ago, after the attack in Mayfair.

He should have kissed her. Comforted her with assurances or promises he kept in his heart. Instead, he'd rallied all of his strength to put distance between them. In the agonizing moment that followed, he'd destroyed all the warmth and affection she held for him because of a promise he'd also made to his father.

They walked at a brisk pace; she matched his strides despite their difference in height and her massive array of silk skirts, which were growing soiled and dingy with dust and dirt from the road. He remained on a heightened alert. It was impossible for them not to attract notice. Diana walked like a queen everywhere she went, and if Ian had gained one thing from his Harrow education, it was how to swagger down a street like he owned it.

The scents of the market wafted from the small square—some of them pungent, others more pleasant, like the spicy aroma of the cheese and curry hand pies from a stall at the end of the road. The seller gave him a nod of recognition as they passed.

"*Il-lejla t-tajba, għeżież,*" she called. *Good evening, dear.*

"*Il-lejla t-tajba,*" Ian replied.

Diana's mouth curved at their exchange. "You know that woman?"

"She's Maltese. When I'm working late, I often buy her pasties."

"They smell delicious. What are they called?"

"*Pastizzi.* Hers are the best I've had in London."

They also reminded him of his mother. She never baked herself. There was no oven in the spartan kitchen in the San Niccolo apartment she let from Alberti, the merchant who'd employed her to translate his business documents into English. So they bought the savory treats from the bakery. Despite complaining that the pastry was too Florentine, not light and wispy like the kind she ate as a child in Malta, she always fought Ian for the crumbs.

He was oddly protective of that memory. And yet, a part of him longed to share some of it with Diana. She didn't suggest they stop to buy a pastry, but her wistful look made him wager she'd enjoy them.

"Looks like that's the place." Diana gestured to the building ahead. "Is it the right address?"

"I've never been here," he said tersely. He remained uncomfortable with the fact that she now knew he'd concealed Jared's mistress from her.

"'Ave you got a penny for me, guv?" A boy stood at the doorway. As he leaned closer, Ian maneuvered Diana away; he didn't want either of them bringing back chits.

"Where can we find Polly Wren?" Diana asked.

The boy eyed them suspiciously.

"There's sixpence in it for you if you tell us," Ian offered. "But it better be the right door. Or I'll return to claim my money back."

The boy swallowed visibly at the threat. He pointed upstairs. "Blue door."

Ian tossed up the coin, which the lad caught neatly before he ran off to spend it.

Diana's bright laugh echoed in the narrow lane. He'd forgotten how infectious it was, how often the sound had filled the summer days they'd spent together by the shore.

It was a lifetime and a world away from where they stood.

He took a moment to reflect on what he was actually doing, allowing things to progress this far. There was too much at stake for him to be anything less than serious in his investigation. Daylight was fading, Jared could have worsened, and there was still the small matter of needing to steal the emeralds.

He admitted to himself that he was conflicted about taking Diana to meet Polly. Only a scoundrel of the lowest order would escort a woman to meet her fiancé's lover.

Even if the woman had insisted on it.

They walked into the building and up the narrow staircase. When Ian knocked on the door, a surprised shout arose from inside the flat.

He pushed at the door, prepared to throw his full weight at it to get through, but the thing flew open, and he tripped inside.

"Get out, you blackguard, or I'll whistle for the police!"

In the manner of a toy poodle guarding a Great Dane, a petite woman stood protectively in front of a taller, curvaceous woman.

"Lady Cora?"

The shorter woman turned to Diana. "Miss Rives?"

She took in Diana's wedding gown, and her eyes widened before they narrowed on Ian. "Has this fiend abducted you?"

Ian's reputation preceded him, but so did Cora Longworth's. She was one of the fiercest bluestockings in London and known to have a low regard for the male species.

So what in God's name was she doing in St. Giles?

"I assure you I'm quite well and here of my volition," Diana said quickly, as she smoothed her hand over her hair. It was a small tic, the closest she came to fidgeting; Lady Cora's presence unsettled her.

This unsettled Ian.

The woman standing behind Lady Cora—presumably Polly Wren—clutched her hands while she stared at Diana's gown. Her lip trembled. There was more than a fifty percent chance she would break into hysterics at any moment.

Ian half hoped she would just to get it over with, and they could move swiftly on to his questions.

He ventured a step closer.

Lady Cora stopped him with a glare that would have torn a lesser man to pieces.

Diana chided him with a slanted look. "Allow me to introduce you. Mr. Ian Holt, may I present Lady Cora Longworth."

Lady Cora sniffed her disapproval. "And this is Miss Polly Wren."

"Holt," Polly whispered. "You're Jared's kin?"

"His brother," Ian acknowledged with a tilt of his head, which he hoped would assure the woman he wasn't a brute.

It had the opposite effect.

Polly broke into sobs as she rushed over to a wooden cradle perched in the corner. "You won't take my son away! You're not taking him!"

"Why on earth would you think we came for your son?"

"Because his father is your brother!"

Ian struggled to process the series of appalling epiphanies.

Jared's mistress had given birth to a son.

The man Ian had charged with watching Polly either hadn't known about the baby, or intentionally kept it from Ian.

And Polly believed Ian was the bogeyman sent to separate them. Because if Jared had told Polly anything about Ian, the woman knew it was his charge to eliminate any threat to the Holts.

Ian observed Diana; her expression remained eerily calm.

Neither of them should have been shocked by Polly's revelation. Jared was reckless, and it was possible the baby in the cradle wasn't the only child he'd fathered. It was also possible he wasn't the father at all, given that Polly had until recently worked at the bordello.

Yet Jared had continued his arrangement with Polly. He'd never shown such interest in any of his other women.

"You lot have some nerve. Wasn't enough for the lout to give me that!" Polly gulped another sob as she gestured to a pile of papers on the small table. "So he sends the Devil of the Docklands to force my hand."

"Hush, Polly," Lady Cora said in the least soothing voice Ian had ever heard.

"Please, Mrs. Wren, your son is safe with you. We only came to talk," Diana added, in a much gentler tone.

"That's what they all say." Polly hiccupped. "Before they take our babies."

Ian had done terrible things to protect his family and their business. Many were necessary; others he regretted. But he'd never rip a mother apart from her child.

He could insist that he wasn't like the men Polly knew, but she'd never believe him. Diana didn't jump to his defense either, which he hoped was a tactic to disarm Polly's wariness. The woman watched them through slitted eyes, suspicious of them both.

They took a collective silent moment of contemplation to process Polly's words.

Eventually, Diana cleared her throat and turned to Lady Cora. "How are you and Mrs. Wren acquainted?"

"The Ladies' Discussion and Improvement Society received a pressing request from Polly for help with legal documents."

"The society is an instructional institute for young ladies, to improve their entrance to society," Diana explained to Ian. "They also provide employment training for working women and other types of support."

"Couldn't read them papers," Polly said in a smaller voice. She retreated to the cradle and lifted the sleeping baby from it. "Learned my letters, but Lord, if I couldn't understand a word of that mess. Someone said that Lady Cora's group could help."

Ian scrubbed a hand down his face. "Were the papers the only reason Jared paid you a visit last night?"

"What's it to you?" Polly drawled. The woman was undereducated, but she wasn't stupid.

"He was missing for a good part of last evening, and when we found him this morning, he was unconscious," Ian replied. "We haven't been able to revive him."

"Good God. Could he di—" Polly's voice cut out in a swallow and her face turned ashen. "You think I'm to blame for it!"

"Not at all, Mrs. Wren. Come here. I know this is most upsetting to us all." Diana's tone was gentle without being patronizing. She gathered a blanket from the settee and settled it over Polly's shoulders. "We only want to piece together what happened. It could make all the difference for Jared. Will you help us?"

Polly heaved a sigh and shared a nod with Diana. There was a shift of energy in the room with their alignment.

Ian had once read a story in *The Times* about a rattlesnake let loose in the lobby of Shepheard's Hotel in Cairo. An Italian monk had strolled among the screaming patrons and staff, taken a firm hold of the snake, and tossed it into a nearby bucket of water. Then the man had walked calmly out the door as if he'd performed such services countless times before.

Ian wondered if the monk's expression had been as calm as the one Diana now wore.

He realized, with a cold certainty, that she must have uncovered the truth about Polly and Jared's child long before arriving in St. Giles.

How had she continued on with the pretense of the engagement, apathetic to the way Jared had treated her? Had she become so numb over the years that nothing wounded her? When they were young, she'd taken the waves at the beach at full force.

Ian couldn't fathom what had snuffed out her passion, her ferocity for life.

As he silently held her gaze, he begged her to tell him, *How much did you know?*

She lifted a shoulder, as if to say, *Less than you're imagining.*

When Polly had quieted enough to take a sip of water, Diana asked, "What time did Jared arrive last night?"

"Must have been close to half-eleven."

"And he wasn't himself."

"He'd been drinking. But I think he took something else. His hands were shaky, like. Usually, when he comes in, he sits with the baby. But last night, he was so cold, so distant," Polly said thickly. "And then he threw down those papers and said he was taking Johnny away."

"Johnny?" Ian murmured.

"That's his nickname for John. Named him after…" Her voice trailed off before she could say they'd given him Ian's father's name.

Ian's head went fuzzy as he tried to reconcile the wildly conflicting information. Naming the boy after their father was no small thing. Jared truly must have cared for the boy. It made his overtures to take the child from Polly completely baffling.

Lady Cora smoothed the papers together on the table. "This is a legal affidavit stating Johnny is Jared's son. It instructs Mrs. Wren to deliver Johnny to the care of Grayson Institute in Surrey."

Grayson was a home where the aristocracy and gentlemen of means sent their bastards for rearing. The previous night, one cretin among Jared's stags had extolled the virtues of the place.

"They can't take him!' Polly wailed. "I'm his mother!"

"Of course you are," Diana said softly. She exchanged an inquisitive glance with Lady Cora.

"By law, the courts favor a father's rights." Lady Cora shook her head. "More so if the parents are unmarried."

When all three women turned to him, Ian had never wanted to run further or faster from any spot in his life.

He had to settle for pacing the length of the small room.

Diana observed him warily, and he glared at her because it was easier than accepting her betrayal and the possibility she'd been toying with him since she'd leaped into the dumbwaiter.

"You need a solicitor who can advise you. An expert in this type of law," Ian said eventually. "I can help."

Polly stopped mid-sob.

"In exchange for some information."

He ignored the hostile looks the women tossed at him. "Mrs. Wren, why did Jared deliver the papers last night? He'd known about Johnny, and you had a long-standing arrangement."

"That's what you'd call this?"

"What changed?"

"He was getting married."

They all avoided looking at Diana.

"Jared said he couldn't afford to keep us any longer," Polly added, her voice hard. "I always thought your kind came into money when you married."

The woman was no dimwit, Ian would give her that. "Do you know of anyone who would have wished Jared harm? Someone he was trying to protect Johnny from, by sending him away?"

"Are we in danger?"

Ian couldn't deny his belief that someone had come after Jared. It could have been whoever loaned him money. Or someone his brother had crossed in the professional sphere; their business was a competitive one, barely removed from the work of cut-throats and smugglers.

He also couldn't discount the enemies their father had made over thirty years ago. Jared might have encountered any of them if he'd been stupid enough to mention the emeralds in the wrong circles.

There was no solid evidence pointing to a suspect, but Ian couldn't lie to Polly about her son, so he turned to the one person who was better at it than he was.

"There's no threat that we know of," Diana said smoothly. "But we are worried about Jared. If you help us find out what happened last night, it could help you. And Johnny."

"He had debts." Polly shrugged. "Most gents do. But I've no idea who held them. Or what we'll do if they come looking for us to settle them."

She started to cry again, this time more quietly, and that was Ian's undoing.

He turned to Lady Cora. "Contact Henry Eden. You can find him at chambers on Fleet Street. Ellison and Carter."

Lady Cora nodded. "Yes, I know the name."

"You may use mine as a reference. We're old friends."

When Polly sniffled again, Diana crossed the room and handed her a handkerchief. She peered down at the baby and asked Polly, "Do you love him?"

A sudden hush fell over the room.

Polly looked quizzically at Lady Cora, who glowered silently at Ian.

There was an unspoken acknowledgment among all three of them that Diana was confronting cogent evidence of the betrayal of the man she was supposed to marry. On her wedding day. Reasonable women would have blazed a trail of scorn and fury in the wake of such revelations.

It made Diana's unfailing composure seem more dangerous than ever.

Polly gave a short cough. "You're asking if I love Jared?"

Diana nodded.

"I depended on him. He's the father of my child. Our time together is always short. Never in the open. He insists on it that way." With a shake of her head, Polly added, "I love him the only way he'll let me."

Ian had never had an amorous affair that lasted longer than a week. Never wanted one either, for exactly the reasons that were playing out in this small flat off a shadowed lane in St. Giles. He'd know what a burden he'd been to his mother in the years before his father's return, and he'd never wanted to exact that on any woman, particularly one he cared for.

Until he dealt with the emeralds, he couldn't promise anyone his name, or his life.

But for the first time in years, he allowed himself to question what would happen if he could. And those thoughts only ever took him in one direction.

To one person.

When Diana caught his eye, and hers widened slightly, he was momentarily terrified he'd revealed every thought and fear as explicitly as taking out an advertisement on the side of a building.

"Thank you for the hospitality, Mrs. Wren," he said stiffly. "I shall send word to Henry to expect your call." He tipped his hat and opened the door to allow Diana through.

She paused by the small window to evaluate a stray raindrop that tracked along the glass. "Mrs. Wren, where did you say Jared was before he arrived here?"

"The Swan's Nest."

"That's the public house down the lane? We passed it on the way."

"I would not recommend it," Lady Cora quipped. "Not dressed as you are."

Outside, a deluge assaulted the cobblestones.

"Should have believed me about the rain," Ian couldn't resist remarking from the doorway. Mostly to assure himself that he was right about something and that his intuition was still functioning.

"It rained last night." Diana studied the wet street. "What time did it start?"

"Around midnight."

"That must have been why Jared ended up at the bordello. When Polly tossed him out on his ear, he wouldn't have been able to walk far enough to find a hack without getting soaked."

She turned to him. "We have to find out what he was doing at the Swan's Nest."

"*We* don't."

If she thought he'd allow her involvement to go any further, she was deluding herself. Not after what she'd concealed, for God only knew how long. She had to be itching for retribution, and he needed to squelch whatever she was scheming at.

"Well, we can't stay here. And before you say it, we're not going back," Diana insisted. "Not until we find out who drugged Jared."

"He could have taken the opium himself. It wouldn't have been the first time."

"It still doesn't explain what he was doing at the pub. Why would he go to the Swan's Nest before he brought the papers to Polly? What was so important he had to stop there before delivering them to her?"

Ian shook his head. Gangs and other less than legal entities conducted business at the Swan's Nest. He'd gone there himself when he needed an off-the-books contract. And as the date of the wedding and his access to the emeralds had drawn closer, he'd played cards there to sniff around for any inquiries about who was searching for the gems. So he'd have a full picture of who might chase after him once he had the necklace.

It was possible Jared had followed Ian one night. And probable his brother was stupid enough to have gambled with unsavory company and lost a prize he wasn't in a position to stake.

"You need to leave this to me now." There was nothing soft about his voice.

"Nonsense. You can't go in there alone. *That* is unwise." She smoothed a hand over her hair. "We both know I can defend myself. I can help."

"You've done enough."

An alluring flush rose over her cheeks. "You're angry I didn't tell you. About Johnny."

"We're not discussing it. Not here. Not now." Not ever, if he had his way.

"I thought you knew."

"And you believed I intentionally kept it from you?" They hadn't spoken openly with each other in eight years, but she must have thought he was a veritable devil if she believed he'd let her marry Jared, knowing his brother already had a son with another woman.

"You didn't tell me about Polly," she argued.

"I thought you knew."

She made an exasperated noise in the back of her throat, and with her pink cheeks and her uneven breaths and the way her attention fixed on him, he had to strangle the umbrella to resist touching her.

Diana registered the motion.

She took a step closer to him.

When her eyes dropped to his mouth, a swell of lust rose over him like a tidal wave.

"You're genuinely furious at me," she murmured. "Is it because I didn't tell you about Johnny? Or do you think, after all this, that I drugged Jared myself?"

She leaned perilously close to him. The scent of her violet perfume set his skin on fire and made his muscles shake. He squeezed his eyes shut and searched for the strength to resist her.

Dampness kissed his cheek before a frigid gust of wind revived him like a cold bucket of water.

When he blinked his eyes open, he was alone.

In the distance, Diana scurried down the street under the shelter of his umbrella.

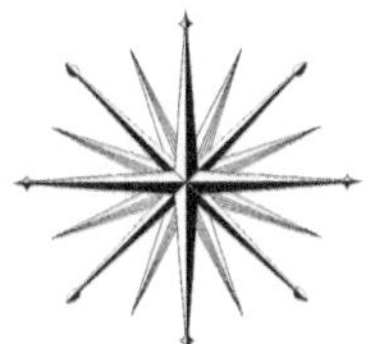

Chapter Six

Everything was more difficult than Diana had planned.

From the time the White Stags had recruited her, she'd expected orders about her betrothal to Jared. When the signal finally arrived, she spent months preparing her crew for the operation.

In her well-plotted scheme, Jared would have drunk himself into a stupor the night before the wedding. Someone would have found him the next morning at Polly's flat, providing a *ton*-approved reason to call off their engagement. Diana would have escaped London for seclusion in Bristol and met up with the ship and cargo departing as scheduled, two days hence.

But plans were only perfect on paper. In execution, they were vulnerable to a traitor's sabotage.

They also couldn't account for the onslaught of emotions Diana had encountered in the space of a day. They couldn't specify how her heart would twist when she met Jared's son. Or the way it had fluttered when she'd grazed Ian's cheek as she'd stolen his umbrella.

He was going to be livid when he found her.

That was, after all, her intent. She needed to determine how far he'd chase her.

The thrill of their future confrontation gave her a renewed strength as she stepped through the door of the Swan's Nest.

It was larger than Diana's sources had described. And more crowded. The dock-workers had ended their shift, and many were cashing in their coin for pints at the wood-topped bar that ran the length of the room.

The scent of hops and tobacco clung to the warm air, along with a salty aroma she associated with the water and ships, and men working. They were impossible to separate from her memories of her father.

In the years before his death, Harry Rives relentlessly indoctrinated her in the running of Rives Shipping. The days in their dockside offices in Bristol and London were often grueling. Many of the men overtly resented her presence in meetings. They called her a distraction. One fool had possessed the gall to suggest she was a pretty little lapdog.

Diana had planned to make his life misery, but her father had repeated the comment in passing to Ian, and within a week, the pig was indentured on a long and unforgiving passage to Hong Kong, without a return ticket, courtesy of Holt & Company.

Ian was the only person who could have arranged it. Diana cherished that malicious act as a gift more precious than the emeralds she wore at her throat. It gave her hope that he'd been lying to himself, as well as to her, when he'd sworn she could never be his.

As a burly sailor brushed past her in his eagerness to reach the bar, a hand tightened around her arm.

Ian's expression was ferocious.

She gave a small sigh. "If you drag me out of here, it will cause more of a scene."

"That's a risk I'm willing to take," he retorted. "Poking around, asking questions here is beyond unwise. It's dangerous."

"Then act like we're here for something else." She wound her arm through his. "Play pretend with me. Like we used to. Or did you forget how?"

To her surprise, he drew her closer. But the way he scowled at her would convince anyone watching that his intentions weren't affectionate.

It was a prodigious effort to keep from confessing everything to him. Diana wasn't above admitting to herself that she was in a precarious position, and Ian's shrewd mind and devilish talents would be excellent assets for the next phase of her operation.

She ached to find out how he'd react if she told him she'd done everything in service of a bigger mission. And he was among the lives she was working to protect.

"There's a bit of room there at the bar." She withdrew her arm. "Let's catch our breath."

Ian trudged forward and paused for her to walk through ahead of him in the path he'd cleared. She pulled her cloak and scarf tighter around her throat to conceal the emeralds. As she scanned the crowd, her eyes snagged on a woman in the corner in breeches and an oilskin coat. A woolen flat cap covered her short, dark curls.

Diana glanced away quickly, irked that Birdie had disregarded the orders to stay clear of the Swan's Nest. Her nerves pricked at the possibility that one of her crew carried a note with yet another change to their mission. Any more alterations would compromise Diana's own plans, which her handler didn't know about and absolutely wouldn't approve of.

At the bar, Ian found a small opening, and a serving maid sauntered over to them. "What can I get ya, luv?"

"A pint of porter and a lemon shandy," Diana answered.

Under his breath, Ian grumbled, "We don't need to prolong our stay."

"And they likely won't part with information without compensation. It's less conspicuous than paying them directly."

"We're already conspicuous here. Which is why we shouldn't stay longer than necessary." As he regarded the room, he casually tucked one hand into his pocket. He had a weapon hidden there.

A small thrill coursed through her before she pondered what would have made him reach for it.

She evaluated the crowd and the stacks of hops haphazardly piled in the corner near the cellar door. A group of men stomped through the door and the table near the center of the room greeted them with rowdy roars. An older man with silver-streaked hair sat apart from the rest. He deliberately assessed the place Diana and Ian occupied at the bar.

Ian deliberately stared back in a more sinister manner.

"It seems you have a follower," Diana teased.

"Never met him."

"Perhaps I'll go introduce myself," she offered brightly.

His hand clamped down on her arm so forcefully she thought it might leave a mark, and this made her skin hum in a startling way.

"Approaching him would be foolish, Diana."

She wouldn't with an entire pub full of rogues and criminals watching. But Birdie's presence compelled her to speed along their investigation.

Ian angled his frame between the bar and the tables to block her view of the room. "What are we doing here?"

"Finding out who might have drugged Jared, and with what. To help him recover."

"If I had recently left the flat of my betrothed's lover—and his *son*—I'm not sure I would possess such generosity of spirit."

He was still irate she hadn't told him about Polly and the baby. She didn't have time to waste on his stubbornness. The instructions in the note she'd received tonight gave her only a handful of hours to find out the extent of the danger Jared—and Ian—were in, and if it could compromise her mission.

"Rives Shipping has a diligent staff of investigators. They told me about Polly and Johnny a few weeks ago." Her tone was perfunctory. "It's clear you didn't know until today, or you would have handled things, like you always do."

"If you've known for weeks, why on earth did you perpetuate the farce of a wedding?" He posed the question calmly.

She wondered how long he'd practiced saying it in his head that way. "Jared owes money to many people who extract payment by force. I couldn't call it off without putting him in more danger."

It wasn't the full truth, and the deep vee Ian's brows formed telegraphed his skepticism. "Running from the altar won't absolve Jared of those threats."

"No," she conceded. "I made a fair mess of it, and I must put things right. We have to uncover who Jared was meeting with and limit the damage."

"If you'd told me sooner, I could have helped you."

We could have worked together, remained unspoken, but she knew he'd meant it.

She met his gaze, gratified and slightly unnerved by the heat she found in his eyes. "The last time I spoke about the engagement and your father's wishes, I had to rebuild my entire life. My entire self. I didn't think I could take that again."

It was the most honesty she could afford to give him, and she wondered if her countenance betrayed any of the terror she felt about it.

Ian studied her a long moment before he leaned closer and rounded his shoulders as if it would shield them both from an imaginary foe. "You're not telling me everything. That puts us at risk."

Diana dismissed the accusation with a sniff; there was no time to bicker with him. She nodded to the table at the center of the room. "The man with the silver hair. Tell me about him."

"He's a new face." Ian slid a glance at the group. "The men at that table run with the Skinner's Lane Lads."

The South London street gang had fingers in many pockets. They held a prominent place on the Stags's watch list.

"That lot handles commissions for hard-to-find items. Antiquities, artifacts. Gems," Ian added. His eyes flicked to the lace that hid the necklace. "There's a rumor they are working for peers who are advocating for Parliament to repeal the Pharmacy Act. Many sitting members of the House of Lords have significant investments in Indian opium. They stand to gain millions if there were fewer regulations on where people can get the stuff."

If the repeal succeeded, it would make the Stags's mission more difficult. And treacherous. "Suppliers who deal in opium often traffic in other things," Diana ventured.

Neither of them said *people*, but the word hung between them.

"It's probable then," she went on, "that Jared could have met one of those men here last night, and they slipped him the drug. By compromising his judgment, they could gain the upper hand in their dealings."

This explanation was preferable to the possibility that one of Diana's own crew was acting off script, for reasons she didn't want to contemplate.

"Now, 'ere ya go, luvies." The barmaid finally returned with their drinks and made a special show of reaching over the bar to wipe off Ian's glass before handing it to him.

When he paid her, he placed an extra shilling in her palm. "My lady friend here lost one of her earbobs here last night. We're trying to track it down. Were you working?"

"Sorry, pet. Had a night out wiv me fella. Took us down to the penny gaff, and we had such a row after, I don't fink I'm in a mind to forgive 'im." She batted her lashes at Ian.

"Was your colleague here?" Diana gestured toward the brawny barman at the other end of the bar.

"Aye, believe 'e was. You want a word?"

"That would be most gracious," Ian replied. He squeezed Diana's shoulder to root her to the floor while he leveled a charming smile at the barmaid. "You'll keep an eye on my hen, won't you?"

The maid winked. "'Course, luv."

Diana forced a lethal smile. "I'm afraid—"

"Mind our drinks," Ian interrupted. He tossed a parting grin at the barmaid.

Diana would have wiped it off his face, had the woman not clamped a hand on her arm.

"Oh, let 'im go see to 'is business, pet. 'E's a fine specimen. You want to 'old on to 'im. Men like that need to feel needed."

How Diana's mother would have *laughed* at that.

Before absolutely eviscerating the woman for even thinking it.

"Stay and finish your drink, luv," the maid insisted. "Let your man help a damsel in distress."

Diana regarded her with the kind of stare that often made grown men cower. "I'm not that kind of a damsel."

The maid released her arm as if it were a hot coal.

As she wove her way through the mob, Diana clutched her cloak to cover her skirts. She kept a careful eye on the silver-haired man. His attention was fixed on the sacks of hops in the corner.

Curious, that.

She risked a peek at Birdie, who scratched her nose and pointed a finger at the sacks, before slowly pulling on her right ear. It was a signal their crew used to convey an important transaction. Or a payment.

Curiouser and curiouser.

The sound of Ian's rising voice pulled Diana's focus back to the end of the bar. She firmly pushed her way in and found the barman leaning toward Ian in a much less friendly way than the serving maid.

"Fought I told ya to leave, before I make ya."

"I just want to know what you saw," Ian demanded.

"Is there a problem?" Diana asked insipidly, hoping to distract them, but both men continued staring daggers at each other until she reached for Ian's jaw and pointed it toward her.

"Calm down," she murmured as her hand dove into his coat in search of his coin purse.

He jerked at her touch and stepped neatly out of her reach. "What are you doing?"

"Buying us another drink to smooth the waters."

"I ain't taking no blunt from *you*," the barman bellowed. "It's a bloody shakedown."

"Eh, Shep, this bloke boverin' ya?" a muscled sailor asked.

"Oi, 'oo's causing trouble?"

"Cagey bugger wiv the dark 'air," another man chimed in. "Says that leary cove 'oo were in last night's 'is brover."

A chorus of rumbles echoed from the bar. Worried glances darted to the table at the center of the room.

Diana stared at the sacks along the wall that she was now certain did not contain hops.

"My mate got nicked today." The barman pointed a meaty finger at Ian. "Because of the dodgy notes 'e got from this snide pitcher's brover!"

Shouts broke out. The men at the center table were on their feet, staggering over each other in their effort to charge.

"On my count, you head to the back stairwell," Ian rasped. "It should lead to the cellar. You can escape outside to the alley. Get a hack and get as far away as you can."

Birdie intervened by darting past and spinning drunk men around. Diana hated leaving any of her crew on their own to handle cleanup from an altercation, but she had to get Ian out.

"I won't make it across the room without a distraction," she warned him.

"Diana, don't you dare—"

She hopped up on a chair, placed her thumb and forefinger in her mouth, and peeled a whistle so loud, the man nearest them covered his ears.

The room went completely still.

Diana's cloak fell from her shoulders to reveal her shimmering silk bridal gown.

The sight of it precipitated more than a few grunts of surprise.

It was, after all, a room populated mostly by men.

And she was, after all, the most drawn woman in London.

No one expected her to reach beneath her skirts for two daggers and throw one at the sacks in the corner.

Five-pound notes cascaded out.

With a collective roar, the mob scrambled for the money.

Ian threw Diana's cloak at her. "Cellar. Go now."

She hesitated. The knife she'd thrown was a particular favorite, and she hated losing it.

Nearly as much as she hated the idea of leaving Ian to fend for himself.

"Go, Diana. I'll find you."

The urgency in his voice forced her to hike up her skirts. She made it across the room and down the winding staircase to the cellar. There, she pried open the doors used to load casks and pulled herself out into the alley.

Years of disciplined training forced her to prop her back against the wall, as her eyes worked to adjust to the dark. The lane was small and she couldn't see well enough to gauge where it led.

She counted her breaths. Then counted to a hundred while she willed Ian to emerge.

He'd never let her go far without him. Not while she still wore the emeralds around her neck.

Unless something had gone horribly wrong.

And today, very little had gone right.

He was so strong; she'd never considered he'd need her to extricate him.

The crunch of broken glass made her whip around and brandish her knife.

"I told you to run." Ian grabbed her free hand and tugged her into the dark road.

"Are you all right?" she wheezed.

"No. I'm being chased by an angry mob, with my brother's intended, and no protection."

"Nonsense. I still have one knife. And you have your pistol. You just didn't want to flash it in there."

He acknowledged this with a garbled laugh as they emerged onto Russel Street.

"We'll never find a hack at this hour," he lamented breathlessly.

"There." She pointed to the end of the street. "Looks like a boarding inn?"

"Or a cathouse."

They never determined which of them was correct because a cab miraculously appeared and delivered a man to its door. Ian flung himself in its path and roared at the driver with a bellow so savage, the poor lad would have handed over the reins if Ian had asked.

His hands came around her waist. She had only a brief moment to appreciate their warmth and weight before he flung her inside the cab, pushed her skirts aside and pulled himself in next to her. He mumbled an address she couldn't hear and offered the driver double the fare if they were quick about it.

The carriage lurched, and Ian fell over beside her. She made no move to push him away. Her blood was singing from the way he'd roughly handed her into the coach and then commandeered the entire space.

When the hack evened out its course, he retreated to his side of the seat. "Forgive me."

She made a cooing noise of acknowledgment and straightened her skirts. She kept her eyes on the road ahead and fought the urge to lean into the waves of heat coming from him as she asked, "Why did you take so long to follow me?"

"I needed to find this."

His hand brushed against hers, and he placed the cold steel of her dagger in her palm.

"The police were on the way. They would have found it," he said. "They're custom-made and weighted to your grip. They would have traced it back to you."

"Yes, of course." He'd thought only of their survival, not that the knives were precious to her. "Thank you."

They rode in silence for several minutes before he murmured, "They're the same ones. From that night."

"Yes." She was elated he'd remembered. "I'm never without them."

"Even on your wedding day."

His voice was low and sardonic. It made her regret that she could no longer hide her duplicity. He wasn't hiding his disdain for it.

"I'll take you anywhere you want to go if you tell me everything," he said.

She almost confessed that would happen no matter what she told him. She could not deviate from the course she had set. Too many lives were at stake.

Including his.

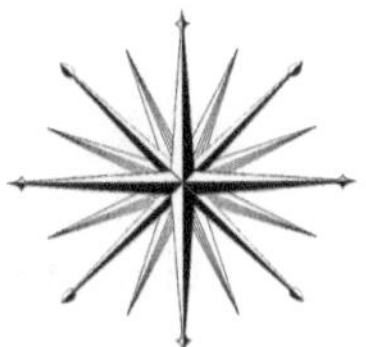

CHAPTER SEVEN

WHEN THEY ALIGHTED FROM the hack onto Holborn Street, Ian didn't offer Diana his arm. He knew she would have refused it.

His heart was still racing from the altercation at the Swan's Nest, but he was as practiced as she was in blockading his feelings, and he would be damned before he revealed how much uncovering her lies had riled him.

"This way," he said roughly. He positioned her on the inside of the path while he walked on the perimeter of the street. Despite his anger, he couldn't quash the urge to put himself between her and any threat. It gave him a satisfying sense of purpose that eased the tension gathering between his shoulder blades.

He led them down a back lane to another street behind the row of townhomes and paused at the back gate. "Come through here. There could be reporters out front."

They crossed the paved back garden, and he unlocked the kitchen door. It was dark inside and the fires were cold. He'd given the cook-maid a day out because of the wedding celebration.

"Sir?" Ian's valet emerged from the hall with a lamp. His eyes flicked to Diana momentarily before returning to Ian. "May I be of service?"

"Hepburn," Ian greeted him. "We could do with some hot water. And light supper provisions." Neither of them had eaten a thing all day.

"Of course, sir." Hepburn hesitated. "I was sorry to hear about the wedding being postponed. Mrs. Turner sent a note and advised you shouldn't return to the house because of the press."

"If there are any skulking out front, I'll need to change." Diana directed her order to Hepburn. "Could you assist me, please?"

"It would be my pleasure, miss. I'm sure we can find something that will suit. If you'd follow me."

Ian didn't object. If journalists were circling, Diana needed to shed the gown. And the emeralds.

He couldn't have dreamed up an easier way to get his hands on them. Given the revelations of the day, and everything he knew Diana to be capable of, he found the happenstance far too convenient. And more than a little alarming.

He trudged up the stairs and into his study, where he poured himself a large draft of whisky. The front bell rang and to his immense displeasure, Hepburn announced, "Mr. Eden to see you, sir."

"You shouldn't be here," Ian grumbled.

"Stop telling me that every time I call. One of these days, I'm going to think you mean it." Henry refused Ian's gesture of a whisky. "The aborted wedding is all over the evening papers. I thought you might require a hand."

"Please tell me none of those rags say anything about Polly Wren, the mother of Jared's son."

When Ian related what they'd found in Soho, Henry's jaw dangled open. He agreed to take Polly's case but cautioned it would be difficult.

"The papers mention nothing about an affair," Henry said. "They do go into excellent detail on Diana's bridal gown. And jewelry."

He paused before adding, "If you're still determined to leave with the emeralds, all of this will make your departure plans sticky."

Ian's stomach clenched. For years, he'd planted false clues and trails to suggest they'd lost the emeralds after his father's death. It was a delaying tactic, until he knew solidly that he could play the dangerous competition for them and win.

He had to approach the players with the necklace before things escalated. He couldn't risk them coming anywhere near everything and everyone he'd devoted his life to safeguarding.

Footsteps echoed from above, and Henry peered at the ceiling. "Diana's here?"

"Momentarily. And before you ask, I don't need any help getting her out of London."

"You're going with her."

"Of course not."

Henry tilted his head thoughtfully. "You could."

His tone implied, *You should.*

Ian stopped short of reminding Henry that the war he was about to battle to win the necklace meant he could never be with Diana. His role in the scheme she'd designed to avoid marrying Jared was quickly ending. And he needed to make his own fast retreat.

Henry cast his eyes upstairs again. "Every day for the past eight years, I think about what would have happened if, instead of telling Beatrix to leave England, I had offered to go with her."

"You can't play that game." Ian placed a firm hand on Henry's shoulder. "If you had, you might be at the bottom of the ocean too, old man. And then where would we all be?"

Henry gave a self-deprecating grunt on his way out the door.

Ian forced himself to partake of the tray of light sandwiches, cheese, and fruit Hepburn had left so his thoughts wouldn't fixate on the ghosts from the past. Or his fears about the future.

"May I have one of those?"

He looked up from brooding over his plate and whisky to find Diana standing by the settee, dressed in his clothes. Hepburn had altered Ian's shirt and waistcoat to fit her. Beneath the shirt, she wore a pair of fencing breeches.

The absence of her restrictive, heavy skirts allowed her to move nimbly across the room. An untamed possessiveness stirred in his gut as he admired how very right she looked wearing his clothes.

She gestured to his whisky, and he finally tore his gaze away long enough to pour her a drink.

When he handed her the glass, he noted her breeches were too closely fitted to be his. They were precisely tailored to Diana's measurements and tucked neatly into a pair of sturdy short boots. "Were you wearing the boots and the breeches beneath your dress?"

"Of course." She flapped a hand to suggest the question, and not her attire, was the ridiculous thing. "I'm afraid you've had to sacrifice these."

As she casually stroked his shirt and waistcoat, he became painfully aware of the fit of his own trousers.

"It's no matter," he said roughly.

"You will make out better in the trade. My dress cost enough to fund a coup in several countries."

Neither of them said a word about the emeralds, which weren't visible beneath the open collar of her shirt.

Diana perused the half-empty bookshelves bordering the fireplace with some interest before she sat down primly on one of the well-worn leather club chairs. "Who does this house belong to?"

"Why don't you think it belongs to me?"

When she arched her brow, he was sorely tempted to do something foolish involving his mouth and hers.

She peered at the books. "Freddie Sterling used to live here. You acquired it from him?"

He respected the careful way she positioned that question. "Lord Sterling was living far beyond his means, which he thought he'd rectify by staking this place in a game of *vingt-et-un.*"

Ian omitted telling her that Freddie Sterling was on a list of men who'd danced with Diana and tried to assume liberties. Sterling had once grazed his hands over Diana's bottom before she'd seamlessly made him stumble onto his face on the dance floor. Ian had vindictively waited for Sterling to sink himself into debt before luring him into a game he had no chance of ever winning.

"Poor Freddie." Her tone was full of mock sorrow. "He should have known better than to play with the Devil of the Docklands."

"Don't call me that."

His voice was low, suddenly grave.

Diana went very still.

They both stared at each other, daring the other to speak first, until Hepburn arrived with a delivery of letters.

"It's from Mrs. Turner." Ian sliced his letter-opener through the seal and scanned the note. "Jared woke briefly, was ill, then returned to his stupor."

"I suppose that's good news?"

"The doctor says it's small progress. Turner says the journalists are still staked outside the house."

Diana hummed as she read her own letter. "Amelia reports they're at Rives House as well. She told Mrs. Turner that I'm staying with her to avoid them."

"What is Miss Hunter's involvement in all of this?"

She kept her eyes on the note and sipped her whisky quietly.

Her silence needled him; she'd chosen reticence rather than overtly lie to him again. "Exactly how long have you been planning all this?"

"That's not the question you want answered," she replied carefully. "You want to know why events unfolded as they did."

He hated she knew this about him.

"Don't deny your hand." If she'd been a man, he would have accused her of behaving unsportsmanlike. "You orchestrated every piece of what happened today."

"I'm neither that talented nor that spiteful."

"So when you found out about Jared's transgressions, you didn't set out to ruin him completely?"

Diana slammed the whisky glass on the table and rose to her feet with such swiftness she vibrated. "We both know that the one person responsible for Jared's ruination is Jared. You've spent most of your life cleaning up after him. To what end?"

As Ian closed the distance between them, he caught the whisper of violets mixed with the scent of the soap Hepburn used to launder his shirt. It roused hot and forbidden imaginings of how else their scents and their bodies could combine.

"Why does it matter to you what I do?" he demanded.

She leaned closer, and his body followed, pulled by some outside unequal force toward her.

"You matter, Ian," she said softly.

His heart soared for a brief, jubilant moment.

Before he realized she'd stopped short of saying he mattered to *her.*

Ian backed away and poured himself another drink. "I never thought you'd go through with marrying Jared. At first, it seemed like a dare. Or a threat. Because of what happened that night you made the promise to my father, and what I said after the attack."

He swallowed. "I hurt you worse than those miscreants tried to. And it wouldn't be far-fetched to believe you needed to hurt me back."

An interval elapsed where the only sound in the room was an intermittent pop from the coals tumbling in the fireplace.

Eventually, Diana murmured, "That night... It wasn't what you thought, what everyone thought."

"A dying man made a last request for you to marry his son."

Ian's voice was icy and detached because he'd learned to become that way about his father. It was the only way to process his grief and frustration over the mess he'd left Ian to handle. "Father must have had some reason for believing you wanted to marry Jared."

"He wanted to unite his business with Rives Shipping."

"There are plenty of other ways to secure that without arranging a marriage."

"Not when the businesses were so unequal in their financial holdings," she argued. "The board of Rives Shipping would never have accepted a merger, and Jared would never concede to an acquisition."

"Then why on earth did you agree to marry him!"

His voice was still reverberating in the room when she lifted her chin and said calmly, "My mother."

It took Ian a moment to check his surprise. Diana's mother had contracted a wasting disease when they were children. It happened three years after his own mother died from a terrible fever. Harry Rives had been so stricken with grief, they'd invited no one to the funeral.

And fifteen years later, no one talked about Diana's mother, including Diana.

That she mentioned it now was weighty. He'd have to treat it delicately.

With care, he took her empty glass and refilled it.

She accepted the drink with a small huff of resignation. "When your father had the first episode with his heart, and then couldn't leave his bed, Papa was so worried. Until then, I never appreciated how close the two of them were."

Ian hadn't either. But when his father's health declined suddenly—and Jared had been unreachable doing God knew what on the Continent—Ian had left his studies at Cambridge to oversee Holt & Company. Harry Rives had generously advised him on more than a few matters. His father had left their business in a dire state. Ian spent months trying to dig out of years of mismanagement.

When Jared finally returned, his brother had forced him out of the boardroom. And he'd refused to pay Ian's fees to finish Cambridge, claiming Ian had a duty to serve the business by overseeing the docks.

"It was easy to convince Papa that I should go to London and call on Mr. Holt. And you know my reasons for coming," Diana continued. "Since your father was feeling well, I offered to read to him, hoping it would buy me time until you arrived. We were only a few pages into a Trollope novel when he stopped me. He said he was glad that I was the one who visited and not my father because he had something to show me."

Her fingers tightened around the whisky glass. She'd barely taken a sip of it because she was a far smarter creature than he.

"I respected so many things about your father," she said softly. "He knew he was dying, and he wanted to put his personal affairs in order. When he was sorting through some files, he'd found a letter that had never been unsealed. It was from my mother."

Ian's mouth parted. "I wager it wasn't some unopened dinner invitation."

"He had it tucked into his journal, and when he showed me..." She shook her head and rubbed her chest a little frantically.

If he were another man and she another woman, he would have stilled her hand by clasping it in his own.

Hell, he would have taken her into his arms.

But he was who he was, and he had a faint sense that if he made one move toward her to acknowledge the slipping of her mask, she'd retaliate. Violently.

"What did your mother write?" he asked gently.

"That she was ill, and she was afraid she wouldn't survive much longer. She wanted to ensure that her family was taken care of, and she had a vision of her daughter having a place beside him and his family one day."

She took a small sip of her drink. "It was haunting, seeing those words in her hand-writing. To be honest, I was stunned."

He would have been. "She'd never spoken of such a thing before, to you?"

"Never. Her departure from us was...abrupt. When I said nothing in reaction to the letter, your father took my hand. He said he'd watched me with his family over the years and he knew my mother was right."

She drew a breath. "'Promise me, lass,' he said. 'Promise me you'll honor our wishes. Marry my son.'"

Ian knew that part was true because he and Mrs. Turner were in the hall, approaching his father's room. They'd heard his father's request, and Diana's soft reply of acceptance.

He'd been so angry about the impending loss of his father. And his own dreams. There was so little in his control, he'd seized on the pledge he'd made to defend the emeralds and protect his family and he'd made it his calling. His father hadn't minced words about what would happen if he failed. Ian knew the man wouldn't have wanted Diana mixed up in any of it.

And he'd swindled her into believing that the promise she made was about Jared, because he'd convinced himself it was.

"I couldn't refuse your father," Diana said. "I was reeling from hearing my mother's wish, from beyond the grave. With all of that spinning through my head, I wasn't thinking clearly when you walked me home that night. If I had, I would have noticed the men in the shadows."

"I should have seen them. And I don't regret what either of us did to defend ourselves."

"Neither do I. But I am sorry about the way we parted, and what happened after."

Diana took a step closer. A faint flush rose over her cheeks.

"I never intended to marry Jared. I planned to call off the engagement, but when someone leaked it to the papers, a miraculous thing happened. Men stopped hunting me." She gave a short laugh. "It was the first taste of freedom I had since my debut, and it was glorious."

He couldn't find relief in her confession because her proximity and the whisky were making his blood heat.

"My father might have been happier than me." She laughed again, this time with affection, as she brushed her eyes. "He wanted Jared nowhere near Rives Shipping. It was his idea to keep up the charade of the engagement until I was ready to call it off. The ruse gave me the chance to learn his business. It allowed me to step in when his own health began to falter."

She'd had years with her father, which Ian envied. "Still, after he died, you had the entire mourning period to end the engagement. There was no need for such a dramatic exit from your betrothal."

Her small sigh carried an edge of exasperation. "I'm not as Machiavellian as you think. I expected Jared to overindulge the night before the wedding, and I'd planned to confront him about Polly this morning. But he went missing, and I needed to know what happened. You did too."

He didn't want to believe her explanation. It made it too easy for him to surrender to his desires, and he couldn't betray his duty to his father.

"Where do we go from here?" he asked.

"I need some time to think through what happens next. Away from London," she replied. "Will you help me with the final stage of my escape?"

She sounded tentative.

He hated that their constant jockeying with each other made her believe he'd willfully refuse her anything. "Tell me where you wish to go, and I shall escort you safely there."

The smile she rewarded him with was so bright and so quick, it momentarily blinded him. "I must visit my man of business at the shipping office."

"I'll have Hepburn hail a cab on the high street, while you gather your things."

Hepburn also produced an overcoat and hat for Diana. As she pulled the coat around her, she squirmed. "I must have missed a button."

"No, it fastens from the inside." As Ian reached inside the lapel, his fingers grazed her breast.

Her breath caught on a soft hiss.

He froze.

With one small motion, he could lean over and claim the kiss they should have shared eight years ago. The one that had consumed his dreams and his waking fantasies.

It would be sweet. Too sweet to stop at merely a kiss.

And if he acted on the impulse, it would make their impending separation unreservedly brutal.

He quickly fastened the inner clasp of the coat, and then the outer buttons, and stepped aside to lead her out the back door.

They darted through the dark street and took turns glancing behind them to ensure no one followed them. At the corner of the high street, Hepburn had a hack waiting. Diana threw the valet one of her dazzling smiles, and they climbed into the carriage.

As the taxi lurched forward, she remarked, "Hepburn is exceptionally talented. I hope you pay him well."

"He's undoubtedly the most overpaid valet in London." Hepburn was also more than a valet. Which he suspected Diana knew.

"I left the dress in your guest room," she said softly.

"Hepburn will see to it," he assured her.

"There was one thing I thought you should look after."

Diana took his hand. He hadn't put on his gloves yet, and the bare touch of her fingers burned his skin as the cold weight of the emeralds filled his palm.

She folded his fingers over to cradle the gems. "Now I can be certain that you're staring at me and not some shiny object."

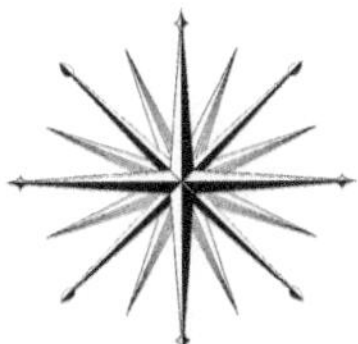

CHAPTER EIGHT

The emeralds sat like an anvil in Ian's breast pocket.

Diana had handed them to him like they were a pair of gloves, or a reticule she'd borrowed from a friend.

Acquiring them with such little effort on his own part left him wanting. She couldn't appreciate how important the necklace was to him, and this rubbed at him, even though he knew he should be grateful she'd never know what he'd planned on risking to possess it.

Defending the emeralds would require immersing himself in a world of orchestrated crime. Ian didn't fool himself into believing he had even a slim chance of ever escaping. Once he left England with the necklace in hand, he could never risk seeing Diana again.

But he would send her off with a proper farewell.

At the docks, he followed Diana along the pier to the warehouse that housed Rives Shipping's London offices. When Diana removed a key from her pocket and unlocked the door, they found the place deserted.

"Damn, we've missed them." She wrinkled her nose at the clock mounted on the wall. "I was hoping to catch my head of engineering before he departed."

"Why is he here in London if he's your head engineer?" Ian asked. "Shouldn't he oversee the building operations in the Bristol shipyard?"

"He goes back and forth. He's training his deputy to oversee construction so he can focus on designing. And representing the business side of things. Contracts, suppliers, and such."

"It sounds like a massive job."

"It is."

"Too big for one man alone."

Her chin twisted over her shoulder. "My team are quite talented."

"As are you."

"If you're implying that my temporary absence will impact the business, you shouldn't fret."

"That isn't what worries me," Ian said darkly. He wanted to know where she was planning to flee to. It amused him mildly that she persisted with any attempt to conceal her destination.

Eventually, he'd find her. After he won the emeralds. When it was safer for him to search for her.

The front office bell chimed, and a breathless messenger rifled through his satchel. "Rives Shipping?"

"I'll take it." Diana ignored the way the man's mouth twitched when he took in her hat and garb as he handed her a parcel wrapped in pink ribbon.

Ian paid the man, locked the door, and checked that the deadbolt lock was sound.

"It's a legal notice," Diana said haltingly. "From the chambers of Bates Holloway."

Ian paused. "They represented my father."

She flicked the ribbon apart with her knife and rifled through the first page. "This is a notice for Rives Shipping to vacate the warehouse and the docks. There's a contract for possession and sale of the building." She passed each page to Ian after she quietly read it. On the last page, she hesitated. "That's my signature."

When she looked up, her face was pale. "It's a forgery, obviously."

"A bloody good one." There were only one or two counterfeiters who could produce such high-quality fakes. "Now we know why Jared was at the Swan's Nest. He must be desperate for funds if he's embroiled himself with the Skinner's Lane Lads."

Diana made an unladylike sound of disgust in the back of her throat. "He knew it would take time after the wedding to get his hands on the bank accounts, so he tried to get a quick sale."

"One of those toughs could have drugged him."

She worried her lip. "But if Jared was paying them, why would they need to?"

A forceful fist pounded at the door. "Open up. City police."

Diana slowly shook her head. They both knew whoever was at the door was not a legitimate member of law enforcement. She motioned for him to follow her into the dimly lit interior office in the back, and Ian alarmingly noted the door had no lock.

The pounding outside grew louder, and the floorboards shook, until the noise suddenly halted.

Then came the unmistakable echo of shattering glass.

They've broken in, Ian mouthed.

Diana darted to the back of the room and drew aside a drape to a small broom cupboard.

"We won't both fit—"

She covered his mouth with her hand, pushed him inside, and pulled the curtain closed.

They fell into each other. As she tried to right her balance, his arms came around her. There was no spare space to turn, nowhere else for him to put his hands without smashing something that would call attention to their presence.

There was a crashing sound of the front door being flung open, and several sets of heavy footsteps clomped across the wooden floorboards.

Diana's breath came in jagged, hot bursts that warmed his neck. He grasped for some action to calm her. But he could only tighten his hold to still his shaking hands. He held her so close he had no doubt she could detect the wild pace of his heart.

When she leaned into his embrace, exultation warmed his limbs. His mind took a brief jaunt into a fantasy where that heat built between them, and their clothes evaporated and they were touching skin to skin. Lips to lips.

A few feet away, the ruffians dragged furniture across the floor, but Ian couldn't make out what the harsh, muffled voices were saying.

Diana's arms tightened around his waist, and his hand instinctively cupped the back of her head. "You have your knives?"

"Of course. Your pistol?"

"At the ready."

The door to the inner office rattled.

He tensed, bracing himself. "If they find us, I will throw the first punch to disarm them. But if I can't—"

"Knives, then pistol," Diana finished.

An inelegant clatter arose in the front office.

"What's going on here?" a familiar voice echoed loudly. "Who are you?"

A muted exchange followed. Furniture thumped and doorknobs rattled.

Then silence descended.

Diana's arms trembled around him.

"Hello? Miss Rives? Mr. Holt? If you're here, it's safe to come out. They've gone now."

Ian relinquished his hold on Diana. He flung back the curtain and yanked open the door. "Hepburn."

"Are you well, sir?"

Diana gave a startled laugh. "Your timing was exquisite."

"The intruders skived off. They claimed they were with the police." Hepburn's lip curled as he took in the mess they'd left.

Ian searched the tumbled outer office for an indication of exactly how much trouble they were in. "What did the fake coppers claim they were looking for?"

"You, sir." Hepburn nodded at Ian. "Two more came to the house. They must have been watching and followed you here."

"Did they take anything?" Ian asked.

"Doesn't appear like it. But they made this place a disaster, the filthy cretins."

"Everything important is in the safe," Diana said. "Did they say why they were looking for Mr. Holt?"

"Allegedly, someone saw Mr. Holt at a tavern that was the scene of an exchange of knives and counterfeit notes."

The odds of the Metropolitan Police Constabulary working that quickly to track them down were as probable as Ian inheriting the throne. The Skinner's Lane Lads had sent the men.

It wasn't anything Ian couldn't handle. But he'd manage it better knowing Diana was out of the fray. She had to leave London tonight.

Hepburn left to summon the port-side guards while Diana surveyed the ransacked room. She shook her head. "Jared is in more trouble than either of us suspected. And if it slipped past both of us, some clever people are manipulating him."

Although she'd included herself in the blame, the observation landed like an admonishment.

"I'll take care of it," he clipped.

"You shouldn't handle it alone."

"Is that an offer?"

Her blush deepened; she hadn't expected he'd call that bluff. Or perhaps she colored because, despite his indifferent tone, he regarded her more openly than he'd ever allowed himself to in the past.

The very act of trying to conceal it seemed ridiculous at this point. Their remaining time together would be measured in minutes.

He was suddenly angry he'd spent their brief interlude in the cupboard terrified for her safety and overwhelmed by holding her. If he had acted more like the scoundrel everyone thought he was, at least he could have touched and tasted her the way he dreamed about.

In a hushed voice, Diana asked, "Do you want me to stay?"

He needed her to be on the other side of the planet, but he selfishly wanted to believe the only way to truly protect her was to keep her by his side. "The safest thing is for you to leave. As soon as possible."

She looked forlornly at the remnants of the room before lifting her gaze to his. "There's a ship waiting. Will you walk with me?"

He agreed before she finished asking.

CHAPTER NINE

As they traversed the docklands, Diana was in danger of losing her nerve.

Her mission had consumed her for years. She'd devoted the best of herself to it; given it her dreams and aspirations, along with a good deal of her fortune.

A few words from Ian could convince her to toss it all away.

As the dim light from the gas lamps gilded his handsome silhouette, she pleaded with him silently.

Ask to come with me.

Ian watched the dark water lap against the dock. He needed to capture every sight and sound and scent of these last moments with Diana to preserve them in his memory.

Hazy lamplight and fog obscured the ship moored in the distance. The wind stirred and bit at his cheeks. As he turned to shield himself from it, the sight of Diana pulling his coat close around her neck roused a deep ache in his chest.

"None of this was about revenge, you know," she whispered. "I wish Jared no ill will. And I do hope Henry can help Polly and Johnny."

Ian refused to think about Henry's suggestion that he accompany Diana. If she'd even allow Ian to accompany her, he'd never extract her from the factions warring over the emeralds, and he wouldn't risk her life out of his selfish desire to be with her.

But he bloody well wasn't letting her out of his sight without finding out some clue about where she was heading.

He squinted at the boat ahead of them and swallowed his frustration that he couldn't make out the name or defining marks from a distance. "When do you make sail?"

"Sooner than I wish."

Imminently, she'd be too far out of reach to touch, and that anxious thought prompted him to draw closer to her. He thrilled as her breath faltered.

"Whatever you're going to ask me, I likely can't answer," she insisted primly. "I know you hoped to interrogate me. I can detect your intention plain as day on your face. When your jaw clenches like that, you're downright sinister."

Confessing that she'd paid such close attention was careless. The very opposite of guarding herself.

His heart wanted to fly, if not for the questions that plagued him.

"We're here in the docklands, and I'm its devil," he said, his voice low. "You seem to be the only person who isn't afraid of what I do here."

"And you seem to be the only person who's afraid of what *I* could do here."

To prove her wrong, he stepped closer. In the cold of the evening, the visible white trails of their breaths mingled. "I could make you talk."

Her smile flashed a brilliant white streak as she slowly shook her head.

"At least tell me where you're going." *So I can find you*, he omitted.

"I can't," she said kindly, as she would to a child.

He detested it because she was trying to be gentle when all he wanted was something forceful to break him away from the need to be beside her.

"The boat doesn't have a route filed with the harbormaster, which isn't entirely legal, and the police will try to question you about what happened at the Swan's Nest," she added. "This way, you won't be forced to admit you were a part of my plot to disappear."

"Merely one of your tools to implement it."

"No. You're the reason I succeeded."

Her cheeks were stained red; he hoped it wasn't just from the wind, that it was because she felt the same restless heat that plagued him.

The dock swayed with the tide, edging them closer together, and he couldn't resist placing his hand at her waist.

"You didn't need to make me a part of this," he rasped. "Tell me why you did."

"You've watched over me one way or another since we were children. I used to think it was because my father wasn't the protective sort, and you needed something to protect. It took me a long time to realize the reason you were paying such close attention was something entirely different."

He couldn't deny it. Not with the way she gazed at him, her eyes clear and calm, and her plump mouth parted.

Slowly, he brushed a knuckle down her cheek; her skin was softer than velvet. She trembled, and the surge of joy and relief at her reaction, at what they were admitting, made his hands shake.

He cupped her face. "You need protecting because you draw danger to you. Everything is drawn to you, Diana. Including me."

"I wish we had more time."

"I wish I could go with you."

She gave a faint moan that collided with his. But now that he'd spoken the desire aloud, he couldn't stop there.

"I wish neither of us were bound to our obligations. And no one else's lives hinged on the choices we made." His eyes traced her face. "And I wish I had the strength to let you go without it feeling like I'm being sliced open and losing the very best part of myself."

Diana reeled him in by the lapels of his coat and pressed her lips to his.

He experienced the impact in every atom of his body.

Her mouth was cool at first, then deliciously hot as friction built between them. The faint scent of whisky lingered on her breath. It made him ravenous for her taste, which was beyond anything his fantasies had conjured over the years.

As his arms tightened around her, he teased her lips open with his tongue. She gave a feverish little groan and responded to his advance by sampling him, adding and releasing pressure. He would have praised her for it and commanded her to apply those clever lips in an array of obscene ways, but he couldn't stop kissing her.

She savored his mouth with equal fervor. There was an underlying urgency in the way she hardly stopped for a breath; it echoed his own desperation. Her hands dove into his coat and began an exploration of his torso, which made him gasp, and he swore she laughed in the back of her throat.

A sharp whistle tore through the air.

It sounded suspiciously like the one Diana had deployed at the pub.

Ian broke the kiss but couldn't bring himself to lose contact with her entirely. He pressed her face into his neck, terrified he'd blurt out the only thought that consumed him.

Ask me to come with you.

His pride wouldn't allow him to beg; his common sense reminded him of the harm that could befall Diana if he joined her.

But his heart didn't care what his pride or his sense wanted.

The whistle blew again, and Diana physically started. Her eyes roved his face with something like wonder, and something like pain, which was the expression he imagined he was wearing.

He couldn't go with her. He needed to leave London himself. And he didn't want her to witness what he'd have to become to protect her, and his promise to his father.

Wordlessly, he gestured to the ramp that led down to the wharf.

"I can go from here. It's not that I wouldn't prefer your company," she added quickly. "But I'm struggling with my conscience at the moment."

He was struggling with everything, but her honesty made him acquiesce. "I'll bid you farewell from here. But I shall stay and watch for a while."

"Thank you." She placed a hand on his cheek. It was gone before he fully registered she'd touched him again, and in the next blink of his eye, she'd darted down the gangplank.

Her trim figure bobbed along the pier. As she swung up onto the boat with alacrity, it resurrected his suspicion until he reminded himself that she'd grown up in her father's shipyard.

A horn blew, and the boat pulled away from the dock. Diana walked around and stood at the stern. Ian wanted to believe she was staring back at him, but it was impossible to tell in the darkness, with mist blanketing the river.

He watched devotedly and wouldn't allow himself to blink until the ship was out of sight. Only then would he accept his last moment with her had ended.

"I can't believe you let her go."

For a frantic moment, Ian imagined the voice was his disembodied conscience before Leo Ashton stepped out of the fog.

"Your...Grace?" There was no rational explanation for the duke's sudden arrival. "What in God's name are you doing here?"

The duke raised a compact spyglass and replied, "Spying, Holt."

Sunderland had worked for the Royal Navy before unexpectedly inheriting his title, and the gossips whispered he continued on in clandestine service. The duke enjoyed stoking those rumors.

As a devil himself, Ian knew it could have served as an excellent cover.

"How long have you been watching my family?" Ian's low rasp was uncivil, but given the events of the day, he was overly enthusiastic to crush something. Or someone.

"Jared isn't the one who interests me," Sunderland said plainly.

Ian stepped in between the duke and his view of the departing ship. "Diana Rives has nothing to do with Her Majesty's military."

"Not true. Her father's company has more shipbuilding contracts with the navy than anyone else in Britain."

"Her company," Ian corrected.

"Yes, and wasn't it supposed to become your brother's?"

"Is that why you were keeping such a close eye on him?"

A trace of a smirk played on the duke's face. "I caught wind of Jared's meeting at the Swan's Nest. Your brother collected some counterfeit papers. But he also made inquiries about selling the Holt emeralds."

Ian paused. "That was foolish of him."

"Indeed," the duke agreed. "Especially since that necklace can never be bought or sold. It must be won. But you knew that."

Apparently, Jared hadn't. Or he'd refused to believe the stories that were more truth than tale. Ian had never uttered the words *Il Gioco* to his brother, but he assumed, wrongly, that their father had warned Jared about the dangerous game and the criminals they'd hidden the gems from for years.

Jared didn't own the necklace because Jared had never had the chance to win it. And suggesting he had a right to sell it, without earning it in the first place, was more dangerous than entangling himself with counterfeit thugs.

"The *Il Gioco* legend is a favorite of mine." Sunderland's grin turned predatory at Ian's silence. "Three *famiglie* who all have historic claim to one notorious set of jewels. It's deliciously heathen to imagine they all played to the death purely for the bragging rights to own it. Once upon a time."

"What an incredible story," Ian said faintly.

"Truly," the duke agreed enthusiastically. "Imagine my disappointment when I encountered a prominent player at the Swan's Nest, and he refused to divulge what was real and what was fiction."

He was referring to the silver-haired man Diana and Ian had seen at the pub. The reprobate could have sent the brutes who ransacked the shipping office.

"Is there a credible threat to my family?" Ian demanded.

"Not that I know of, but we haven't ruled it out. Of course, this," the duke gestured to Diana's departing vessel with his spyglass, "is a complication."

When Ian's silence offered a tacit accord, Sunderland gave a low laugh. "Why did you let her go?"

"She was never mine to lose."

Good Lord, he sounded pathetic.

It was enough to draw a louder laugh from the duke. "No, you clodpate. I meant why did you let her escape with that fortune in emeralds around her neck?"

Ian's hand dove into his waistcoat. And found his pockets empty.

His head snapped toward the river. There was hardly a ripple left from the boat; it had receded into the fog.

He swung back around to Sunderland.

The duke lifted his spyglass as proof of his accusation. "Now why would one of the richest women in Great Britain need to steal the Holt emeralds?" Sunderland mused. "She might know some of the legend, but does she know what's attached to them?"

Blood beat loudly in Ian's ears, and he expelled a string of curses in every language he spoke.

With that searing kiss, Diana had betrayed him. And put herself in more danger.

Sunderland, damn him, was standing in the middle of the dock, watching intently. Ian brushed past him, but the duke halted him with a commanding grip on his arm.

"Your show is over for the evening, Your Grace. Let me go." He had no time to clean up a puddle of aristocratic blood tonight. He had to find out what course they were charting before Diana was halfway to France or Flanders, or God help him, the Antipodes.

"Easy, old man. The tug she boarded is bound to Bristol." Sunderland lifted a battered silver pocket watch from his pocket. "If you hurry, you can catch the nine o'clock out of King's Cross. You might beat her there."

This helpful suggestion was insipidly convenient, which gave Ian pause. He evaluated the duke and his sly spyglass before he reached into his pocket to palm his pistol. "Why have you made this your business, Duke?"

"I enjoy amassing favors. And make no mistake, Holt, I will collect on it. Your Miss Rives is part of something that could threaten the Crown and its allies abroad. She's put herself in the crosshairs of some nasty people who are looking for that necklace. You know how to reclaim it and keep her safe. And I need to know whose side she's playing for."

So did Ian.

Diana had entwined him in her escape to prevent him from stealing the emeralds himself. The kiss they'd shared was the perfect distraction; he couldn't have concocted a better ruse himself to cover her theft of the necklace.

And yet...

The way she'd kissed him hadn't felt like a goodbye kiss. On the contrary.

It had felt like an invitation.

Perhaps he was deluding himself, but the only way he could make sense of her actions was to believe that she wanted him to follow her.

She was practically daring him to.

"Any of the *famiglie* could have targeted Diana and coerced her to take the necklace," Ian said.

"The alternative is that Miss Rives could be as dangerous as the other scoundrels vying for the necklace," Sunderland replied. "You can either leave it for us to find out...or you can go after her."

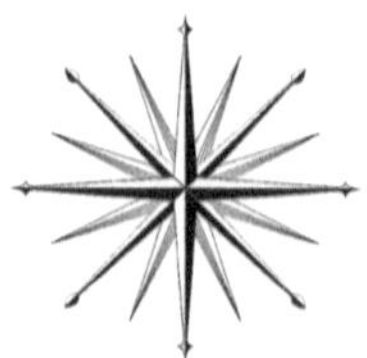

CHAPTER TEN

As the sun set over Bristol Harbor the next evening, Diana stared out the window of Rives Shipping's wharf-side offices and tried to appreciate the small joy of a beautiful view.

The plush chair she sat on and the bitter hot coffee she sipped at were temporary comforts. She hadn't slept on the journey from London, and there had been too much to do when she'd arrived in Bristol to stop for rest. Widow's new orders compelled them to depart two days earlier than planned. Diana couldn't sleep until her crew was ready to make sail.

Birdie knocked on the open door. "Miss Hunter and Captain Virgil are here, ma'am."

Diana motioned for them to come through and rose from her desk. "Will we be ready to leave by midnight?"

"All-a-taunto. The crew has signed on to the special conditions," Amelia confirmed. They were paying the sailors handsomely for their silence about the first voyage of the company's newest ship, the *Ever Hart*.

"Her Majesty's Navy is keen to understand how the ship will maneuver along the Channel Islands," the captain added. "They're giving us a long leash on our navigation plans. And paying a generous incentive if we can prove *Ever Hart* will surpass fifteen knots."

Diana nodded. She'd written the contract herself. Payment from the navy offset the costs of the Stags's operations and would make the ship more attractive to potential commercial buyers. "Well done, sorting this out so quickly. How are we on cargo?"

"Ready to load after sundown," Birdie said. She managed a crew of women trained as sailors and deckhands, but their first duty was guarding the precious shipment the *Ever Hart* carried.

Diana massaged the back of her neck so her head would stop throbbing. Normally she was clearheaded before departure, but following her tumultuous escape from London, she found herself vacillating between hypervigilance and feeling completely dazed. "Make sure there's enough light at the pier so no one trips over the gangway, but don't blaze the place up. We don't want to draw unnecessary notice. I'll meet you on deck within the hour."

Virgil ducked out quickly, but Birdie lingered in the office. She observed Amelia for a long moment before addressing Diana.

"Holt's on the move from the hotel. He's headed to the docks. Alone."

Diana made a concerted effort to keep her expression from revealing any overt signs of relief. She'd been on pins and needles throughout the night and most of the day, dreading the possibility that she'd pushed Ian too far with that kiss. "We were expecting him to follow the emeralds."

Birdie crossed her arms. "He'll want onboard."

"If so, we'll interview Mr. Holt, exactly like any of our hands." A steamship the size and scale of *Ever Hart*—even when running with a fraction of its occupancy—depended on a cadre of staff: cooks, maids, and the strong men who performed the back-breaking work of feeding the coal boilers were as important as the sailors who manned the lines.

"And will Holt pass inspection?"

"Is it your job to question if he will?"

Birdie ducked her head. "It's a risk, ma'am. He's not one of us. Widow won't like it."

Their handler would, in fact, hate it.

After years of proving her loyalty to the Stags, Diana now oversaw her own operations. Her frustrations with the secrecy and the blind allegiance the Stags demanded of her faded every time she shuttled women out of danger, to a place where they could flourish.

But this mission would be different. Diana couldn't comply with Widow's strict orders to leave Ian Holt behind.

"I will manage Mr. Holt. Please let Virgil know to expect him. He'll be arriving any moment."

On her way out, Birdie stole another furtive look at Amelia before she slammed the door.

Amelia made a throaty noise that sounded surprisingly aggressive. "She really dislikes me."

"Nonsense. She doesn't trust you."

"It's what happens when one asks too many pointed questions."

Amelia and Diana each had their own reasons for passionately taking to the mission of the White Stags. And they both knew the danger involved with rescuing women from abusive situations and helping resettle them in new lives.

But last year, Amelia had uncovered a disturbing pattern. Funds that were supposed to be dedicated to specific Stag operations vanished. The missing money correlated with the dates and locations of targeted acts of violence. Against criminals known for trafficking people.

Diana placed her hand on Amelia's arm. She would have embraced her friend, had Amy not been so uncomfortable with hugging. "Dear, if you hadn't asked those questions, we could still be oblivious to the fact that there's a traitor in the ranks."

"It took a while to convince you."

"I was furious with you, for doubting the cause," Diana admitted with a faint wince. "It felt like a betrayal, which was so childish. Other than Beatrix, you're the closest thing I've had to family."

Amelia's soft smile made her violet eyes crinkle. "Thank you for saying that. I feel the same about you. That's why it was so hard to tell you about what I'd found."

"I didn't want to believe it."

"Neither did I. It's world-shattering to discover the reason one gets out of bed in the morning is a complete charade."

"We won't let it be. We're going to track down and obliterate the turncoats. It's the only way we can ensure the mission continues. It has to."

Amelia glanced at the door. "What do you intend to tell Ian?"

Diana was relieved, and encouraged, that he'd followed her. But he'd want retribution for her deception. "He's too furious with me for stealing the emeralds to think straight. I'm worried if he comes aboard, he'll lash out and terrify a passenger."

"Despite his devilish reputation, I find it hard to believe Ian would become...forceful with a woman or a child."

"No. But he'll want his pound of flesh for what I did, and he may not care who stands in the way of it."

They both contemplated this as they evaluated the tranquil waves in the harbor.

"If your suspicion about the emeralds is right..." Amelia ventured.

"He has to come with us," Diana finished. "For his own good."

"He'll be less angry if you tell him why we're doing this."

"Can't risk it before we set sail. When he's calmer, there's a better chance he'll believe me."

"And what about San Genaro?"

Diana hesitated. "When it's safe, I'll tell him."

Amelia remained quiet as she ran the length of her finger along the velvet seam of her sleeve in a rhythmic motion. Their schoolmistress had rapped Amelia's knuckles countless times, but it hadn't curtailed the habit.

"Is anything else bothering you, Amy?"

"We're not putting Ian at more risk by taking him with us, are we?"

The same thought had chased Diana all the way from London. "The emeralds have nothing to do with our mission to protect women. Someone in our organization is using the necklace as a pawn to entrap criminals who want to claim it. And Ian can't extricate himself from the chase." She dropped her voice. "I think the Stags want him to become collateral damage."

Diana wouldn't allow it. And she'd never forgive herself if her efforts to capture the traitors in her own organization jeopardized him.

"Then I shall interview Mr. Holt about his interest in the ship," Amelia resolved. "Let's hope he has enough sense to pass inspection."

Compared to London's docks, Bristol's floating harbor was practically quaint.

It made Ian's skin crawl.

The narrow lanes and hundreds of workers employed in various ends of the shipping trade made for a densely populated square mile along the riverfront. As he strode along the docks, more than a few heads turned in his direction.

In London, he was used to people staring at him. On the occasions he found himself in a packed ballroom, or on the streets in Mayfair, the olive shade of his skin and the thick, dark hair and eyes that he'd inherited from his mother made him stand apart. But in his corner of the docklands, people knew him. He'd taken the security of that infamy for granted.

He ducked into the narrow alleyway between two large warehouses belonging to Rives Shipping. Thankfully, he did not have to wait long before Hepburn made his way through the sea of bodies. Revulsion painted his features as he picked through the crowd to meet Ian.

"I packed the essentials." Hepburn handed him a saddle valise. "Did you figure out which ship it is?"

"There's only one moored at the pier. Everything else is in dry dock. It has to be that one." Ian nodded to the nearest ship in the distance. "I take it the harbormaster did not confirm a sailing?"

"Nothing filed. But he said if it's a commission from the Royal Navy, they wouldn't alert them until after they set sail. The lad pulling pints at the Angler's Arms was much more forthcoming."

"Barmen usually are."

"There's talk at the tavern that a new ship pulls out tonight, at midnight. And not everyone's happy about it. Apparently, the captain's selective about who they take on as crew."

"The smith in the yard said the same."

If Diana wanted Ian to follow her, he wouldn't stroll onto her ship easily, which he appreciated. It made it feel less like a trap.

More like a lure.

A little like a seduction.

"There are some letters I need you to attend to."

Ian withdrew a stack of notes from his pocket and handed them to Hepburn. Even if he retrieved the emeralds from Diana quickly, he wasn't returning to England. He buried the thought that if things went poorly, he'd never see its shores again.

"The first one is for Henry Eden. He's in desperate need of a valet, although he will never confess it. Don't worry, he's got plenty of money to pay your demanding salary. It will benefit both of us to have you placed in his household."

It would provide Ian with a back channel for Henry's legal counsel, should he need it.

"The second note is for Mrs. Turner." The carefully worded missive informed Jared's housekeeper that Ian had been called away on urgent business and instructed her to send word through Henry if there was any change in his brother's condition.

"And one last thing," Ian added. "When you return to London, there's a bank draft to pay off the bill at Sunderland's. I'd prefer you handle it personally."

The amount was a cipher that would set up a protocol to communicate with the duke directly. In exchange, Sunderland would apprise Ian if the duke's sources uncovered information about the players hunting the necklace.

"Consider it done." Hepburn nodded. "It's been a privilege, sir. I wish you safe travels."

Ian cleared his throat, which had grown suddenly tight. "Thank you, Hepburn. And best of luck to you with Henry. You will need all the patience you gained over these last few years with me."

When the clock tower in the distance chimed ten bells and the crowd had thinned, Ian emerged from the alley and walked toward the dock where the liner rose from its harbor mooring. The ship was smaller than the other hulking vessels in port and designed for both speed and to accommodate the new canal in Suez.

He contemplated how far Diana intended to lead him on this pursuit for the emeralds. Was she bound for Calcutta, or all the way to Melbourne?

"Oi, you." A burly man stepped in front of him. "Why you hangin' about here?"

Ian scanned the dock for other shadows, but the man appeared to be alone. "I heard at the Angler's Arms that this ship is taking on crew."

"Ya heard wrong." The guard gave him a shove and sputtered a rough laugh when Ian hardly moved.

Ian placed his valise on the ground. "I'm not here to cause trouble."

"Then leave."

"I only want—"

A meaty fist came at his jaw. Ian ducked the blow before it could meet its mark and delivered a right hook that snapped the other man's head back.

"You'll regret that, you bloody little—"

Ian socked him in the kidneys.

As the man doubled over in pain, Ian circled him with his fists raised. "Listen, mate, I don't want carnage here. I only want to talk to the captain of that ship."

His assailant came from his left side and caught a swipe at his cheek. In doing so, the fool left his own right side unprotected from Ian's left hook. The force of the punch made the guard stagger back. He fell onto the dock, and his head landed with a thud.

Before he could confirm if the man was temporarily or permanently knocked out, a shrill whistle sounded in the distance.

Six figures emerged from the shadows. Each of them pointed a gun at him.

A tall woman wearing a mariner cap and oilskin coat greeted him with a jagged smile as she snatched the pistol holstered inside his coat. "You've stirred up trouble, pet."

While they marched him into an empty warehouse, Ian silently upbraided himself for not going for his pistol sooner.

He wouldn't make the mistake again.

A man as brawny as the guard he'd felled searched him for hidden weapons and shoved him through a door.

"Well, you've caused quite the palaver," Amelia Hunter greeted him pleasantly.

Ian's jaw hinged open before he snapped it shut. Demands perched on his tongue—all of them having to do with Diana—but his attention quickly fixed on the man who sat next to Amelia at a spartan wooden table. He was neatly attired, with a groomed mustache, which made Ian think of every military officer he'd met.

"Won't you sit down, Mr. Holt?" Miss Hunter asked in a genteel voice.

The nicety grated on his nerves. As he clenched his teeth and slowly sank onto the chair, he hoped he appeared as menacing as Diana accused him of looking.

Miss Hunter nodded at her companion. "May I introduce Captain Virgil."

Unlikely the man's real name. But he had the mien of a mariner about him, and Ian tipped his head respectfully.

"Now, Mr. Holt. I believe you were making inquiries about a vessel."

Miss Hunter's gaze was evaluating. Unnerving, Ian realized. He'd never noticed her stare linger long on anyone. If she had a clue how disarming her ethereal violet eyes could be, she'd have half of London on their knees.

"I hadn't realized you were in the shipping business, Miss Hunter," he said slowly. "Is the ship yours?"

"No. But I own the title to the cargo on board. It's of great value to me. So naturally, I'm concerned when a person of my acquaintance has displayed such a violent interest in the vessel."

Ian pursed his lips together and tasted blood from his scuffle with the guard. Diana was taunting him with this pretense of an interview, and the admonishment of his less than gracious manners was trying his patience. He hated having his back to the room; he had to shift his eyes constantly to keep watch over his unfamiliar surroundings. He wanted to ask Miss Hunter plainly where the hell she was hiding Diana, and if they'd lost their minds completely by making off with the Holt emeralds.

Neither Amelia nor Diana needed to sell the necklace for money. They were not women who'd stake their lives on a set of pretty gems. Other than the outright animosity she'd shown occasionally to the Duke of Sunderland, no other woman in Ian's acquaintance had tried harder to blend in with the wall than Amelia Hunter.

Yet here she was, coolly and confidently managing him.

Like an expert negotiator.

Ian braced his arms over his knees. "Perhaps I can be of service ensuring the protection of your valuable cargo."

"Forgive me, Mr. Holt, but if there are others pursuing you, you'll endanger it. Gravely."

"Only one person knows of my intent to board the ship." *At the moment.* "They won't follow me. And there's no need to be concerned about my brother. Jared will chase whatever breadcrumb trail you've scattered leading away from Miss Rives."

"What will you do when you meet her again?"

His attention snagged on her use of the word *when*, not *if*. He would have grinned had he not been so furious it was evidence of Diana toying with him. "I would never harm Miss Rives."

"No man ever keeps that kind of a promise."

The low steadiness in her tone made his chest tight. He was the Devil of the Docklands. He might convince Amelia Hunter he'd never turn a fist on Diana, but she expected him to hurt her in other ways.

"The last thing I want is for anything to happen to her," he said as evenly as he could manage.

For a long moment, Miss Hunter searched his expression for any sign that would belie the responses he'd given her.

Eventually, she turned to Virgil. "I believe that answers all my questions."

The captain tilted his head and inspected Ian in a way that made him feel like livestock. "In your enthusiasm to board my ship, Mr. Holt, you've disabled my best coaler. I'm now down a hand with less than an hour until we set sail. Do you make it a practice of assaulting men to extract information?"

"Your associate attacked me. I was merely defending myself."

"Yes. I wonder why you didn't use your pistol. It would have sped things up considerably."

"It would have escalated the situation beyond what was necessary."

"Tell me one good reason I shouldn't contact the police about a man in possession of a gun, sniffing around my ship."

Every time Virgil referred to the vessel as "his" ship, Ian had to suppress the urge to laugh. He could practically hear Diana coaching the man on what to say. "Your crew also possesses firearms. There's no law against it."

"Still, it would put me at ease to know why you and your pistol want to set sail on this voyage."

Virgil was graciously tenacious in his questioning. In another life, Ian might have liked the fellow. "I am eager to leave England for new horizons. You're the only ship casting off tonight."

The captain folded his arms across his chest. "If you were to join my crew, Holt, our rules are more than requirements. They are the law when we're at sea."

"I expect I would have no trouble with your charter."

"And I cannot return your pistol to you until the journey is complete."

"Understood." Ian nodded. He'd track it down within a day.

"Then I believe we're finished here. Welcome aboard, Holt." Virgil rose from the table. "Birdie's outside. She'll get you sorted with a bunk."

"Aye, sir." Ian stood and offered a conciliatory bow of his head.

Amelia gave him a final piercing look that Ian took as a blatant warning before she followed the captain.

Outside, the woman in the oilskin coat, Birdie, leaned lazily against the warehouse wall. She watched Ian like a gull scanning the shore at low tide. "Have you agreed to behave yourself? 'Cos if not, I enjoy renderin' a bit of the old discipline, now and again."

At Ian's silence, she pushed herself off the building and led him to the gangplank. He searched the dark foredeck for some sign of Diana, but only spotted deckhands moving about. At the stern, one of them hung up a lantern. It bobbed back and forth, and the light cascaded over the port side of the ship, where they'd painted the vessel's name in neat, white letters.

Ever Hart.

Ian released a rough laugh.

Birdie rolled her eyes. "It ain't a mistake. Thought a toff like you would know what a hart is."

He smirked, unwilling to let on that he knew bloody well that a hart was a more poetic name for a red stag. "Haven't read much Homer, have you, Birdie?"

"No, pet. Been meanin' to, after I have the ballroom redecorated."

Her sarcasm was original. Ian was beginning to enjoy it. "He's the ancient Greek poet who composed the *Iliad* and the *Odyssey*. They say Homer was the first person to transcribe the oral tradition of Greek myths. If you know how to navigate by the stars, I reckon you've heard about the Greek gods and goddesses."

"Aye, I know my constellations and some stories."

"There's one goddess in particular you'd like. Artemis, goddess of the hunt." He jutted his chin to the ship. "Her symbol was a deer. An ever-faithful white stag."

Birdie's skeptical frown faded. "Didn't know that."

"The Romans had a different name for Artemis." Ian peered up at the bridge of the ship. "They called her Diana."

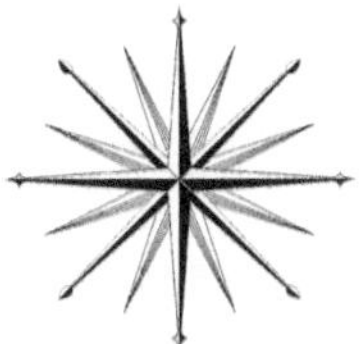

Chapter Eleven

Diana waited three insufferable hours before she began her inspection of the *Ever Hart* at the bowels of the ship.

In the dimly lit corridor, she held herself back from descending the narrow ladder leading all the way through to the boilers. She didn't want her presence to raise suspicion and unnecessary turmoil among the crew working the most grueling and important job onboard. The arduous work demanded not only physical strength but resilience to the scalding heat and careful attention. One stray movement, one toss of a burning coal, and the entire ship could go up in flames.

When the operating shift came up for the mandatory water break, Ian was the last to emerge.

Like the other crew members, he wore nothing but the cotton drawstring trousers and linen undervest they provided to keep the men cool as they worked. The fine fabric was damp and clung to the well-formed muscles of his chest.

Her sharp intake of breath reverberated in the narrow confines of the corridor.

Ian's eyes snapped to her corner of the hallway. His nostrils flared and his jaw clenched in that way that was supposed to scare her.

Instead, it stoked her arousal.

She drew her posture to its full height and ignored the wild patter of her heart as she turned away and strode down the corridor.

She proceeded through the steerage deck, which they'd assigned to the crew for *Ever Hart*'s first voyage, to further incentivize them for their silence about the cargo and the ship. Then she stopped in the galley to confirm the food on board was enough to supply them for three days before they docked in France. When she reached the promenade deck, she assessed that all twenty passengers—women and children—had settled into their quarters without issue.

Finally, she made her way outside to the weather deck and worked her lungs to find the even pattern of breathing she'd lost the minute Ian had locked eyes with her.

Amelia found her standing beneath the eaves of the foredeck as she futilely searched the cloudy sky for stars.

"Rain's on the way," Diana murmured. "We should let the passengers know the sea may turn choppy."

"I'll handle it. Have you spoken with Virgil?"

"Yes. Everything's sorted for the navigation exercises tomorrow. We have a chance of making it to Guernsey tomorrow evening. If that storm doesn't slow us down."

"The crew are all settling in?"

"Your idea to house them on the steerage deck was brilliant. Let's hope they play nicely with our newest recruit."

"I thought Mr. Holt was more like a hostage." Amelia's smile was sly, bordering on cheeky.

Diana had a smart retort perched on her lips, but Birdie landed on deck and offered them a curt nod before strolling along the rail to inspect the lines.

"What does Mr. Holt know about the voyage?" Diana asked carefully.

"That it's a test run on the new triple-expansion engine," Amelia replied. "We're conducting exercises in Guernsey to assess its capabilities, then going on to La Rochelle for restocking and coaling."

"And the cargo?"

"Birdie told him we were offering passage to a small group of papists as part of a passenger trial. Those nuns are convincing. Even I'd believe they're headed on a pilgrimage."

"The nuns always deliver. Must give Widow credit for that one."

"There is some other news." Amelia's tone was too calm for it to be anything but good. "I decoded the message that you received from our source at the bordello. The cargo from Australia will arrive in five days. But it didn't say where."

"We'll have to check all the drop sites in La Rochelle to confirm." With Birdie's crew all around them, Diana couldn't risk asking Amelia if Widow had signaled anything about the emeralds. "Anything else I should know?"

"One of the passengers says someone followed her to the ship. She told our harbor guards, but no one found the man. Birdie's team did an extra sweep to make sure he wasn't on board before we left port. No one found anything, but that doesn't mean they won't follow."

"Did we get a description of the man?"

"She said he was well-dressed. Older, didn't wear a hat. He had gray hair."

He fit the description of the man they'd spotted at the Swan's Nest. Diana had hoped they could have bought more time before the Skinner's Lane Lads tracked them.

Ian's insistence that no one would follow him was, as they all believed, bravado. He was lying to himself if he thought he was clever enough to slip out of London unnoticed. That kind of cocky blindness was exactly why Diana had lured him onboard the *Ever Hart*. If he continued acting like a lone wolf, he was going to get himself killed.

Somehow, she was going to have to convince him he needed her.

The contemptuous glare he'd given her confirmed he trusted her less than ever. Since they'd set sail, he'd peppered Virgil, Birdie, and other members of the crew with myriad questions about the ship's layout. He didn't bother to conceal that his aim onboard was to steal the necklace.

But Diana couldn't suppress the budding hope that he had other motives for following her.

Despite the choppy weather, a woman appeared on deck. She carried a child whose crying was loud enough to rise over the roar of the waves. Several of the deckhands cringed at the sound.

When the rain started, Diana was surprised that the mother remained outside with the child. Perhaps she hoped the whipping wind and splashing mist would cool the baby's temper.

A movement stirred from the starboard side of the deck, and a tall silhouette cut into the lamplight.

Diana wondered if Ian could identify her shadow as easily as she recognized his. Over the years, she'd memorized his shape: the breadth of his shoulders, the length of his torso descending into a trim waist.

His long legs treaded across the deck before he paused, pivoted, and retraced his steps. He marked neither Diana's presence nor that of the mother and child. When he stalked closer to them, the woman cowered back. A muffled yelp rose above the wind.

Ian stopped dead in his tracks.

The child's screaming cries—which had quieted—resumed in a piercing shriek.

Diana rushed between them. She gave the mother an assuring nod, then swung back to Ian and pointed her arm to the other end of the deck.

Thankfully, he didn't hesitate long before he marched off in the opposite direction.

"He's one of the crew," Diana told the mother. "He's here for everyone's protection."

The mother hugged the child closer.

Diana gestured to Birdie and the other nearby crew hands to assure the mother other women were looking out for her. "If anyone on this ship makes you feel uncomfortable, you only have to say the word and we'll come running. We have a secure brig for troublemakers, and other means to defend ourselves."

In a softer voice, she added, "You have my word, you and the baby are safe here. Why don't you take him below, out of this weather. While I remind my crew about the code of conduct on my ship."

She channeled her father's arrogant swagger as she crossed the deck; it was far more powerful than the gliding gait her governess had drilled into her.

Ian marked her arrival with a glance over his shoulder before he returned his attention to the black water. "If you mean to wear me down with physical exhaustion, it won't temper my anger about what you did."

There was a healthy dose of gravel in his voice. The underlying threat in it roused a sensation of delight Diana forced herself to tamp down. "It would be foolish of me to try to dictate your emotions. But as long as you're aboard my ship, I will have a say in how you behave."

He whipped around and drew closer to where she stood. He'd washed and changed after his shift, but his overcoat was wide open, and he wore only a clean shirt, half unbuttoned, as if he were still trying to cool his body from the exertion and heat of the boilers.

His proximity made her breath stagger again.

Ian registered it. His eyes glinted as he perused her fitted wool jumper, oilskin coat, and trousers. They differed from the breeches she'd worn during her escape, with a wider leg and narrower waist that was more feminine and less revealing.

The fraught silence between them broke when the child's cry rose from the other end of the deck as the mother tried to wrestle the toddler below deck.

Ian pinned his arms across his stomach. "I frightened them."

His unease about it disconcerted her. "You startled them. And the poor woman couldn't get the baby to settle. She was already frazzled."

"Will you send me back to the boilers for punishment?"

"It's a punishment now? I thought you said nothing would wear you down."

He scoffed and turned back toward the dark view.

She desperately wanted him to look at her instead. "Working as a coal-firer to gain passage is an extreme gesture. You agreed to take the job with no negotiation. Why?"

"Why did you kiss me?"

She reared back. His question was an unusually direct confrontation compared to the way he typically sparred with her.

The kiss they'd shared had been necessary for her to pilfer the necklace. It had also been something she'd wanted for longer than she could remember.

None of her plotting could have prepared her for the impact of her fantasy becoming reality. The way Ian had ravaged her mouth and wound his fingers through her hair, the weight of his body as she'd pressed against him, had made her so giddy she'd almost forgotten her intent to rob him.

Now that she knew the truth of what it was to act on her desires, if there had been any other way to take the emeralds without betraying his trust, she would have.

She huffed a terse laugh to cover the way his suspicion pained her. "If you're looking for an apology for the kiss, you won't get one."

"I'll accept one for the theft instead."

There was no heat to his tone. Someone could have construed his dryness as a subtle jab, a tease. But Diana wasn't foolish enough to read into it. He hadn't forgiven her for it.

Tomorrow, she'd find some way to tell him she could never surrender the emeralds to him. If she did, she'd put his life, and countless others, in jeopardy.

The wind gusted suddenly and pushed a loose line off its cleat. One of Birdie's hands brushed past them to tie it down.

"There's weather coming in. You should go below," Diana said.

Ian shoved his hands into his coat pockets. "I've withstood plenty of storms on the open sea. I'm not worried about it getting rough."

"I am," she admitted.

Rives Shipping's engineers had designed *Ever Hart* with luxury in mind.

While its technical engineering had the navy salivating, the ship was also built to ferry four hundred passengers and over fifteen hundred tons of cargo. Determined to corner the commercial market on the Kangaroo Hop between Britain and the Antipodes, the company had not sacrificed comfort for innovation and speed.

Diana occupied the captain's quarters, which were as plush as the saloon-class staterooms. To avoid disturbing the passengers in the dining lounge and the crew belowdecks, she took her meals at a small table beside a tufted banquet in her cabin.

The cooks on board—students from the Ladies' Discussion and Improvement Society—prepared breakfast, lunch, tea, and dinner that would have rivaled the service in any great aristocrat's house.

For three long days, Diana served as an inmate in her pretty prison, trapped by the fear of another encounter with Ian.

Hiding didn't sit well with her. She concealed so much of her true self from the world to perpetuate the role her parents had carved out for her among good society. It had allowed her to protect and grow a fortune she could put to use for the Stags's mission.

But now, years after committing her life and her inheritance to serve them, deciphering a way to upend the organization consumed her. By the time they docked in La Rochelle, she had no more clarity on how they were going to thwart the traitor's next attack. Or what the emeralds had to do with it all.

"Everythin's sorted for the coalin'," Birdie said as they marched down the gangplank to the pier. "Miss Hunter and the passengers will stay on the promenade deck lounge."

"Safer to have them all in one place while they stock the coal," Diana agreed. "Were we able to take on any local coalers for the rest of the sail?"

"Aye. No one pays as well as we do."

"Excellent. Remind the crew that R&R ends at five o'clock." Diana ignored the way Birdie was cataloging her movements as she pulled on her gloves. "Do you have someone tailing Mr. Holt?"

"Got my two sparrows followin' him."

They'd tail Diana too. Her support of Amelia's inquiries had made Birdie visibly wary of them both.

Diana left the harbor and headed to the *centre-ville* of the city. It took the entire morning—and stops at four different drop sites—before she finally dodged the sparrows and made her way to l'Eglise Saint Sauveur. The holy water font in the back of the church was the last of the established places where Widow dropped messages. When Diana found it empty, she became properly nervous.

Widow had never gone silent during an operation. It had to be a passive-aggressive reprimand for flaunting her orders to leave Ian behind. Diana hated being treated like an insubordinate child, but there was little she could do to rectify it, until Widow signaled.

She cut back across the city. At the office of her merchant bank, she retrieved a summary of her account statement, which Amelia had wired ahead to arrange. Diana took the folder—along with newspapers the manager had collected over the last week—to a small private office.

The funds in the account were in order, and she tucked the paper into the hidden pocket of her skirt so Amelia could verify it later. She perused the newspapers carefully, relieved the only account of her and the emeralds was speculation about the canceled wedding.

When she read the headlines of the previous day's paper, her momentary relief evaporated.

"Investigation Continues into the Death of Il Corno Heir."

The bank manager tapped jauntily at the open door. "Mademoiselle? The bank will close in five minutes. Shall I take the papers for you?"

"What a tragedy about this poor man." She nodded to the broadsheet. "It was a fire?"

The manager's expression darkened. "Yes. Thankfully, no one else was hurt."

"Thank God. The *gendarmes* think it was arson. Who would do such a terrible thing?"

"His enemies, of course." The manager lowered his voice. "These men, they are their own society, eh? We do not speak of such things."

Diana was surprised the newspaper was bold enough to print a reference to the Il Corno crime syndicate. The Stags had monitored several of their members for years, but information about the shadowy network was scarce and dangerous to procure. She prayed the manager was correct, that Clementi's enemies had started the blaze; she would not linger over the fact that the fire had all the hallmarks of a White Stag operation.

As the cathedral bells pealed for evensong, Diana headed back to the harbor. Her failure to find the coordinates for where they needed to deliver the women who traveled aboard the *Ever Hart* made her stomach churn. There was one last place where Widow might signal, and when she reached the cobblestone lane outside Tavern L'Etoile, she gathered a breath. And her mettle.

Birdie and her sparrows knew Widow left messages at the tavern on rare occasion, which meant one of them might observe who Diana was meeting there and overhear what was said. She wished that, for once, she wouldn't have to calculate what an honest conversation would cost her.

The *maître d'hôtel* ushered Diana to the quiet table she'd requested. A carafe of water and one of wine waited for her.

Along with Ian.

In his immaculate gray suit and a blue waistcoat, he hardly looked like a man who'd been at sea for three days, much of which he'd spent shoveling coal. He must have slipped off to a hotel for a bath. The only hint he'd spent time away from shore were the whiskers darkening his face. Birdie had confiscated his razor, and without it, he'd have a full beard within a matter of days.

As Ian rose from the table, his eyes traced her plain wool skirt and fitted coat, and lingered on her flushed cheeks. "You're late."

The clock tower chimed in the distance, and she smirked. "I'm perfectly on time."

"Admit it. You didn't think I'd show."

Although Amelia had assured her Ian had received her message, Diana had perseverated over whether he would accept her dinner invitation. "I'm very glad you did."

His fury was buried somewhere beneath the calm expression he wore on his handsome features. He didn't offer to help settle her into her chair, which was for the best. If his hands had brushed her shoulders, she didn't think she could stop herself from leaning into him.

When he took his seat, she asked, "Did you enjoy your shore leave?"

Ian scanned the menu card. "It's like that, is it? Are we to talk about the weather next?"

"There's no reason to begin a perfectly nice dinner with antagonism."

"I don't believe you. You're itching for a fight. Look at the way you're clenching your hands."

Defensively, she buried them in her napkin.

The waiter arrived with a tray of fresh oysters in mignonette sauce, and Diana boorishly seized one so she'd have something to swallow along with her annoyance.

Ian reached for an oyster with less ferocity. He ignored the perfectly good fork on the table and slowly lifted the shell to his lips before tipping the oyster into his mouth. It was the vulgar way that ship hands ate fish.

Diana found it wildly seductive.

He polished off three more oysters in similar fashion. "You enjoy having a *tête-à-tête* with me. I'm the only one who opposes you, and you find that novel."

"I don't enjoy being at odds with you. I'd rather be allies."

"Allies who steal from one another?"

The perfunctory nature of his tone was more irritating than his accusation. She preferred his anger over his icy detachment because at least that didn't leave her feeling cold and floundering over how to respond.

The awkward silence persisted until the waiters cleared their plates and reset the cutlery. "Mademoiselle, we have something delicious tonight. A seasonal specialty."

"Indeed." Diana attempted to sound bored so Ian wouldn't suspect she was listening attentively. The "seasonal specialty" was a code Widow had used in the past. When it was too dangerous to put orders in writing.

"What is the dish?" Ian asked with forced politeness.

"Langoustines in a fresh butter and vermouth sauce." The waiter kissed his fingertips. "We only have the ingredients for a short time. Our supplier says there will be nothing left in two days."

The message confirmed the timeline Amelia had decoded to rendezvous for the cargo exchange.

"Well then," Ian murmured. "These must be transformative langoustines."

"Can one buy them here, in La Rochelle?" Diana asked.

"*Oui*, mademoiselle. There is one specific shop." In a stage whisper, he said, "The man you need to ask for is Monsieur Donastia. Friends like me call him Sebastian."

Ian fixed Diana with a hard stare meant to attack her composure. She hoped he enjoyed disappointment; he would not rattle her enough to confirm the name was the signal of their next destination. San Sebastian—Donastia, to Basque speakers.

When the waiter darted away, Ian's glare didn't relent. "Are you going to tell me why you invited me here tonight, or are we dashing off to track down the illustrious Sebastian Donastia? I have a sneaking suspicion he's left La Rochelle for parts south. The northern coast of Spain, methinks."

The transformative langoustines arrived along with brioche and butter, and a plate of steamed greens.

Ian paid the food little notice. "Go on, Diana. Confess your sins. The seasonal specialty can wait for whatever it is you dragged me here to say."

She arched her brow and enjoyed the small catch of his breath, and the confirmation she could still render some emotional reaction from him other than disdain. "Let's enjoy dinner and test your theory on my preference for challenging conversations."

"And when we finish?"

"I will give you a bank draft for the appraised value of the emeralds, plus ten percent."

His eyes widened fractionally. He hadn't anticipated she'd come right out and mention the necklace, and she braced herself for his anger, or at the very least, a cold rebuttal.

He looked thoughtfully down at the food, drew a long breath, and quietly began to eat.

The tepid response gave her pause. Perhaps she should have gone on the attack, prodded him into an argument so he could finally unleash on her, and she could retaliate, and they'd both have a small taste of satisfaction.

Eventually, she capitulated to following his lead and took up her own fork and knife while she ruminated over how she was going to persuade him to take her offer.

The miraculous properties of the fish were over-embellished. Ian still ate with fervor. And if he was going to devour the entire thing, Diana would too.

He didn't utter a word or offer her a glance until he'd finished and finally lifted his head. In a low voice, he rasped, "You have the necklace?"

She didn't tell him she was wearing it beneath her high-collared blouse, but she conceded a nod.

He folded his hands across his lap. "I decline your offer."

"I'm prepared to pay more."

"And I'd still decline."

"You've never been foolish about money before. There must be some price—"

"The emeralds cannot be bought or sold!" he snapped.

"No, they can only be won," she finished calmly.

As he sat back in his seat, his eyes narrowed with suspicion. "Is this some game for you?"

"I assure you this is anything but trivial to me."

He made a low nonverbal protest from the back of his throat, and she saw the cold detachment creep into his expression again.

She couldn't stand it. "I can never give you back the emeralds. If I could, I would because I know what they mean to you. But they are now part of something much bigger than you and me."

"They've always been a part of something bigger, but that something is nefarious and treacherous. You don't know what you're playing at, but you *will* give them up if you want to protect the women aboard your ship."

"Tell me about this dangerous game."

"Tell me about the women."

"If it were up to me, I would. Hell." She drew a breath. "In another life, you might have wanted to be part of it. But I can't. It would put every life on the *Ever Hart* at risk."

He studied her. "You're afraid."

She raised her chin, refusing to confirm his accusation, unable to deny that she was most afraid for him.

"Someone else has entangled you with the necklace to force your hand in this," he said. "Who's controlling you?"

When she didn't respond, he banged his fist on the table. "Answer me honestly, one bloody time. Who can intimidate you enough that they would take away *your* choices? Is it Virgil?"

He leaned across the table and glowered at her in a way he'd never done before. Something lurked beneath the anger in his gaze. It seemed almost like possessiveness.

And it was tinged with desire.

Diana was used to men wanting her. Their pursuit was acquisitive. She was one more thing they'd accumulate, like estates or thoroughbreds, or stakes in a trading scheme.

But Ian Holt was angry that someone had the audacity to manipulate her. And he looked prepared to act disproportionately to spare her from it.

"If lives are at stake, including yours and mine, I have a right to know," he pressed. "So help me, Diana, name the man."

"Stop accusing me of some devious attachment. You're behaving like I'm under someone's thrall." She was offended that he thought some paramour would have such power over her. "The only man who's compelling my actions is you!"

She stood, threw down some coins in payment for the dinner, and made a rather dramatic exit from the tavern.

Unfortunately, the pouring rain halted her at the door.

"I wasn't implying you were under anyone's thrall," Ian rumbled from behind her.

The scent of the rain and wet leaves mingled with the soft fragrance of his soap. Despite her temptation to lean into his warmth, she refused to turn around. "I'm not under anyone's thumb. I'm a cog in the wheel of a much bigger machine, and I'm trying with all my strength to protect those we serve."

"Who are you working for?"

She shook her head; he hadn't earned those secrets from her yet.

"Diana. In this moment, it may seem impossible for you to believe me, but I don't want us to be at odds."

The gentle assurance in his voice made her relent. When she turned around, concern pulled at his brow.

"The men who followed us to the shipping office the night you left London were after the emeralds," Ian said. "There are dangerous factions hunting them."

"I know," she whispered. "My orders were to take the necklace and leave London. Amelia and I believe there's a traitor within our organization who wants them for some other agenda beyond our mission. The dangerous game you won't tell me about."

She swallowed the knot rising in her throat. "Ian, whoever asked me to steal the emeralds wants you to risk your life to win them back. They want you dead. That's why I took them, and why I can never return them to you."

Chapter Twelve

Ian believed her without reservation.

Her wide eyes and pinched brow revealed the emotion she'd ceased hiding behind her beautiful mask.

Diana was terrified.

For *him*.

She hadn't stolen the emeralds to taunt him, or as some cocky attempt to win a competition she thought she could best, like everything else in her life.

It had been a way to lure him on her journey, so she could protect him.

The only man who's compelling my actions is you.

It didn't lessen the sting of her deception. Or make him want to hand over his trust completely.

But God, if it didn't make his heart swell.

With a little time, she'd tell him who she was working with. She'd need his help to ferret out the traitor, and once they identified them, it would clear her from Sunderland's suspicions.

Eventually, he'd have to tell her who he was working with, too. She'd risked a great deal trying to save his hide.

"Evenin', ma'am."

Birdie materialized before them and handed Diana an umbrella. "Came to find you when one of the hands didn't return. But I see you've found 'em."

Here, her suspicious glance said to Ian.

"Thank you. Mr. Holt and I were discussing a proposal," Diana clipped. "We'll be right along. Please tell Virgil I have the coordinates."

"I can relay them—"

"Thank you, Birdie." Diana's voice rose as she gave a curt nod.

Birdie took the abrupt dismissal rather too calmly for Ian's liking. She summoned her hands with a sharp whistle and melted into the misty evening.

Ian took the umbrella from Diana, opened it, and offered her his arm. "Shall we?"

She hesitated. "You haven't given me an answer to my offer."

"We'll discuss it on the way to the ship. We can't stay here. Birdie's waiting for you."

Understanding crossed her face. They had a few moments where no one would be listening.

As she threaded her arm through his, Ian fought the instinct to pull her closer. At the restaurant, right before she sat down at the table, he'd momentarily forgotten there wasn't a gulf of past mistakes and present perils between them. He wanted that moment back.

"If you refuse to accept my proposal," Diana said, "you must know I cannot allow you to stay aboard my ship if your sole intent is to steal the emeralds."

"That would put me in a tight spot."

"There is a room for you at the inn across the way." Diana paused at the edge of the harbor and nodded to the row of taverns. "You can stay there while you decide your next move."

"And if there's a traitor among your mission comrades, who will help you in San Sebastian?"

The message the waiter had delivered wasn't difficult to decode—Ian would have to scold her for that later. San Sebastian was a two-day sail on the *Ever Hart*. Diana's organization could ferry the passengers there before they traveled on somewhere else. It was possible many of them didn't have papers; papers left a trail. And laws were unkind to women, as Henry constantly reminded Ian. His own mother had been trapped in a dangerous marriage before she'd met Ian's father.

"Amelia and I can watch out for each other," Diana countered. "We've been in this together from the start."

"She has a brilliant mind, like her father. But we both know there are situations where Miss Hunter can't defend herself. Or you. And the longer you hold on to the emeralds, the more likely one of those scenarios will occur."

Diana observed the ships in the harbor for a long moment before her eyes found his again. "I don't know how to solve this while keeping everyone safe."

"You can't." He gentled his voice, hoping it would make her listen. "Too many things are in motion. Keeping the emeralds makes everyone around them a target."

"It's nothing we can't handle."

"With respect for all you do, it is. And it's something I very much want to handle."

He didn't downplay the threat from his tone, and when Diana's cheeks turned pink, he couldn't help himself from pulling her a fraction closer. "The only thing either of us can do now is prepare ourselves for what may be coming."

"Offering to protect us while we complete the cargo exchange won't make me any more inclined to hand over the emeralds. Without them, I'll never uncover the traitor."

"I understand," he conceded, so she would know that he'd heard she wouldn't surrender the jewels. "Let me help you."

"You'll only try to take the necklace later."

When he didn't deny it, she gave a faint growl. "It doesn't matter. My organization will never allow it."

"They would if I were part of it. What would it take to join your cause?"

Diana uttered a low laugh before her expression sobered. "You're serious."

"I am."

She hesitated. "You'd have to take a vow. An oath of loyalty to our organization."

"What if I pledged my loyalty to you instead?"

The rain drummed against the umbrella. Ahead of them, the *Ever Hart* rose above the pier like a beacon in the inclement weather.

After a long, contemplative moment, Diana said, "Amelia and I will need to talk before I divulge any more details about our organization."

"I would expect nothing less."

A *pffft* noise sounded from her throat. "Uncovering who wants the emeralds will involve an operation. The unwise kind."

The dangerous kind, she meant. A hot thrill ran through him. "As I mentioned before, I have a unique set of skills that could be of value."

"A wise man would take the money and bolt. A wise woman would question why any man wouldn't."

Ian stared at her, willing her to recognize what neither of them could put into words. With all the hazards surrounding them, he couldn't leave her.

It was an easier argument to swallow than admitting he was indulging his selfish desire to keep Diana close.

Birdie's whistle sounded from the bow deck of the ship.

"They're watching," Diana said in a rasp. "Let's convince them of your loyalty."

She took his free hand and cupped it between both of hers in a firm grip. "Do you, Ian Genaro Holt, in devotion to the memory of your parents, pledge your fidelity and service to the passengers and crew of the *Ever Hart*?"

Her small hands squeezed his in a surprisingly strong grip, and Ian fought off a smile. "I do."

"And do you also vow that while onboard the *Ever Hart*, you will make no plans or overtures to intimidate or persuade others to steal the emerald necklace? That by doing so, you would risk your own life?"

"I do," he echoed softly.

A black-bordered envelope was waiting for Diana in her cabin.

Amelia accompanied it, but before Diana could tell her what had transpired with Ian at the tavern, Birdie joined them.

"No one saw this being delivered?" Diana lifted the envelope between two fingers.

Both women shook their heads.

"That does not inspire confidence in our security."

Birdie slouched against the wall with her arms folded over her chest. "My best hands were watchin' over other villains."

"Then make sure everyone else gets another lesson on our protocols." Diana kept her tone cold, which she'd found much more effective than raising it. "We're bound for San Sebastian. But now we have another extraction we'll need to transport with the Melbourne cargo. A gentleman wants to pay us a small fortune to rescue his two daughters."

Amelia's forehead wrinkled. "Who's the target?"

"Enrique da Costa."

Birdie let loose a curse. "He took over Clementi's operations for Il Corno. Word is he's twice as unhinged."

"He's the one who auctions women, isn't he?" Amelia said in a low voice.

Diana curled her lip. "We've wanted to take him down for years but can't work a scenario where we don't all lose our hides."

Birdie issued a choked noise of protest. "We don't have time to plan for this."

"No, we don't," Diana agreed calmly. "That's why we won't disrupt the auction. We will only extract the cargo."

"And leave the other women to the mercy of those shagbags?"

When Diana and Amelia exchanged a quiet look, Birdie sneered. "It's a stupid move. Any action with that lot's a declaration of war. What makes these girls so special? Why should we leave the others behind and risk so much?"

"Money," Amelia replied.

"Their father is paying us to get them out," Diana added. "We will put the funds toward rescuing other women who don't have rich families willing to pay a ransom."

They contemplated this staggering reality for a tense, quiet moment before Birdie asked roughly, "So what's the play? Standard shell game?"

"It's the only thing we have time for," Diana replied. "Our source in San Sebastian should be able to supply us with wardrobe and an extra hand or two."

"Aye, she can get us costumes, but staff may be an issue. Two of her men were pinched last week."

"That's ominous timing," Amelia said.

"We shouldn't be tryin' to pull this off now. We're too close to the cargo handover."

Diana shared Birdie's concern. Widow never justified her directions to them, but they'd never had cause to question their previous orders. Their handler had always given them ample time to plan, especially when taking on something as dangerous as infiltrating a nest of criminals at Costa's auction.

"None of us are comfortable with this, but there are two women depending on us," Diana argued. "If we stick to our protocols, we can pull it off."

"We should ensure all parts of the operation have a backup," Amelia said diplomatically. "Perhaps Virgil can play the role of Diana's escort?"

"He has to meet the Australian cargo lighter at eleven hundred hours. It's too close." Diana rubbed her chin. "We'll have to use Mr. Holt."

"No," Birdie protested. "Widow would never allow it."

"There's no one else," Diana countered. "And we won't forgo the mission."

"We can't trust Holt."

"No," Diana conceded. "But he's the option that carries the least risk. I will mitigate it."

Two days later, when they ported in Pasaia, Ian took an abbreviated shore leave to bathe at a nearby *mesón* and inquire about the quickest routes in and out of San Sebastian. He gave Diana some credit for docking the ship away from the city. *Ever Hart* would have stood out conspicuously in Donastia's small harbor.

Upon returning to his quarters, he found a note in Amelia's hand, instructing Ian to dress in dinner attire. He was still fastening his necktie when Birdie summoned him with a loud knock.

She led him down the narrow corridor of the ship to a door near the entrance to the bridge. After giving Ian a once-over, taking in his suit and a rumpled shirt that would have made Hepburn break out in hives, she rapped at the door and fled the moment Diana's voice beckoned them to enter.

Ian strode inside and leaned back against the door to ensure it was closed.

The setting sun filtered through the windows of generous quarters twice the size of his cabin. The scent of violets permeated the room.

"I suppose that suit will have to do."

Diana moved smoothly around the large bed covered in snowy linens and approached the mirror that hung on the far wall. She gave her reflection a small frown and adjusted the sleeve of her sapphire silk gown.

"It's the best I have with me. I didn't expect I'd need dress blacks in the boiler room."

Ian studied the movement of her hand so he wouldn't gawk at the exquisite way the dress gathered at her breasts and waist.

Carefully, she threaded a jewel earring through each earlobe. "I'm glad you trimmed your whiskers at least."

Ian's skin grew uncomfortably hot as he realized she'd invited him into her chamber while she was still completing her toilette. Evidently, she thought she could distract him from asking too many probing questions.

It was working; he was having a hard time focusing on anything but what her skin might feel like. Or what she'd do if he placed his lips at the crook of her neck, where it met her shoulder.

"How was your trip to the telegraph office?" Diana asked.

The feigned mildness in her tone made him stifle a laugh. With Birdie's crew on his tail, he'd only risked a terse signal to Sunderland.

"Diana, what am I doing here?"

"Deploying the special talents you pledged to my service. Now, put those on." She nodded to the freshly starched shirt, blue silk waistcoat, and tie lying on the bed.

Ian braced both hands on his hips and made no move to follow her convoluted command.

In the mirror, she regarded his stiff posture and gave a terse sigh. "Two women are being kept against their will. They are lucky—or unlucky, depending on how you examine it—to have a very wealthy father who will pay us handsomely to extract them. As part of the operation, we need you to help put on a performance, and possibly improvise."

"These are orders you received from the people you work for, or the traitor who wants me dead?"

"If you do well tonight, I could be more forthcoming with information."

He gave her a sardonic smile. "Why not use someone whose loyalty you don't have to question?"

She brushed at an imaginary spot on her skirt. "We are in a pinch with very little time. There is a narrow window for a cargo exchange later tonight."

"How do you know these orders aren't a scheme from your traitor? If they suspect you suspect them, they might be setting you up for a fall."

The cool stare she gave him in the mirror confirmed she had the same fear. And his heart jumped at the fact that she was afraid enough to show him her confidence wavered.

He wouldn't discount what it took for her to admit she needed his help.

"Who is the target?" he asked.

"A wine merchant from Porto who recently assumed control of one of the largest smuggling operations on the Continent."

Ian paused. "Please tell me you're not planning to strike Enrique da Costa."

"I have a plan," she insisted.

"Are you completely mad?" He kept his tone lethal, his jaw clenched in the way she claimed she found frightening, so he could scare some sense into her. "Costa is a member of Il Corno, one of the factions who want the emeralds. Strolling into the same room with that man while wearing the Holt necklace is like waving a red flag before a bull."

In the mirror, both their gazes dipped to the emeralds.

Ian kept his there fractionally longer to appreciate the swell of her breasts.

"Are you saying you won't help?" Diana asked.

It was a definite taunt. He glanced away long enough to draw a breath.

When he looked back in the mirror, he noted how closely she was watching him. It was more than an assessment; her eyes lingered, as if she enjoyed the view.

He had an inappropriate urge to press her about their kiss again, but he needed to wait for a better time. He could be patient.

Up to a point.

"Tell me everything you know about this," he ground out. "I won't go in there blind."

"And in exchange you'll tell me everything you know about Il Corno and the others hunting the emeralds?"

"Only Costa. If we get out of this unscathed, we can negotiate the rest." He was still operating under the foolish hope that he'd disentangle her from those who were chasing the necklace.

"For the good of the operation, I'll agree to those terms," Diana said cautiously. "Costa has been on our list for years. He's leveraged in opium, and we've had accounts of him trafficking women and forcing them to labor in workshops that fabricate cheap cloth and notions."

She paused before adding, "There are also rumors he takes women as payment for debts and auctions them off at elaborate soirees."

The laws governing such things had as many holes as a sieve. Ian had made everyone in London believe he was a scoundrel so he could wield his own notoriety to keep that kind of illicit trade from Holt & Company's docks.

"Your orders are to infiltrate one of these parties?" His voice rose, the only outward sign he hated everything about the idea, and the harm that could befall her if she set foot in the same room as Costa and his jackals.

"Yes," she confirmed pragmatically. "Now tell me what you know about Costa."

He took a moment to swallow his fury at her blasé attitude about such a treacherous situation. "No one can stop talking about how quickly Costa moved in on Clementi's businesses. Which means he either orchestrated his murder or knew someone else was planning it."

"Why do you believe he's coming after the emeralds?"

"With his rival dead, he now has rank."

A furrow appeared on her forehead. "What does that mean?"

Out of habit, Ian hesitated. In Italy, people only spoke of such things in hushed voices and whispers. "How much Italian history do you know?"

Her mouth quirked. "Do you mean ancient Rome?"

Her teasing smile would not beguile him. Not even a little. "For centuries, the Italian city-states ruled themselves. Although they are now united under the Italian flag, each region is home to several unofficial...militias. The men who run them also hold monopolies on certain enterprises. They succeed by secrecy and intimidation, and their reach now extends well beyond Italy."

"And these...militias want the emeralds?"

"Since the crusades ended, three of them have competed for it. To them, the necklace is more than a trophy. It's a chance for them to bet huge stakes of their business against each other. An excuse for a turf battle."

"And how do they—"

"We don't have time for all that now." If he had his way, that was all she'd find out about the emeralds. "What are the plans for tonight?"

Diana cast down her eyes and fiddled with the gloves on the table. "You should change."

The feigned modesty irked him. She'd seen him without a shirt often during summers at the shore. She refused to look him in the eye because she was withholding something from him.

He was going to enjoy prying it out of her.

Slowly, he shed his coat and vest. He took his damn time unfastening his tie, and the buttons of his shirt, and let it fall from his shoulders. As Diana watched him undress in the mirror, her gaze traveled the length of his body in a way he'd dreamed about.

He thought of a thousand different things he could do to distract her with his mouth and his touch, so she wouldn't dream of leaving the cabin.

In the mirror, she raised a delicate finger over the ink tattooed on his heart. The motion was something akin to an imaginary caress.

Her reaction heated his skin and stroked his ego. He slowly closed the distance between them and stood behind her, facing their reflections. "You're holding back something. It's more dangerous for me to go in there without knowing everything."

"You won't like it."

The blush rising over her cheeks was the best form of encouragement. He inched closer. "Tell me."

"Put your shirt on," she whispered.

Diana kept her eyes on him while he reached for the shirt, but she averted them when he tucked it into his trousers.

"Tell me the part I won't like," he insisted.

"Our orders to extract the two women from Costa also included a specific request that I wear the emeralds."

He swore. "It is obviously a trap!"

"Of course it is." Her voice shook. "But we have to go. There are lives at stake. And this could be our best chance to uncover information that will lead us to the traitor."

Ian expelled a breath, and in a somewhat calmer voice, said, "When you walk into that auction wearing the necklace, it will signal Il Corno and other factions to set chase for us. We might manage a clean escape tonight, but as long as you have the emeralds, they will pursue you."

"I know. We'll have to splinter off after the cargo exchange. I'll take the necklace and the others will take the new passengers back on the *Ever Hart*."

He hated the pallor that had replaced her flush. "There must be an easier way to find out who betrayed you."

"Probably. But there are still two women we can help protect tonight. Their father is offering an outrageous sum for us to move them to safety. Amelia believes if we follow the payments, we'll uncover the traitor."

"And the other women?" Ian asked. "The ones who have no wealthy fathers to pay for their rescue?"

"There isn't enough time to get them out. Attempting it with limited resources will get everyone killed." Her throat bobbed on a swallow. "The organization I pledged my loyalty to would never allow me to leave them behind. There is some other agenda at play."

The uncertainty in her voice made Ian take a protective step closer to her. One of the back buttons of her dress was only partially done, and his fingers found the fabric and pushed the shell of the button through the slippery silk.

His hand grazed the bare skin of her neck, and something like a low moan sounded from her throat. He rested his fingers against her throat for a moment longer than needed, stopping just short of stroking the necklace.

"If I prove faithful to you tonight, and you find the trail that leads to the traitor, give me the emeralds," he murmured. "You said yourself you can't put the women you're supposed to be protecting at risk."

Diana reached for her reticule. "And what about you?"

His hand clasped her wrist. "I can take care of myself."

Her free hand spread protectively over the necklace. "Is this worth such a lethal gamble?"

"They won't hurt me as long as I play by their rules."

She responded with an emphatic scoff.

Reluctantly, he released her arm.

Diana brushed past him and seized a cape from a hook on the door. "If tonight proves a success, we'll negotiate the return of the emeralds."

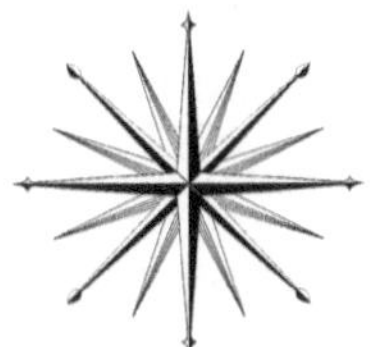

CHAPTER THIRTEEN

THE CARRIAGE LEFT THEM on the corner of the Calle Major in the old town, so they could approach Costa's exclusive casino by foot and blend in with the throngs of people crowding the narrow street.

Ian examined the guards outside the ornate doors at the rear and side of the building. He noted at least four different ways they could get caught. "Are we planning to leave by the front door?"

"Unless you can come up with another alternative." Diana flashed a society smile at the servants who collected their cloaks and their forged invitations. "It will cause the least disturbance."

For the hundredth time since they'd left the *Ever Hart*, Ian resisted the urge to throw her over his shoulder and parcel her onto the next ship bound for England. He hesitated only because she was at more risk out of his sight.

When Diana had relayed their scheme to rescue the women, he'd admired the simplicity of it, while knowing that, at best, their odds of success were fifty-fifty. And even if they rescued the women without incident, Il Corno—and whoever else attended the soiree—would pursue them until Ian made himself their sole target.

They followed the sound of voices and music through a corridor to a small receiving room that was far too cozy for the size of the crowd.

"Goodness," Diana murmured as she flicked out her fan. "The casino is certainly...popular. Makes one question the meaning of the term 'exclusive.'"

Well-dressed, middle-aged men crowded the room. The few women who accompanied them wore the bright face paint and low-cut gowns favored by paid courtesans.

"Stop scowling at everyone." Diana slid her arm through his. "It's hypocritical for you to be so disapproving of a salty crowd."

Ian's discomfort grew as they progressed to the dance floor, and he took in the whirling of the other dancers.

"Let's dance and we can reconnoiter the layout," Diana said lightly. "Please tell me you know the bolero. It's practically all they do here."

His heart sped up in the same manner it would have if she'd suggested he walk unarmed into a pit of hungry lions.

How many times had he watched her on the dance floor with other men, wanting to be in their place and hating himself for it? When he'd first come of age, he'd avoided anything to do with ballrooms. But after the thugs attacked them in Mayfair, he refused to leave Diana unguarded. With Jared away on the Continent, he accepted his brother's invitations to every party he knew she'd attend and bribed his way into the others.

The prospect of finally holding her closely—in front of so many people—was disarming. Their plans couldn't afford for him to be so distracted. "Perhaps we should watch."

"We need to survey the room." Diana rested her hand on his arm. "You'll figure out the steps."

She was baiting him gently. He resented how much he wanted her to continue. The weight of her hand made every one of his muscles stand at attention.

But it was her slow smile that finally prompted him to lead her to the dance floor.

All of those nights watching her must have imprinted the steps onto his brain; they fell into the turns, easily negotiating the narrow space between them. It was not unlike the way they'd moved together to defend themselves at the Swan's Nest.

Ian couldn't grow accustomed to it. They needed to complete the operation, and he needed to convince Diana to give up everything related to him and the emeralds.

"I count two guards at the entrance," Diana murmured.

"Two more at the stage," he confirmed. "How do we get downstairs?"

"There." She nodded toward the staircase at the far end of the room. "That must lead to the wine cellar. Our contact will meet us there and take us to the women."

The music halted, and a burst of applause broke out. As the crowd pushed around them, Diana stumbled into him.

Instinctively, his arms locked tightly around her waist.

A knock sounded from a platform at the front of the room, and a man—short of stature but large on muscles and dark hair—greeted everyone in a mixture of Portuguese and Spanish.

Ian slowly rotated their position so that the shadow of his body obscured Diana's face.

"Do you recognize him?" she asked, her voice breathy from dancing.

"It must be Costa. See his tiepin, the gold twisted horn? It's a *cornicello*. Clementi wore one for luck. Costa's wearing it now that he's taken his turf."

Costa summoned another man to the stage, and Ian tried to decipher the mix of Spanish and Portuguese. "It sounds like they're going to start the auction. They're talking about jewels."

"They must mean the women." Diana cringed and placed a hand over the necklace.

A man standing nearby was eyeing the emeralds far too carefully, and Ian covered her hand with his own.

Her glance slid to their observer before locking back on Ian.

"Remember the plan." She leaned into his hand. "The casino has rules against avid displays of affection. We need to pique enough interest to earn an escort out the back entrance."

Once there, the Stags had bribed the serving staff to lead them to the room where the girls were being held.

Ian hated the plan more now than when Diana had first told him about it.

Except for the part that allowed him to suspend reality so that he could touch her, like she belonged to him.

"This is going to backfire," he warned, before his fingers languidly traced the front of her necklace where it dipped into her décolletage.

"It won't if you convince them you can't keep your hands off me."

Her hushed voice urged him to forget everything but the point of contact where his bare hand met her warm skin.

Music erupted again, and the tide of people moving about the dance floor forced them toward the edge of the room. As Ian steered them out of the fray, their bodies remained entwined. Diana's eyes fixed on his mouth.

He forgot everything but the need to taste her lips again.

"*Senores.*" A young woman wearing a white carnation in her hair stood at Ian's elbow. She wore a close-fitting dress of scant lace and nearly transparent silk.

Diana's eyes locked back on him as they both took a moment to comprehend the girl's sudden arrival.

"There is an exclusive wine tasting in the cask cellar," the woman said. "It would be more intimate for you, I think."

"I would adore something intimate. And a taste of something special," Diana said quickly.

The woman didn't wear the uniform of the casino staff, and Ian didn't trust where she might lead them. "Are you sure we won't be missed here, darling?"

"Don't be silly, my love." Diana laughed and gave him a little shove, moving him to a different view of the door. One of Birdie's sparrows stood in the wings, wearing a dress identical to Diana's.

Ian had to admit she was an effective stand-in for anyone watching out for Diana and the emeralds.

"Shall we?" Diana placed a firm palm on Ian's cheek.

He pressed her hand to his mouth and gave it a small nip to warn her to remain on guard.

The woman with the flower guided them through the crowd and down a dark set of stairs into the basement. Diana proceeded him while Ian followed behind to ensure no one else trailed them into the room.

When the sturdy door snicked closed behind them, Diana had the woman back against the wall with a blade at her throat. "Where are they keeping the white flowers?"

The woman frantically reached for the carnation pinned to her hair.

"*Flora e Blanca, las ninas*," Ian clarified. "The girls."

"*Gracias a Dios*." The woman's breath shook on a sob. "Papa sent you to get us out?"

"Flora?" Diana eased her knife away. "Where is your sister?"

"Upstairs, the third story." She swallowed. "Costa separated us so we wouldn't conspire together to escape. He has some of us walk around the party, pretending we are free, but if anyone tries to lay a hand on us, Costa forces them to bid on us to drive up the money he receives."

Ian's stomach churned. Diana kept her expression carefully blank; she'd probably heard countless stories like Flora's. He wouldn't let himself think about the ones that were worse. "Where's the back stairway that leads to where they're keeping your sister?"

Flora shook her head. "There isn't one."

Before Ian could express his vehement disapproval of this development, Diana's head snapped to the door. She clapped a hand over his mouth and whispered, "Someone's coming."

Her knife disappeared into the bowels of her reticule before she pulled Flora into their embrace.

The cellar door flung open. Costa swaggered through the entrance with two burly guards behind him. "What have we here?"

Diana glanced at the men under hooded eyes. "I'm afraid you caught us in a passionate moment, *senor*."

Costa clucked his tongue against the back of his teeth. "Flora knows better than to offer private tastings without asking."

The filthy scoundrel's attention locked onto the emeralds before he perused Diana's breasts. The man's eyes were red-rimmed and drooping; with any luck, the blackguard had over-imbibed, and his defenses would be weak. Ian calculated that if he went right for Costa's throat, he had a thirty-second window before the guards retaliated.

Diana squeezed his hand in warning.

"Perhaps, *senor*," she drawled, "you would care to join us?"

"I don't fuck men."

"Neither do I." Ian retreated an inch to snag a better view of Costa's guards, who he was happy to note were swaying on their feet. Nearly as drunk as Costa. "But I enjoy watching."

Costa barked a rough laugh. "You'd let your woman fuck a stranger, and this whore?"

"Yes," Ian said in his best *of course* tone.

The smuggler curled his lip. "You are a bold woman, *senora*, to walk into my house wearing something that doesn't belong to you."

Costa shoved Ian out of the way, which Ian tolerated because it gave Diana the chance to slip him the knife she'd hidden in her skirts. He was grateful he had cold steel to grasp hold of when Costa stroked a long finger down Diana's neck and pressed his palm on the emeralds.

"Tell me, did you steal these pretty gems yourself?" Costa rasped. "You have an enemy, *mi amor*, if they sent you here to tempt me. Who would do such a thing?"

Diana's eyes held Costa's. Ian waited an eternity for them to flick to him.

And then he moved.

He whirled around and hurled the knife to take down the guard closest to him.

The second guard was so slow to react, Ian had him unconscious with one hard punch.

When he spun around again, Diana had the blade she'd kept hidden in her reticule pressed between Costa's legs, and handed a cloth to Flora so she could smother his nose and mouth with it. Costa wheezed a muffled protest before he collapsed with a thud on the cellar floor.

"We have five, maybe ten minutes before he revives." Diana grabbed her skirts and stepped around the bodies.

Flora muttered something incoherent around a laugh or a sob; Ian couldn't distinguish which one. She evaluated Costa's prone body, then flexed her fingers.

Ian made the same motion when he itched to punch something.

"We must leave," he said forcefully.

Flora looked up with a tear-stained face. "This could be the only chance to end him."

"It won't end it for the others." Ian shook his head. "He has brothers-in-arms who will take his place. When they don't find you, they'll claim retribution from whoever they can find. Your parents. The rest of your family. Even your close friends."

"Come now," Diana urged. "We must get upstairs."

"But how will we get everyone out?" Flora asked.

Diana placed a gentle hand on her shoulder. "There's only enough time to get you and Blanca."

"No. They have to come with us. Blanca and I can't leave them, knowing—" Her voice cut out before she added in a whisper, "I couldn't live with myself."

Diana looked at Ian in silent supplication.

"You cannot help anyone if you stay here," he said frankly but softly. "Tonight is the only chance you have to get out. Once you're free, you'll have more power to help them."

"I need you to take a big breath, Flora, and try to clear your head," Diana said. "How do we find Blanca?"

The girl blinked. She gazed down at Costa, and her chin wobbled. "There's no time to make it upstairs. We'll have to wait for Blanca to come down with the other girls. They're supposed to circulate, offer dances to the gentlemen."

"With the guards watching," Ian rasped.

"Which we planned for," Diana reminded him with a glare. "Flora and I will slip into the ladies' withdrawing room and exit the window there. You will find Blanca and dance her out of the room."

He barked a laugh. "This is insane."

"You knew it would be."

He murmured for Diana's ears only, "There are others out there who will follow the emeralds."

"That's why we've given them emeralds to chase. Now go. This cretin will wake soon."

Diana darted upstairs with Flora. Ian followed and watched them filter into the crowd before cautiously rejoining the party. A second set of musicians had arrived, and the music became rowdy. More wine and spirits continued to flow while a partially dressed woman on the stage performed an evocative dance.

Then two phantom Dianas swirled onto the dance floor.

Ian blinked as they drew up their skirts and began a seductive flamenco.

The crowd stirred again as scantily clad women wearing carnations behind their ears descended the central staircase. The last one to enter the room had the same thick-lashed, hazel eyes as Flora. Her head swiveled as she observed the room like a hare sniffing an open field.

Ian elbowed two men out of the way and sent a third scampering with his best devil's glare. He made a small bow before the trembling girl. "*Senorita*. You have your sister's eyes."

Her mouth parted on a small squeak.

"Shall we dance?" Ian gently took her in his arms, thankful the music had shifted to a waltz. "Flora is outside waiting for you. Shall we go meet her?"

"I cannot l-leave." Blanca's voice shook.

She was smart to refuse him, but it was damned inconvenient. If he swooped her up, she might kick and scream in protest.

He cast his eyes toward the cellar door, but there was no sign of Costa.

Punters danced around him. The men without partners watched the dance floor with carnivorous gazes that made Ian's stomach roil.

"You can come with me, Blanca. Right now, we can walk right out that door."

"Do not tease me, *senor*."

"I'm not. I'm here because your father sent me."

"If that's true, why didn't he have the courage to come himself?"

Ian had wondered the same thing. He'd never allowed himself to think of a future family, but if Costa had taken his child, he'd have killed the man himself. If he hadn't been raised with his mother's fear of Il Corno—and known what they could do to Diana—Ian would have ended Costa tonight.

He scanned the room again to ensure the guards weren't watching closely, and slipped Diana's blade into Blanca's hand. "This is on loan. It belongs to a very lovely, very dangerous lady who would not be happy I am surrendering it. But it is yours for the time it will take us to walk out of this room and meet your sister."

The girl's eyes glistened as her fingers curled around it.

Behind her, the door to the cellar opened.

"Now, will you come with me, Blanca?" He strained to keep his voice steady. "We're running short on time."

When she finally nodded, Ian spun them around the dance floor and used the cover of two dancing Diana doppelgängers to escape from the room into the dim corridor. Blanca struggled to walk on her shaking legs.

Footsteps approached. Ian pressed a finger to his lips and drew them behind an open door. Two guards stood by the front entrance to the casino.

A footman noticed them waiting. "Do you need a carriage, *senor*?"

Above the music and the noise from the crowd further down the hall, Ian heard the faint rumble of Costa's voice.

He cleared his throat. "No need for a coach. I think we shall walk."

The footman nodded to confirm the signal. He reached into his pocket and withdrew a small straw, which he used to expel a dart into the back of the necks of each of the guards.

A moment later, they crumbled to the floor.

Ian swept Blanca up in his arms, leaped over the prone bodies at the door, and ran out into the side alley.

"Here!" Diana called from a wagon tucked in the corner.

Blanca trembled like a leaf in his arms as Ian placed her inside, but when her sister called her name, they both dissolved into jubilant, screaming sobs.

"Hush!" Diana hissed. "Don't breathe a word or move until the wagon stops. Someone will show you where to go next." She covered them with a burlap blanket and knocked on the side of the wagon. It jerked forward and clattered off into the night.

Without a word, Diana reached for Ian's outstretched hand, and they tore down the narrow lanes of the old town to the carriage.

"Did anyone spot you?" Diana huffed once they were inside.

"No immediate followers, but I heard Costa's voice before we left. Let's not dally."

"The wagon will snake around the old town. We'll follow behind."

It was the safest way to protect against an ambush. "No problems getting Flora out?"

Diana hummed an affirmation. "My blade?"

He pressed it back into her hand. "Blanca was shaking so much she could barely hold it."

"You were quite gentle with her. Thank you."

The events and the emotions of the evening came upon him in a sudden flood. He tried to sift through it all, and ultimately landed on familiar anger. "Why must you risk your life with this...mission? There are hungry children you could feed in St. Giles. Or take the poor wretches from the workhouse and pay off their debts, give them a decent way to earn a wage."

He heaved a ragged breath. "Why this, Diana?"

"These women are trapped," she volleyed back. "They are abused, locked away, unable to govern their own bodies. And indentured to a life of trauma. Some of them choose death over spending one more day in that existence."

"This won't stop Costa and Il Corno. It only signals what you want from them."

She scoffed. "Someone within the Stags thinks the necklace will persuade them to end their trafficking of women."

"It won't."

Diana didn't argue with him.

If she had, it would have allowed him to press his case that she needed to give it all up. Flora's broken voice haunted him. As did the fear in Blanca's eyes.

And the man who'd put that terror there wanted something Diana possessed.

"Your comrades dangled you like bait in front of Costa," Ian hissed. "Why would an organization bent on saving lives consider yours any less worthy of protection?"

Her mouth curled in a protest, but as he glowered at her, she wordlessly shook her head.

The carriage pulled up to the pier. When Diana placed her hand on the carriage door, Ian stopped her. "Who asked us to put so many people in danger? You trusted me as your partner tonight. Trust me with this. Please."

"When the cargo has left harbor safely, I'll tell you what I can," she replied slowly. "And you'll tell me what you've been holding back about the other factions vying for the necklace."

The blast of the ship's horn forced him to open the door. They alighted, and he was relieved to see Birdie escorting Flora and Blanca to the *Ever Hart*. But before any of them had made it up the gangplank, a commotion arose further down the dock.

Next to the ship's mooring, a small boat had taken on enough water, it was listing. Several women stood with their skirts dripping wet on the pier.

Diana ran, with Ian on her heels. At their approach, a tall woman directing the group stood protectively before the others. There was something about her silhouette that made Ian's blood freeze.

As she stepped into the lamplight, familiar red curls cascaded down her back.

Ian blinked. It was possible he'd fallen asleep in the coach and was sleepwalking through some nightmare. With the mists rolling around them and the full moon overhead and Diana hovering out of his reach, he felt very much as if he'd lost touch with reality.

It was the best explanation he could gather for the apparition that stood before him.

"Diana! Thank God it's you."

The specter's voice made Ian shudder with horror and disbelief.

When Diana threw her arms around the ghost, he stifled a cry.

"We're all right, Di. There was a leak in the skiff. Only a few of us got wet."

Diana made a garbled noise, and the tears in her eyes gave Ian the courage to approach and make certain that he wasn't hallucinating.

"Beatrix?"

His voice was hoarse and threatening, which made the other women retreat from him.

"Jesus Christ, Beatrix Wilde, is that actually you?"

Before Beatrix could dart out from Diana's embrace, Ian snagged her by the arm and pulled her into the lamplight.

And when he saw for certain what his mind told him was impossible, he barked a strangled laugh. "You have some bloody gall standing here, alive and well, while my oldest friend—one of the few truly decent men I have ever known—has mourned your death for eight years."

Diana wedged herself in between them. "Ian, not here."

Birdie's shrieking whistle sounded.

"The passengers must board." Diana's voice climbed. "There's no time to waste. Costa is on our trail."

Ian's glare shifted from Beatrix to Diana. "I'll call for the harbor watch myself if you don't tell me exactly what this is all about."

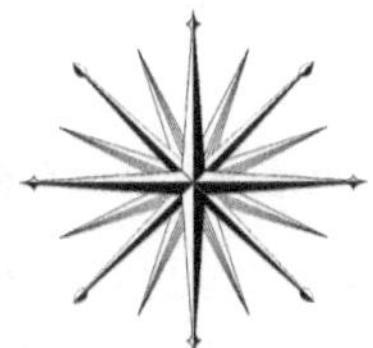

CHAPTER FOURTEEN

"LEAVE BEATRIX ALONE," DIANA ordered.

She paid no mind to Ian's thunderous expression. He was itching for a fight, and she wouldn't give him the satisfaction of acquiescing to so hostile a demand. "I will explain what I can when your temper cools. Take a walk."

Ian stood stock-still, as if contemplating a challenge to her proposal, and she casually reached into her pocket for her blade. She'd no intent to use it, but he knew what the gesture meant, and his eyes widened a fraction before he marched off to fume along the length of the pier.

"I take it things aren't going as planned," Beatrix commented.

Diana scoffed and placed her woolen scarf around her friend's shaking shoulders. "Forget him for the moment. Are you truly well?"

"It's only damp at the bottom of my skirts. I don't need to go inside yet. Luckily, this didn't get damaged." Beatrix handed her a black-edged envelope.

They studied it for a quiet moment.

"How was it delivered?" Diana finally asked.

"The skiff pilot. The poor man thought it was a real mourning note. He looked at me so sadly."

"Perhaps he felt guilty about ferrying you in a boat that would leak."

"I don't think anyone interfered with it." Beatrix sighed. "It's my natural ability to attract disaster."

"It is one of your greatest strengths." Diana tried to hold back a laugh and failed. Beatrix caught her giggle and in short order, the two of them were wiping tears from their eyes.

During their debut season, the ship Beatrix was supposed to travel aboard sank en route to France, and Diana mourned her friend deeply. Years later, the quest to find a better treatment for her father's illness took them to Melbourne. A Stag missive had led Diana to Beatrix.

When Diana had discovered why Beatrix had remained hidden on the other side of the world, she knew the Stags's mission would resonate with her, and she'd recruited Beatrix to join them.

She reached out and gave Beatrix another hug, to assure herself that her friend was now well and flourishing. "Lord, it's so good to see you."

"And you. I've missed you and Amy so much." Bea's eyes shone. "I confess, I didn't think it would take me this long to work up the nerve to leave Melbourne."

Diana glanced over her shoulder to confirm Ian was finally out of earshot. "There's been no other news about Henry's uncle. Our sources say the engagement is still proceeding."

"So Henry hasn't stopped it."

"Not that I know of. But I've been considerably preoccupied."

"Fleeing your wedding with the groom's brother," Beatrix teased. "Are you returning to England with us?"

"Not tonight." Diana clutched Widow's note. "I have a terrible feeling about all of this, Bea. We're one wrong move away from disaster."

Beatrix looked back at the ship. "Nothing firm yet on any of your crew linked to the payments or the attacks?"

"The terrible thing is, other than you and Amelia, I trust no one."

"What about Ian?"

At Diana's groan, Beatrix flashed one of her impish smiles. "Oh, it's like that, is it? And don't tell me he's only here for the emeralds. I've been gone eight years, but there is no force—neither earthly nor divine—that could make Ian Holt's feelings for you change that dramatically."

"I think I have to trust him. Which means I'm going to have to tell him everything, and it will make things worse between us."

"When I came up with my crazy scheme to win Henry back, you insisted it would be worth the risk."

"And it will be," Diana assured her. "But this is different. Ian and I—we haven't been honest with each other since we were children. There's no way I can conceive of for this to end well."

"It will if you both want it enough to work for it. Women like us, Di…we have to fight for our happiness."

Diana gave her friend another squeeze.

"I'm not sure I'm doing the right thing either," Beatrix said softly. "If Henry is as affected as Ian said, how can he ever forgive me?"

"You'll find out in London."

"It could all blow up in my face."

"Nonsense." Diana flapped a hand. "But Henry's diabolical uncle does concern me. You are taking precautions?"

"Yes. Amelia made all the arrangements. Poor dear, she's working herself ragged for both of us."

"I've dragged her into this mess with the emeralds. Luckily, she's safe in France until we need her elsewhere."

"She's a smart woman. If she's involved, it's because she wants to be. And you're too protective of all of us. We all need looking after sometimes."

They both stole a glance at Ian pacing the docks.

Diana regarded the letter. She didn't want to be alone with whatever it said. "Will you wait with me while I read it?"

"Of course."

She opened the note and scanned it several times. "They want me to hand over the necklace. There's a meet here, at sunrise."

"But that would mean a delay. The women—"

"*Ever Hart* will depart as planned. You'll have to take them with Virgil. It's too risky to stay here."

Beatrix narrowed her eyes. "I don't like it."

"Neither do I." Diana kept her voice steady. "But I can handle it."

"Not by yourself, Di."

"I won't."

They both turned back to Ian. He halted his pacing and paused beneath a lamppost. His expression was darker than the evening.

"He looks a little too murdery to be alone with you," Beatrix murmured. "Take Birdie with you."

Diana gave a low whistle and beckoned Ian with a dip of her head, which made him glower. He approached them carefully, with his hands buried in his pockets.

At least he wasn't overtly reaching for his pistol.

"The *Ever Hart* must make sail now," Diana said. "Beatrix will take the cargo to Bristol with Virgil. For the safety of the women, you and I will not be on board. We have other orders."

Ian remained suspiciously silent, which disappointed her; it was easier to know what he was thinking when he was growling and sniping.

Diana gave Beatrix one last hug. "Safe travels, dear. I'll meet you in London soon. With Henry," she added in a whisper.

Beatrix tossed her a grin before she scrambled up the gangplank.

"Come with me." Diana flicked her eyes to Ian before she marched in the opposite direction down the pier. Over her shoulder, she added, "Perhaps we can find something for you to hit."

They ended up in a dockside *mesón* that catered to sailors making port and shipping out at all hours.

Diana's stomach rumbled at the savory scent of *marmitako*—stewed bonito with sausage and potatoes. She signaled the barmaid for an order and two glasses of local cider.

She was always ravenous after an operation, and it was a relief to concentrate on the small act of fulfilling that need rather than plot out their next move. Ian demolished his food. She envied how he ate with such quiet and efficient zeal.

He leaned back in his chair and eyed her neck, as if he was trying to see through the thick scarf she wore to conceal the emeralds.

She mirrored his posture. "Go on, ask me."

"How long have you known Beatrix was alive?"

"Two years," she replied without hesitating. "And I'm not telling you any more details about why she did it. It is not my story to tell. If you want to protect Henry, you'll keep silent about it until Beatrix reaches him."

"He grieved her. Henry never moved on from her death." He sounded affronted by Henry's pain. "When Beatrix drops out of the sky, back into his life, it's going to break him."

"It won't. I know what he's about to face, better than you can possibly imagine."

"Just because you've forgiven her doesn't mean he will."

"They hunted her, Ian. All Beatrix wanted was to stay safe."

His scowl softened. "Then how did you find each other?"

She hesitated while she debated what she could reveal.

Without Beatrix or Amelia, Ian was the only person she could rely on to help track down the Stag traitor. But if she brought him with her to the meet to exchange the emeralds, he'd find out everything about why she'd joined the Stags.

And she'd finally be free of the burden of hiding so much from him.

Diana recalled the brush of his fingers along her throat earlier, and the seamless way they'd disarmed the guards together.

It was foolish to continue denying the true reason she'd made him part of her endeavor.

She couldn't let him go; she wanted him alongside her.

"Eight years ago, a covert collective known as the White Stags recruited me," she began. "And before you say something biting which you'll later regret, it's merely a coincidence that both my name and the organization's are associated with the goddess of the hunt."

"If you say so," he replied with mock solemnity.

"When I agreed to join the Stags, my handler emphasized that secrecy was a necessary part of our mission to help and protect women in trouble."

"There are plenty of organizations with the same mission that don't operate in the shadows."

"They don't need to if their sole purpose is to convert the poor and downtrodden into righteous Christian soldiers. The members of those organizations seek to rationalize their own indulgent lifestyles by forcing others to adopt a set of values and morals that are as far away from London's rookeries and slums as Arabia is."

Ian made no comment on her summation of good society, which was wise of him since she was in no mood to entertain any misogynistic counterarguments.

"The Stags help women leave dangerous and abusive situations and place them in communities far away, hidden from their abusers. But that is only one part of our mission," Diana went on. "We also work with them so they can live independently. They come from all walks of life. Some have no money, connections, or skills. Others come from what society would deem as respectable homes, but they know nothing beyond how to manage a household. All of them need help to support themselves and navigate a new world."

"And Flora and Blanca?"

"They're an exception."

"Which is why you had cause to suspect the traitor arranged for their rescue." He drummed his fingers against the cider glass. "Do these women do well in their new lives?"

"Yes. We are clear from the start that it won't be perfect, that there are sacrifices involved. None of them go into this expecting utopia."

"I understand," he said softly.

"Of course. Your mother had to do the same thing. She left Malta to escape her first marriage. My mother told me about it."

Ian's gaze hardened. "Whatever you think you know is most likely wrong."

Diana was tempted to ask if that entanglement had something to do with the emeralds, but it would only anger him more. "You know what her life was like, what she had to do to start again in a new place. With no one she could trust or depend on. She made a new life from the ashes of her old one, and you were witness to it."

"And you're telling me all of this to protect the people you're working with?"

"I'm telling you so you'll understand how difficult this is for me."

Ian leaned forward with a glint in his dark eyes. "I'm tired of smoke and mirrors. We barely scraped our way out from that mess with Costa. Your ship—the one center of security in this storm of madness—is setting sail without us. Who the hell are you working for, Diana?"

"Are you saying you want to meet them?"

"Are you saying I have a choice?"

He said it so dryly, it made her laugh. The momentary release of tension made her fatigue settle on her.

Her eyes sought comfort in the familiar, handsome planes of his face. His dark whiskers hid the cleft in his chin, and she pondered what it would be like kissing him now, with his beard.

Sitting across the table from him, arguing like this, felt so right, so close to a sense of belonging. She wondered if this was how married couples settled into each other at the end of each day.

Diana would never capitulate to some cliché sense of destiny. But she was tired of pretending that she could easily push Ian out of her life.

It was the last thing she wanted.

"I've received orders to deliver the emeralds at sunrise," she said. "I can't refuse. It's the best chance to find something that will expose the traitor. If you come with me to the handover, you'll know everything I know about the Stags."

"If the extraction operation at Costa's wasn't a trap—and I'm still not convinced it wasn't—this certainly is," he insisted.

"There is a time for stealth. And there is a time for calling someone's bluff." She rose from the table. "I'm tired of being manipulated."

Diana wove her way through the tables, but before she reached the door, Ian caught her arm. His hold was surprisingly gentle.

"It would have taken little to convince Jared to give you access to the emeralds. You had the bloody key...you could have stolen the necklace any time," he murmured. "The Stags could have swapped it for paste without blinking an eye, and you would have remained in the clear. Running from your wedding and flaunting Costa so publicly has drawn attention to your clandestine collective. They can't like it."

He leaned in and crowded her against the door. She could have brushed her lips against his if she wanted.

If he'd let her.

"Why did you do it, Diana?"

He wasn't an obtuse man; she had to conclude that it was sheer stubbornness that kept him from seeing why she'd dared him to chase after her.

"When I received the orders to steal the necklace, I knew the mission could only bring harm to you, and that—" She drew a breath. "That made me see red."

He echoed her sentiments with a faint growl.

"Whoever is leading the White Stags doesn't want to protect women. They want to punish the men who harm them. I have to stop whoever is threatening our true mission. Maybe I'm a terrible person for not telling you this sooner. It was the only way I could think of to protect you."

"You can't. I'm in this up to my neck, exactly like you."

"I know." She studied his face and tried to summon her wavering courage to answer his question truthfully.

"There was another selfish reason I orchestrated it this way." She reached one hand for the door. "I needed to know where we stood. If you were only after the emeralds. Or if you wanted to find me."

She flung open the door and stepped out into the darkness, with Ian bellowing behind her to wait.

His words were drowned out by the sound of triggers unlocking as half a dozen men surrounded them.

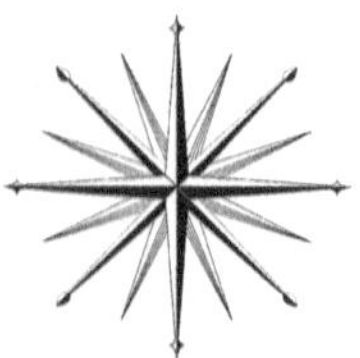

CHAPTER FIFTEEN

It took four men to wrestle Ian away from Diana, and he'd only complied because the bastard who held her with his gun cocked against her head also had a grip on her throat. Ian couldn't see straight from the panic of what could happen if she tried to free herself.

Their captors had tied the knots binding them well and tight. Diana's were already chafing, marring her delicate wrists, and he silently vowed to take blood from every person who left a mark on her.

The thugs shoved them on board a tugboat, which hugged the coast back to San Sebastian. Then they dragged them through the narrow alleyways of Calle Santa Korda. The street was barely wide enough for the two men to walk abreast as they hauled Ian between them.

Diana handled the capture stoically. Anyone watching closely could surmise from the way Ian watched her she was his weakness, but he couldn't hide it. Not after she'd confessed her scheme to entwine him in her play to steal the emeralds wasn't only for his protection.

She wanted him.

After all these years. All the lies he told to make her think he could never want her, and the ferocious reputation he'd cultivated to keep everyone at a distance. Over time, Ian had convinced himself he'd sacrificed everything to protect her from *Il Gioco* and his father's enemies, and she'd kept her promise to marry Jared because she didn't want him.

But that was the lie he'd told himself.

Diana. Wanted. *Him.*

Their current dangerous predicament notwithstanding, Ian perseverated over what her revelation truly meant for them. He could accept she considered him a valuable partner in her crimes, whom she also enjoyed kissing. Would she surrender her thoughts and her desires to him, as well as her body?

And what did she want in return? Commitment to her cause, or commitment to her? And for how long?

He wanted to forget all the reasons he couldn't abandon his own plans for something so long forbidden to him.

The forced march through the old town ended at a townhouse guarded by a strapping sentinel, who waved them inside. Their captors coerced them through a narrow staircase that held the lingering scents of tobacco, heady perfume, and something sour.. Voices echoed from the floors above them. Their cries and shouts made Ian cringe.

They'd landed in another brothel. But this one made the Soho bordello appear as plush as Buckingham Palace.

"*Si, mi amor*, it's what you think it is," wheezed the bastard holding Diana. "First time in a bawdy house, fine lady? Won't be your last!"

Diana glared at Ian in a silent warning against doing anything stupid, which he would have done had he not been bound so tightly.

"Ah, our visitors have arrived." A rail-thin woman with a painted face, wearing an atrociously ugly red wig, welcomed them. She nodded her head toward a door at the far end of the hallway. "Put them there."

The men shoved Ian and Diana into a shabby room barely large enough to house a brass bed frame and thin mattress, covered by a threadbare counterpane.

"The bed," the madam ordered.

One tough poked the barrel of a gun between Ian's ribs to force him onto the bed. He fixed Ian's bound hands to the bed frame with precise knots. The filth must have worked aboard ships and knew what they were doing.

They tore Diana's arms out of her cloak and bound her next to Ian. They tied her hands over the bedpost, for reasons he was too overwhelmed to understand.

One of them pulled Diana's shawl away with a fierce yank.

A collective hum hit the room. Every eye fixed on the emeralds at her throat.

Not one of their captors made a move to snatch them, and this made Ian more nervous than being without his pistol.

"Whatever ransom you're expecting, I can pay more," Diana smoothly addressed the madam.

"The protection Costa offers me is priceless." The tart grinned a ferocious smile. "From what I hear, you're trying to destroy the good living he brings us."

"He is selling *women*," Diana volleyed back.

"No different from my trade."

"They didn't have a choice."

"Women don't have choices." The madam sneered. "They have options. Some, better than others. Any of those girls and mine would tell you they'd prefer a full belly and roof over their heads to starving on the streets. Some," she drawled. "Love their profession. There's no shame in that."

"When men like Costa control them, they'll never be safe. Or free to work however they wish."

"You." The madam's attention flicked to Ian. "One more try at those ropes and we'll start shooting."

The goons who remained in the room flashed them their holstered weapons.

"Costa is on his way to collect you. Alas, I can't stay to keep you company. Duty calls." The madam batted her lashes. "But I have a feeling you won't be alone. This is a dockside cathouse. Patrons pay to enter, and most take more than their due, especially when the doormen are distracted." She nodded at the men with the guns. "And yours are *so* easily distracted."

The men trailed her into the corridor. One guard remained outside the partially open door to monitor the hallway.

"Blades?" Ian whispered to Diana.

"Gone. It will take weeks to have another set made," she complained. "Their knots are excellent. Truly, I would have them train my crew if they weren't the filth of humanity."

When footsteps echoed down the hall, Diana turned to Ian. "Good God, she was serious about the patrons? I thought she was trying to intimidate us."

The tightness in her voice made him redouble his efforts to escape the ropes. "It will take a few minutes, but I can work free of the knots."

"What if they find us first? We need a ruse to distract them. Can you sing?"

"Have you lost all sense?"

"Yes." She hiccupped a laugh. "My mind keeps spinning."

Her voice was drowned out by amorous cries and screams as a couple in the room above them met their climaxes.

Diana's cheeks turned pink. Her forehead glistened with perspiration, and despite their harrowing circumstances, Ian's entire body went hard.

He shook it off with a rattle of his head. "As long as you're wearing the necklace, they'll keep their distance."

"Not everyone thinks it belongs to Costa." Diana frantically tugged on her binds. Dots of crimson blood spotted her porcelain skin.

"Careful," he cautioned. "The harder you pull, the tighter they tie. You need to loosen the center with gradual movement."

"Of course. I knew that."

When her eyes caught his, he read pure terror in her gaze.

Somehow, she'd forgotten that she herself was a force of nature. A champion who rescued women and felled criminals with a toss of her wrist.

A goddess of the hunt.

"Breathe, Diana," he murmured. "I swear to you, we'll get out of here."

A rowdy, drunken chorus heralded sailors in the street below.

"If the guard lets that lot in this room, even the emeralds may not distract them from what they came here for," Diana hissed. "We have to find some way to stall them."

As loud footsteps and jeers approached, Ian knew she was right; they needed a distraction to buy them the time to get free of the ropes.

"We will have to perform," he said in a rush, because to linger on the words would put enough thought into them to make him change his mind, lose his courage. "There's only one thought on their minds if they come here."

Her throat bobbed on a swallow. "Ian—"

"Oi, my friend, what have we here?" a slurred voice called out. A man craned his head around the guard. "Looks like a pretty package all tied up for us."

"Must be a precious gift," another said to the guard. "How about you let us in?"

"There are no good options left, Di." Ian moved closer to her. "We will have to pretend. We both know how to put on an act."

"Not this kind."

Her voice sounded so unsure; it nearly undid him. "It signifies nothing."

"It won't work."

Ian leaned into her. "Yes, it will. You and I will be convincing. We will make them understand you're mine for the night."

Her eyes flared, and for a moment—a sacred half second—he actually believed she was his. And that equally, he belonged to her, and what he was suggesting was the inevitable culmination of Diana confessing she wanted him as much as he'd desired her.

The men outside the door taunted the guard. "Let us in, boy. We've paid our fee."

Diana's head frantically bobbed between the door and Ian's face.

"Please," he begged in a whisper. "Play pretend with me."

With a small squeak, she shifted on the bed and straddled him.

They locked gazes. He couldn't even think to apologize for his erect cock, because the place where her legs cradled it was absolute perfection. He would have begged her not to move, for fear of spilling himself, but the fear on her face stopped him.

"You're in charge," he whispered.

Someone shoved the door open.

Diana's mouth descended as he surged up to meet her kiss.

She made a small noise, possibly a yelp, that dissolved quickly into a groan as he took her mouth and devoured it like a starving man tasting his first morsel of bread. He'd said they needed to put on a show, but this felt like the most genuine thing he'd ever done.

"She's a tasty one, is she," slurred the man who'd burst through the door. He and his friend were too drunk, or too transfixed to move, which was exactly what Ian needed.

Diana moaned again, and he took her mouth with more pressure. He wasn't holding back. Neither was she. She met him stroke for stroke, tasting and nipping. It was so indulgent, and his blood was high with the danger and anxiety of needing to secure their escape. The sailors who'd entered the room would not be content to watch for long.

"That's it," Ian murmured as he grazed her jaw with his tongue before tracing circles on her throat. She groaned louder, and he wished he knew if she truly liked what he was doing. Or if she was amping up a reaction for their audience to keep them at bay.

"They're only watching, love," he coaxed in English. It was unlikely that the thugs understood much. "They enjoy watching you move, trying to slip through those knots."

In response, Diana rolled her body against his, as if acting out their scene, while she twisted her hands. Anyone would think she was in the throes of their passionate encounter, not trying to loosen her tie and his.

"Stupid cow," the sailor said. "Thinks she can get away."

"You don't want to escape, do you, darling?" Ian teased in Spanish, for the benefit of the goons. His tongue circled her collarbone. "You love it here. With me. Show them what you want me to do for you."

Diana hinged toward him to offer him her beautiful breasts, and the pleasure that flooded through him was pure fantasy. He kissed her luscious curves and blew on the hard peak of her nipple through the silk of her gown before taking it in his mouth.

As her legs squeezed around him, she rasped, "I must give the devil his due."

And then she moved on him.

She rocked against his hips. The friction against his stiff cock was torture. He was going to spend in his pants and he didn't care who saw it. It was going to be worth it.

"I'm so close," Diana moaned.

It took him a full minute to realize she didn't mean her climax. Her knots were finally loosening.

"What about you, darling, are you there?" She panted.

Ian tested his own bindings, which were nearly undone. The amazing woman had been working both sets of knots the entire time.

"No. You don't get to come until I do," he barked, with one eye fixed on the men. They were watching Diana ride him with glazed expressions and didn't notice the ropes loosening. "You need to take all of me, love. And you're so tight, I'm the only one who can undo you."

"You're wrong there, mate," slurred one goon.

"Think I should help," his accomplice added, unfastening his belt. "This bitch needs to be fucked before she gets to ride someone else."

White light exploded across Ian's vision. With a growl, he rolled across the bed and shoved Diana behind him. He hardly registered that the movement was tearing off his skin. It didn't matter; his hand was free.

Diana pressed a hairpin into his palm.

"Throat," she wheezed.

He flung the pin into the open mouth of the man who stood before the bed. The sailor staggered back and gasped before he collapsed, blue-faced.

Ian caught the other bewildered man by the throat. "Don't say a word. You leave quietly and we're both safe. You stay, you'll be on the wrong side of Costa. I took what's his." He glanced over at Diana on the bed; she was staring at the ceiling, which he hoped was part of her performance. "If Costa finds you here, you're as good as dead."

The sailor paled and glanced at his mate, unconscious on the ground.

"Go now. While you can." Ian gave him a shove, and the man needed no other urging. He tripped out the door and slammed it closed behind him.

Ian returned to the bed to free Diana's other hand. "That was brilliant. I hope you've more pins to use on the way out."

When he loosened the last tie and she still didn't move to follow him off the bed, he saw she was trembling. "Diana?"

She didn't respond. The need to draw her into her arms was overpowering, but as he leaned closer, she shuddered.

"Forgive me." He sat back on the bed, afraid to touch her. "I took things too far—"

"No." She seized the lapels of his coat. "The only thing keeping my fear at bay is your hands on me."

The desperation in her voice cut into him. He was hard again; his breath sawed in and out in raw gusts that burned his dry throat.

Diana was equally winded. The neckline of her gown had frayed during their performance, and the tops of her breasts spilled out of it as they rose and fell.

"What can I do?" he begged.

She swallowed. "Help me—help me finish. Please."

He folded her into his arms. Relief washed over him as her curves melded against him. She met his mouth with a searing kiss before letting him take the lead.

His hands, now free to do their will, stroked her breasts and caressed her waist through the silk bodice. "Having you tied up above me aroused me beyond com-prehension."

She gave him one of those unintelligible moans, and he rejoiced silently in the confirmation that her cries of pleasure before had been genuine. "But I prefer you this way, free to hold."

He stroked his hand down her silk-clad leg and hooked it around his waist to fit her against him, which she approved of, judging by the frenzied way she rocked into him.

"Do I feel as right to you as you do to me?" Ian's words fell as softly as snow as his hands gentled her. "I cannot wait to touch more of you."

She responded by kissing him passionately, grazing her teeth against his lip.

With a tight clasp on his hair, she breathlessly demanded, "More."

He thrust his hips against her and drew the tip of her breast into his mouth. He sucked on her bare nipple and traced it with his teeth until she cried out.

"Now." She gasped. "Touch me now, Ian, please. Make it fast."

He growled as he kissed her deeply and rucked up her skirts.

"Yes," she purred into his mouth when he found her drawers. He plunged his hand through the slippery ribbons and lace and pressed against her mons.

"Please," she begged again.

Ian caressed her entrance. He gently traced her lips, found them achingly smooth and damp. As he delved one finger inside her, Diana's hips bucked to meet his movements, and he sensed his own climax stir at the base of his spine.

"How luscious you are, Diana. What I would give right now to taste you here."

He thrust his finger to demonstrate; she responded with a seductive whimper.

"Is that enough to fill you?" he teased as he burrowed in and out in a taunting rhythm. "Or do you need more?"

"More, more, more," she pleaded. "Hurry, please. I can't stand it."

He added a second finger and twisted them inside her. He relished the way she writhed on him. "God, do I want to soothe this sweet ache of yours with my cock. It's only ever been this hard for you, *tesora*. Only you."

The bawdy scream from her throat as she exploded around him drew his own swift, mind-shattering release.

A moment of silence followed before cries above them resounded their passion.

Diana sat up and looked at him, flushed and stunned.

He cupped her chin and shook his head in quiet, amazed agreement.

Footsteps drew them both back to reality.

As they bounded off the bed, Diana grimaced at the body blocking the door. "We can't exit the way we came in."

Ian's blurry eyes clapped on the window. "We're one story up. Too far to jump, but we could scale the side of the building so that the drop isn't too far."

They worked together to pull open the window, and Ian tried to ignore the heady scent of sex that was permeating the space between them. The stain on his trousers was a painful reminder that they'd lost precious time. And that Diana could unravel him with little more than her proximity and her kiss.

As long as he lived, he wouldn't regret it.

When the window finally creaked open, the shriek of mating cats made Ian recoil. "I hope to hell those vermin aren't mating in the alley. It will make for a terrible landing."

The shriek sounded again, and Diana placed a hand on Ian's arm to still him. "Wait."

She gave a low whistle, which spurred another punctuated shriek from the street below.

"Not cats, a barn owl."

They poked their heads out of the window and found Birdie standing below them. She tossed them a rope and turned to the end of the alley before she repeated the low whistle Diana had made.

"We're clear," Diana confirmed.

Ian secured the rope around the bed frame, and Diana was already over the window sash before he finished tying the knot. He followed her down. His knees nearly buckled when they hit solid ground.

"Costa has the police looking for you," Birdie reported as she ushered them through the lane.

"We can't risk staying for the meet tomorrow. Do you have transport?" Diana asked.

Ian expected a vehement protest from Birdie about abandoning orders, but she only tilted her head in affirmation to Diana's question and led them down to the beachfront, where she dragged a rowboat out from under the pier.

"Tell me you've checked for leaks," Diana insisted as she boarded while Ian and Birdie shoved off into the water.

"This ain't my first passage." Birdie handed Diana a blade, which Diana accepted with a grateful smile.

"Good woman. You can return Mr. Holt's pistol to him as well."

With deliberate slowness, Birdie reached into her pocket and handed Ian the gun.

"How did you find us?" Ian asked as he inspected the pistol to confirm it was still loaded.

"I was across the street, sorting this out." Birdie flapped the oars. "Saw them surround you, so I followed at a distance. Took me bloody ages to double back for the rope."

"We must make note of that oversight so we don't let it happen on future operations," Diana remarked.

After a beat, Birdie said, "We've never ignored orders before."

She delivered this observation casually, but Ian made no mistake of the accusation buried beneath it.

If their situation had been less precarious, he would have enjoyed correcting her view of their predicament with his usual terrifying means.

"The situation requires it." Diana employed the same commandeering tone she used aboard the *Ever Hart*, which bore a striking resemblance to the way she addressed volunteers at a charity fete. "We'll signal when we're clear of Costa."

Her shift back to that cool, contained society heiress was remarkable. With the detached way her glance shifted between Ian and the harbor, no one would suspect that she'd been wild in his arms merely moments before.

Diana was too intelligent to deny the signs that the Stag traitor had penetrated her own crew and could have arranged for Costa's lookouts to nab them. And yet, remarkably, she maintained her perfect mask of composure.

If only he could tell her to surrender it. He'd draw her onto his lap, close enough that he could match his breaths with hers again. She'd look at him the way she did at the brothel.

Like she needed him.

Tonight, she'd saved his life. Again.

With a hairpin.

Tomorrow, he would tell her why he chased her on this journey. And why she needed to let him leave with the necklace. Alone.

As Birdie rowed, Ian registered they were heading north. But he'd never been more adrift in his life.

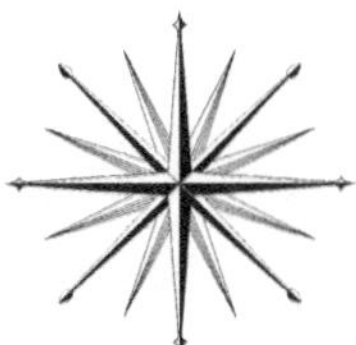

Chapter Sixteen

The next leg of their travels was decidedly less comfortable than the first.

Ian asked where they were going once, nicely. When neither Birdie nor Diana responded, he asked two more times with less charm. Eventually, Diana murmured, "France."

He finally stopped pushing for more details when Birdie flashed her pistol at him.

The crew hand arranged for them, along with two of her lieutenants, to travel with tramp cargo as far as Biarritz, where they caught the train to Toulouse. Their first-class carriage afforded them some privacy. One of the sparrows handed Ian a paper to hide behind while he sat watch over the compartment. They knew he wouldn't leave Diana's side, and he appreciated this unspoken understanding of their situation.

As Diana sat across from him, with her eyes pointed out the window, he perseverated over how much of their interlude at the brothel consumed her thoughts. Even in his panic to flee San Sebastian and determine their next move, he couldn't stop thinking about it.

The way she'd trembled. The softness of her skin, at odds with the edge of pain he'd felt when she'd bitten his lip.

He'd said filthy things, things he'd only imagined telling her, and never in those fantasies had she responded with such fervor.

The unmarried society women of Diana's acquaintance might be ashamed of such a transgression. That was the mores she'd been raised to follow. While her secret life with the Stags empowered her freedom, such moral judgments were hard to shake.

It took a fair amount of his strength to resist reaching across and tipping her chin so he could meet her gaze, so he could assure her she shouldn't possess an ounce of shame about what had happened between them.

At sunset, they reached Toulouse and caught another train to Béziers. Birdie directed them out of the station and set off across the street, where a wagon waited.

Ian raised a brow at Diana.

She gave him the ghost of a smile. "It's a short drive."

The forced lightness in her voice betrayed the lie.

They ended up at a port south of Marseille hours later. Birdie led them through the narrow wharves to a well-fitted yacht. The sparrows boarded the vessel while Birdie hailed the port attendant. The man sneered at her, and Diana intervened, firing off in rapid French about an immediate need to reach Monaco. When Ian reached for his pistol, Diana held up her palm in warning before settling the bureaucratic matter with a less than subtle exchange of notes from Birdie's pocket.

Diana turned to board, but Ian stopped her with a gentle pull on her arm. "I thought I was a part of this now."

"You are." She wriggled. "Ian, we don't have time. We must make sail."

"To Monte Carlo?" He kept his hold firm so he could spool her in closer, while he gently stroked her other arm.

"What do you want from me?" she asked hoarsely.

"No more secrets, Di. It's foolish."

"And you'll tell me yours?"

"When we reach our destination."

Her glance drifted to the yacht. At the bow of the ship, Birdie whistled a shanty tune as she tightened the jib sheet.

Diana watched the ship for a moment before she sputtered an exhale. "Yes, we're going to Monte Carlo. And yes, I know this is the most obvious way to travel, which makes it less safe. But it's the fastest. We must get there by tomorrow evening."

"Why?"

"I'm following protocol." Her eyes flicked to the boat again, and Ian pinched her chin to draw her attention back to him.

"Diana. What is it?"

"If I don't make it to the signal point in Monte Carlo tomorrow, my handler is going to make assumptions."

"They'll think I've turned you into a rogue." The apprehension in her eyes made tension build between his shoulders. "I can help clarify the circumstances. I can be very persuasive."

"It doesn't matter," she said softly. "We can't undo what happened. But we also can't delay another minute."

She led him onto the boat, and Birdie stepped in his way to prevent him from trailing Diana to the bridge. "You know how to man a line?"

"Mainsheet or jib?"

"Start on the jib until we clear the harbor. Two hours on, two hours off."

"Aye," he murmured as Diana's skirts disappeared below deck.

Shortly after dawn, they made port in Saint-Tropez to take on supplies. With only an hour of shore time, Ian didn't bother stopping in at the dockside tavern for a bath—he'd be working lines again on his return to the ship. He bought a coffee and a fine buttered croissant at a café and made his way to the telegraph office.

When he returned to the yacht, Diana was waiting for him, wearing a detached expression. "Someone will track that wire."

"Probably."

"You at least have a code?"

"Do you have to ask?"

"Yes," she said indignantly. Her lower lip protruded.

He couldn't resist swiping it with his thumb. "You said I was in this. Trust me to work my end of it"

His fingers curled around her chin and, to his immense pleasure, she gripped his hand fiercely.

"Ian, you don't know—"

"And whose fault is that?" He strained to keep his voice gentle, his caress tender.

It was worth the effort when she looped her arms around his neck.

"I'm trying to protect you, you stubborn devil," she murmured.

"It's more dangerous keeping me in the dark."

"*I'm* in the dark."

"I know. And it's terrifying you."

Her mouth twitched around a silent protest, but it never rose past her lips. Instead, her eyes took on a shine that made Ian feel things he didn't think still lingered in his heart or his soul.

She met him halfway in a kiss. The wind had chilled her lips, but the swipe of her tongue brought heat and spice, and he let her take control because he knew she needed it. And because he was lost in her, too easily.

Gently, he ended the kiss, but continued holding her. Knowing he could defend their position gave him a small sense of assurance .

"We're in this together now," he declared. "If they want you, they'll have to come through me."

When they finally arrived at the Monte Carlo townhouse tucked at the end of a quiet lane near the tranquil harbor, Diana felt no less exposed than she had on the open water.

Fatigue weighed her down. Ian battled exhaustion bravely, but she hated the dark circles that hung beneath his eyes. Almost as much as she hated retreating to a separate room upstairs after murmuring she'd take a tray for dinner and go straight to sleep.

She fought every instinct to invite him to follow her. It would have taken few words to convince him.

Neither of us should be on our own.

Lie beside me. It will be safer that way.

We won't do anything but sleep.

The door to his bedroom on the floor below hers slammed shut. She hoped he was fighting his own battle to remain apart from her.

Inside her room, Diana found hot water, a freshly laundered nightdress, and two envelopes. One was bordered with black. The other had the seal of the local telegraph office.

She pulled off her sodden cloak and shawl and worked her way out of the ruined evening gown and corset. Her shift and drawers were damp and clung against her skin, setting a chill into her bones. As she peeled off the cloth, she caught sight of herself in the mirror above the dresser.

Lamplight fell against the swell of her breasts, and she brushed a cool hand over one. Slowly, her fingers reached for the hard peak of her nipple. She grazed it with the tip of her nail to reclaim the sensation of Ian's teeth teasing her through the fabric of her dress.

Despite the seedy surroundings of the brothel in San Sebastian, and the fear that had choked her, the way he'd caressed and kissed her as he stoked her pleasure had been the most erotic experience of her life.

She'd *begged* for more. He hadn't hesitated one second debating it before giving it to her.

After all her imaginings, all her plotting, it was disorienting to act on the desires she'd stifled for years. On some level, she'd hoped that it would curtail the feelings she'd fought off. But it had rendered the opposite effect.

It made her hunger for all of him.

It made her dare to dream she could have it.

Her attention turned to the letters sitting on the dresser, and she remembered the obstacles between them.

With a shiver, she pulled on her nightdress and locked the door against her temptation.

As Ian wove his way through the city center the next morning, Birdie trailed him. He was too tired for subterfuge and took coffee and a croissant at a market stall while he waited for the telegraph office to open.

Although physically exhausted from days of grueling travel, he'd slept lightly and little the night before; he'd wanted Diana in his bed more than his next breath. In the crisp morning air, he resolved to spend the day reconnoitering the city, since returning to the townhouse would be too tempting. If they found themselves alone together, he'd try to finish what they'd started at the brothel in San Sebastian.

Until a few days ago, he would have taken whatever access to her delicious body she'd offered without question. Now, he couldn't separate the physical act of pleasure from the potential cost to his sanity and his soul.

When the telegraph office opened, there were two wires waiting for him. The first from Hepburn, confirming that Jared had departed for France. The second wire gave an address for a meeting point at a café in Monte Carlo's Old Town.

Thankfully, a pair of matrons usurped the telegraph attendant's full attention, which enabled Ian to duck through the back-office entrance and outside to the alley behind the building. He turned the new frock coat he'd found in his wardrobe inside out and covered his head with a soft cap he'd bought in Saint-Tropez before he jogged from the Avenue Main to the cathedral. Behind the church, he found a small square and a café. The tables outside only had one occupant.

As he glanced up from his newspaper, the Duke of Sunderland took a long draw on his cigarillo. "Bonjour, monsieur."

Ian sank down on a chair. Their position in the square was more exposed than he'd prefer, and he pulled the cap over his forehead. "We have less than ten minutes before my tails catch up."

"That is one of the few drawbacks of Monte Carlo," Sunderland drawled as a waiter delivered two cups of coffee. "So few places to hide. But so close to the French country-side. A wonderful place for hunting stags."

After the waiter retreated out of earshot, Ian asked, "You've confirmed the details I sent through about the organization?"

The duke nodded and tapped his cigarillo thoughtfully. "Authorities across Britain and the Continent have been monitoring the Stags for the last decade or so. They all turned a blind eye to their propensity for skirting the law. The police don't have the time, inclination, or money to dedicate to serving and protecting women."

Ian swallowed his scalding coffee in one gulp. "When did things change?"

"About a year ago, they began leaving collateral damage. A string of vicious arson attacks, all of them targeting dangerous criminals."

"Diana's uncovered two related to her past operations. And Amelia Hunter tracked secret financial withdrawals connected to the attacks. They both believe there's a traitor in the ranks."

At the mention of Miss Hunter's name, the duke's tiger-like eyes sharpened on Ian. "Could this traitor be one of them?"

When Ian responded with an eviscerating stare, the duke flashed his white teeth. "Didn't think so either, old man. But their entanglement with the emeralds is a problem. Especially now that Costa knows you have them."

For years, Ian had guarded the secrets of *Il Gioco* alone, so no one else would have to carry the burden of it. In a matter of days, the truth of it had spiraled out—like the djinn from Aladdin's lamp—and there was no stuffing it back inside. He resented the duke for the way he could speak about it all with such calm detachment.

"What exactly is your interest in all of this, Your Grace?"

Sunderland gave a low laugh. "Don't worry, I'm not after the emeralds. There's nothing I could stake to win them. I have no shame in holding the title of the poorest aristocrat in Great Britain. Unlike you, I want nothing to do with my father's legacy. The only thing he left me was his staggering debt, and it was no hardship to liquidate every tainted asset he owned. Nothing I can do to shake the title, but I enjoy the status it lends me."

With a dark grin, he added, "I could live off favors for the rest of my life."

"How many does the Crown owe you?"

"Not enough to balance my debt to them. Hence, my current employment." Sunderland leaned back in his seat. "Her Majesty's government is concerned about what's at stake when the factions convene to battle for the necklace. It is no simple *gioco della fortuna.*"

The players simply called it: *Il Gioco.* The Game. "And if I could assure the Crown that I could play with their interests in mind, what would I get?" Ian asked.

The duke blew out a ring of smoke in a perfect O shape. "What do you want?"

"No prosecution for any of the parties playing on our side."

"That would include Miss Rives and Miss Hunter."

"And you and I."

Sunderland tilted his head. "You, and, naturally me, I can guarantee. But I can't promise anything about anyone connected to the Stags until we prove neither Miss Rives nor Miss Hunter had anything to do with the attacks."

If their positions were reversed, Ian wouldn't have made the promise either. "It won't be difficult to prove." He held Sunderland's gaze and added, "When I win, I want to take back what I stake."

"That's only fair."

The matins bells pealed from the church tower and warned Ian he'd already risked too much time with Sunderland. As he rose to his feet, he asked, "Who owes you favors in Florence?"

"A silk merchant with a lovely townhouse near the Duomo. Among others."

Beyond the square, a familiar cry of a barn owl made the hairs rise on the back of Ian's neck. He gave Sunderland a parting nod and fled into the maze of the market stalls.

Ian ducked beneath the brightly colored canopies and hid behind stacked wheels of cheese and apples. It was better to camouflage himself than risk darting out in the open so his tails could find him again.

As the wind stirred, it brought with it the scents of *dejeuner* preparations from the restaurant. Garlic and oregano permeated the air. It instantly transported him to Florence, and his memories of sitting on his mother's lap in the garden while Alberti picked his tomatoes off the vine and the Duomo's bells clamored.

An elderly couple sat on the bench nearby. In the middle of a protracted argument, the man leaned across and planted a passionate kiss on his wife's mouth. She gave a brief squeak before surrendering with a breathless laugh. The fruit vendors applauded and cheered.

The soft way the woman looked at her *mari* made a weight settle in Ian's chest.

When Sunderland had asked him what he wanted in exchange for risking his life to play *Il Gioco*, he'd only been half truthful when he'd named the emeralds.

He also wanted Diana to look at him like that woman had looked at her husband. With irritation and love, and acceptance.

And he knew it was impossible for him to have both the necklace and her.

Chapter Seventeen

Diana sat in a hired coach parked in front of the Grand Casino, contemplating the possibility that she was the biggest coward alive.

Uncertainty had never plagued her before. She'd always excelled at compartmentalizing powerful emotions, like fear. Her fencing instructor had taught her that in the moment of an attack, she couldn't afford to be afraid. He told her to build a vault inside of herself to hide it away. So she could stay in the moment to assess and destroy her assailant.

After that lesson, her blood high from the enthusiasm and the power she'd experienced, Diana had recited the words to her mother verbatim. Her mother had regarded her contemplatively. Then, in a rare display of affection, she'd taken Diana's face by the chin and said, "I could not give you any better advice for your life."

They were the last words she'd spoken to Diana before vanishing from her life.

As she waited in the carriage, she brushed aside those memories, and the others that would corrode her resolve. She searched the street again for some sign of Ian. When Birdie had reported Ian had lost their tails during his foray into town, Diana knew he must have signaled his co-conspirators about his plans for the emeralds.

If she'd waited for his return to the townhouse and demanded an explanation, the confrontation would have stoked his anger. She couldn't afford to alienate him; she needed him at the meet to exchange the necklace. Rather than risk his fury, she'd left him a note instructing him to meet her at the Grand Casino. And she'd fled the house.

The cathedral bells chimed eight. Diana reluctantly abandoned her surveillance and strode into the casino alone. When she passed under the gilded ceiling of the main entrance, something pricked at the back of her neck and drew her attention to the gallery hallway.

Ian locked eyes with her.

If she was another woman, her body would have sagged with relief at finding him there, and she would have flashed her brightest smile solely at him.

But Diana was her mother's daughter. And it took a long moment to decipher which feelings had to go into the box in the trunk in the vault in the cavern, buried deep below her heart.

Because Ian Holt was devastating in his dress blacks.

As he strolled toward her, the flare in his eyes was mesmerizing. It was, in fact, more of a glare than she cared to admit, and reminiscent of the way he used to stare at her when she believed in his resentment. Now, she saw it for the echo of what she suffered: frustration at their circumstances. Smothering an underlying need to be near him.

Her heart pounded as he drew up beside her and dragged her into an alcove behind a trio of potted palms.

"I don't expect you to have any regard for me. But you must have no care for your own life if you want to walk into this situation blindly." The fire in his dark eyes was a striking contrast to the coldness in his tone. "Once you knew the meet, we should have spent the afternoon strategizing."

"So you could return to the telegraph office?"

He blew out a breath. "We agreed to be partners on this. I understand that trust has to be won, but this won't work if you withhold information. It puts us both in danger."

She couldn't argue with him. "I know. I want to trust you. It may not seem like it, but I'm trying."

"Tell me what you know about the meet. Everything."

She caught herself smoothing back her hair with her hand and quickly dropped it. "There will be an approach in the main ballroom. An invitation to one of the private table salons on the other side of the gallery."

"Birdie and her sparrows?"

"The sparrows are at the front and side entrances. Birdie is standing by with transport if things do not go according to plan."

"And they probably won't." He scoffed. "You trusted them with the meet details, but not me, even though you know they could be betraying you."

"That was purely timing. And my need to convince them I'm keeping you at a healthy distance."

Their eyes dipped to where Ian's hand gripped her waist.

Diana glanced at the gilded clock on the wall. "If we don't walk into the ballroom soon, they're going to get spooked."

"Talk fast."

He pulled her arm through his and steered her through the crowd, into the ballroom. Ian guided them through the maze of tables covered with crisp white linens and hot-house flowers, past the sumptuous buffet of savory dishes, to the parquet dance floor.

"What are we doing?" She swiveled her head at the couples dancing around them.

His arm came around her waist. "Dancing and plotting."

"This is going to make an approach a thousand times more difficult."

"Then you're not as good as you think you are."

Her foot stumbled. She would have tripped if Ian had not caught her, which drew her indignant anger; she refused to appear anything less than graceful in public. And she knew they were being watched.

"Who are you supposed to deliver the emeralds to?" Ian pressed.

"You truly are a devil if you're doing all of this solely to interrogate me."

He didn't deny it. "Who are we meeting?"

"I don't know."

"Bollocks. You know every other important detail of your operation, down to the fabric of this suit and the menus on your ships."

"I don't *know*," she repeated.

"But you suspect it's your handler."

The music shifted into a slow waltz. More couples gathered onto the dance floor.

Ian drew her closer. "Why won't you tell me who is behind all this?"

She was terrified of Widow or another Stag observing them entwined around each other like lovers. Diana pressed her hand on his chest to carve out some distance. "You won't understand."

"Did someone hurt you?" He relaxed his hold on her. "Did they threaten to hurt you? I'd end them for it."

To her horror, she gasped.

"Why does that surprise you?" His voice softened. "You killed for me once."

She was prepared to do it again if circumstances demanded it.

"Everything changes when we walk into the room for the meet," Diana rasped. "I'm not afraid of who will be there, or what might happen. I'm afraid of what comes next."

A couple brushed against them before Ian deftly twirled them to the edge of the dance floor. She seized on the movement to pull away from him. His embrace was too intoxicating; she needed the separation to rally her strength.

Ian shoved his hands in his pockets. A frown pulled at his brow as he withdrew a silver token.

"That chip is for the private gaming room." Diana plucked it from his open hand. "It must be the drop point."

Ian curled his hand around hers. "We go in together, or not at all."

"Of course," she said softly. "I can't do this without you."

"And when they try to disarm us?"

"They will. As a precaution. But it won't matter." She held his eyes. "They won't leave with the emeralds."

When he spoke again, his voice was like gravel. "Not everything will change."

In her entire life, Diana never wanted to believe a lie more.

They darted out of the ballroom to the gallery, where they came close to colliding with a waiter carrying a tray of champagne coupes. Diana lithely ducked out of the way but caught the edge of her dress on the nearby settee.

"Damn," she muttered as she lifted the fallen hem.

"Leave it," Ian said.

"I can't, I'll trip. Bloody ready-made gowns."

She glanced up and saw the ladies' retiring room was a few doors down. "There should be some pins there. It will take half a minute. I'll hurry."

Usually, public retiring rooms were well-lit, so ladies could examine their wardrobes with attention. But when Diana walked inside, the room was exceptionally dim and exceptionally quiet. Only one other woman stood in a shadowed corner, at the far end of the room.

Even in the darkness, she recognized Widow's silhouette.

"You can't be surprised I'm here, Diana."

"Of course not," she agreed smoothly.

"Then you know why I had to come myself."

Diana kept her voice low so Widow wouldn't detect the threat of it trembling. "For the necklace."

"It's about more than that now. You raised too much interest in San Sebastian."

As Widow took a step closer and half of her face emerged from the shadows, Diana swallowed the knot rising in her throat. From the beginning, she'd known that in all of her plotting, this would be the hardest part of the operation.

If it killed her, she would keep her composure as she confronted the hate and vitriol in her mother's gaze.

Ian pressed himself up against the wall behind the door of the retiring room.

He hoped to hell Diana realized he'd followed her. There was no chance he'd let her go off by herself when they were this close to a handoff, and she'd left the door open behind her, which was too careless not to be intentional.

"We were compromised," Diana said in a deferential tone he detested. The low lighting in the room obscured the murky figure she spoke to.

"You went off script," came their biting reply. "Because of Ian Holt."

"That's not why we had problems."

"Don't sass me." The shadow stepped forward into the small pool of light from the sole lamp.

Ian choked back a breath.

He was grateful for his years of stealth along the docks, and the self-possession beaten into him at Harrow. Without it, he would have cried out at the woman who looked and sounded exactly like Diana's deceased mother.

"How many times have I told you?" Mrs. Rives reprimanded her daughter. "Men are a trap."

"Ian's not. He doesn't want me that way."

The conviction in her voice made pain slice through his chest. Could she truly believe that, after the last few days? After what had happened between them in San Sebastian?

Her mother gave a harsh laugh. "No, Ian wants the emeralds. It was a mistake to tempt him with them. You miscalculated, and now we must deal with the fallout."

He understood now why Diana had concealed her handler's identity, and why she was so frightened about her mission to uncover the traitor within the White Stags. If she had to unravel the network to rebuild it, she might have to destroy her own mother.

"I can manage it. Ian proved himself in San Sebastian," Diana countered. "Without him, we wouldn't have saved those women."

"Debatable."

"Please." Diana's voice caught. "Reconsider."

"Pleading is beneath you," her mother chided. "Don't degrade yourself for him."

Ian frantically searched the dark room for any trace of others hidden in the shadows who'd pounce if he made a deliberate move to silence the poison words Mrs. Rives spewed. It seemed impossibly lucky she'd come alone.

"My patience is growing thin." Mrs. Rives approached her daughter. "Give me the necklace, and I shall forgive this little revolt of yours."

The shrew's tone was colder than stone, and Ian had had quite enough of it. He withdrew his pistol and checked the deck of cards he'd slid into his pocket. From his angle, he had a partial shot of Diana's mother, but not one that would clear Diana.

"Why did you have me take it?" Diana gripped the necklace as if she would break it apart herself. "It has nothing to do with our mission."

Mrs. Rives scoffed. "There are dangerous men who would do dangerous things to claim the emeralds. They play for more than the necklace, Diana. And we must stop all of them. Including young Mr. Holt."

"Please—"

"Ian is an unnecessary liability. We serve a greater mission. You must remind yourself that none of us are essential."

"He's essential to *me*!"

The startled expression on her mother's face gave Ian an opportunity to fling the deck of cards to open the door all the way, which illuminated the dark room with the light from the hall.

Diana spun around. Her mother jerked her head up.

"Mrs. Rives." He cocked the pistol. "A pleasure to see you after so many years."

A whistle shrieked. Diana's mother darted away as Ian shouted at Diana to duck. Glass shattered, and something doused the outside corridor light and the lone lamp in the room.

Darkness engulfed them.

Ian shouted Diana's name while he hurled furniture aside to cross the room.

The dim light of a wall sconce flickered, and as the hazy light spread through the broken glass shade, he saw Diana's hand quiver as she gripped the gas valve.

He paused with one eye on the door, the other on the room, until he confirmed they were once again alone.

A horrible sense of foreboding rose within him as he remembered the fear Diana had voiced about what would happen next. The tenor of her voice as she'd shouted at her mother was still reverberating in his ears.

He's essential to ME.

"Diana."

At the soft call of her name, she blinked, registered his face, and sprinted across the room.

Ian opened his arms to receive her, but halfway there, her legs folded beneath her. Before she hit the ground, he caught her in his embrace.

167

Chapter Eighteen

Diana's thoughts fogged in. The only thing that kept her grounded to consciousness was Ian's warmth, and the weight of his arms around her.

She blinked to clear her vision and her mind. After a hazy moment, she realized Ian was carrying her up the staircase of the hotel next to the casino. Their progress was smooth; the transition from one place to the next was almost dreamlike as he walked through a hallway and into a small suite of rooms.

A sudden hush descended. In the stillness, a dam burst within her chest, and she lost the battle to restrain her sobs.

It only took a few fraught minutes with her mother to shatter her into pieces.

Widow had denied none of Diana's accusations about betraying their mission. She had no remorse about betraying her own daughter.

A spike of rage cleared away some of her bewilderment. She batted her eyes and blinked as she examined the smart furnishings of the luxurious hotel suite.

Ian stood a foot away from her perch at the edge of the bed. He watched her carefully; his posture was strung tight as a bow.

Everything felt fragile: the air between them, the closeness they'd built together over these few weeks...even her raw emotions.

She assessed the way his strong shoulders filled out the fine wool of his black jacket before she met his eyes.

"We're safe here," he assured her. "I arranged for the room."

"Arranged or swindled?"

"Does it matter?"

"No." It wouldn't make telling him any easier. She buried her face in her hands.

He pried one away and cradled it between his. "Do you want to rest?"

She shook her head. He was behaving so patiently, which was a balm of sorts. Though if he'd been agitating her, she could have blurted it all out. Then it would be over. Done.

With her hand in his, he said, "I thought Beatrix was the only walking ghost I'd ever meet."

"I told you I knew what it was like."

"You did," he agreed. "I can only imagine how difficult it was. If my mother returned to my life, I'd do anything she asked of me."

For so many years, Diana had schemed and manipulated and lied, exactly as Widow had directed. She never allowed herself to consider the repercussions, or question if the outcome justified the means to achieve it. "I'm sorry I couldn't tell you. And I'm sorry for everything I did, trying to fulfill her wishes. None of it warranted my lies."

She swallowed. "I understand why you'd never trust me again."

"I'm not giving her the power to drive another wedge between us," he argued, a threatening edge to his voice. "And I wouldn't be here if I didn't trust you. Now it's time for you to trust me."

When shame choked her throat, he sank down next to her on the bed and stroked her hand encouragingly. "Tell me all of it. Starting with when she resurfaced in your life."

"She was never bedridden," Diana whispered. "One day, she simply disappeared. Without a trace. My father spared no expense searching for her in secret, while maintaining the charade that she was ill to stave off scandal. He was so ashamed. And when he accepted she'd abandoned us, her desertion became our shameful secret."

"He should never have asked that of you."

"For all we knew, she *was* dead somewhere. I'd thought of her that way." It had been an easier way to accept her loss. "Eight years ago, around the time you stopped writing to me, the Stags began recruiting me. They communicated by clandestine notes from someone who called herself Widow. A year later, when we were in Switzerland, searching for another treatment for Papa's illness, Widow finally wrote for me to meet her face-to-face. I followed the address to an old convent."

"Where your mother was waiting." He sounded disgusted by the ploy.

"When I saw her in that wretched basement, I thought I was going mad. And then I was so furious, thoughts of violence flitted through my brain."

"I can't imagine that," he said dryly.

"Before I could find the words to ask why she'd abandoned us, my mother revealed that she'd sacrificed her old life to serve a higher calling. She told me about the women she was helping. The stories of the horrors they escaped still haunt my nightmares." Her voice cut out as she fought off a shudder. "When the police wouldn't help them, my mother and her allies founded the White Stags."

"And to keep you quiet, she told you that a network that relied on secrecy and worked outside the law would have put you, your father, and Rives Shipping in danger."

That threat kept Diana from breathing a word of it to anyone for years. "When my mother said the success of their mission hinged on me joining them, and that my destiny in life was to be more than an heiress and a society wife, I'd never been happier. I instantly forgave her abandonment."

"Because she wanted you."

"And because she needed me."

Ian nodded empathetically. His family had conscripted him to defend their business. He must have borne a similar sense of obligation.

As horrible as it was, Diana liked that they shared something of such magnitude. "I haven't been in the same room with her since she found me in Switzerland," she admitted. "Widow usually communicates through notes or other agents." Allegedly, for their safety and protection. Now Diana knew it was nothing but a cover for her mother's deception and cowardice.

"Clearly, she came to Monte Carlo for the necklace." Ian paused. "And yet she didn't take it from you tonight."

"I don't know why."

"She's controlled you your entire life," he murmured. "Perhaps she can't fathom that you wouldn't do what she commanded."

The indignity of it made Diana cast her eyes to the elaborate carpet. The room must have cost a fortune. She wanted to figure out how Ian had swindled it, rather than deal with the mess of the evening. "After tonight, I know my mother betrayed me, and everyone who's worked for our cause. I intend to take the Stags apart, brick by brick if I have to. Our work is too important to serve some vigilante agenda."

For her entire adult life, the work of the White Stags had consumed her. It was an escape from the pretensions of the *beau monde* and her responsibilities as heir to a shipping empire. At her mother's direction, she'd taken her wealth and her privilege and forged them into a weapon that she no longer knew how to wield.

And now, she felt catastrophically lonely in her mission.

Diana longed to confess this to Ian, but it sounded so absurd in her head, she couldn't imagine giving voice to the words. In her struggle, she sought comfort in the way the firelight danced over his fine cheekbones and cast gold streaks in his dark hair. She'd watched him closely for so long, she couldn't remember a time when he hadn't fascinated her.

"I heard what you said to your mother. When she told you to cut me loose." He cupped her face before she could turn away. "You defended me. Hell." His voice grew hoarse. "You subverted her orders to protect me."

Slowly, he lifted his hand and stroked the necklace with his thumb. "Why did you refuse to give her the emeralds?"

He was daring her to reveal her true feelings. Diana resented the way he'd asked her with such calm.

But when he drew a breath, his chest shook. The hand that rested on her neck trembled.

The same way her hands quaked with the longing to touch him.

She covered his hand with hers. "I thought by now you would have figured out that I wanted...I want—"

When the words stuck in her throat, she laughed at the absurdity of her fear.

She was not a cowardly woman. Neither in her actions nor her feelings.

"You want?" Ian echoed.

"You, Ian. I want you."

He uttered a low groan as his fingers laced through her hair to draw her closer. Against her ear, he whispered, "You want more of what happened between us in San Sebastian?"

"Yes." Heat flooded her, from his proximity and from the memory. "And this time I want to reciprocate."

His mouth skated across her throat. "Are you sure?"

"It doesn't—" Her voice cut out as his hands stroked the sensitive skin at the back of her neck. "It doesn't have to mean anything."

The warmth of his fingers brushed down her shoulders as he deftly unfastened the back of her dress. "Do you think what happened at the brothel meant nothing?"

"No," she admitted softly.

"No," he agreed.

The contrast of his hand moving across her skin and the friction of the fabric set fire to her blood. Perspiration broke out on her forehead.

"I wanted it to only be physical," she whispered.

His lips met the exposed skin of her shoulder as he murmured, "It isn't purely physical."

It won't ever be, she conceded silently.

She opened the buttons on his waistcoat with the same slow precision he was relieving her of the rest of her clothes. His muscles tightened beneath her hands, and she was breathless at the prospect of tracing every inch of his well-formed torso without the barrier of clothing. "The thing is, I enjoy adventuring with you."

He laughed roughly, but his expression turned more serious as his hands traced her throat. "I like the way your mind works around a problem. How fiercely you attack it."

"You're fierce too. Though you fight so hard to contain it. You don't have to with me."

Ian's mouth finally descended on hers. She wanted to drown in his taste and became giddy with the way he nipped at her lips and tangled his tongue with hers. She continued to play along with his slow seduction by lazily unwinding his necktie.

In between long kisses, his fingers explored her hair. Gently, he removed her hairpins so her thick locks wouldn't tangle. When her hair cascaded over her shoulders, he leaned back.

The scent of linseed oil and his soap was so intoxicating, she needed him closer and looped her arms around his neck. "We're two intelligent, capable people. If we make up our minds, this doesn't have to be more than this moment."

"You think once this happens, we won't want to repeat it?"

"It doesn't have to be anything more than giving each other...physical pleasure."

"Are you saying you don't like plotting and talking with me?"

"Fine. We can be scheming friends who also enjoy each other's bodies."

Her face was on fire with her daring words, but she would be damned if he thought she was too embarrassed or afraid to say what she wanted.

His large, warm hands circled her waist and drew her over his lap, bringing her flush against his hard cock. "We haven't been friends for years."

She seized the open neck of his shirt for support. "Rivals, then."

"For what?"

They both looked surreptitiously at the emeralds around her throat.

Slowly, Diana pried her fingers away from the soft linen of his shirt and unfastened the necklace. She lifted his warm hand and placed the jewels in his palm.

For a long moment, they stared at it, both quietly contemplating her surrender.

Ian stretched his arm and placed the necklace on the bedside table. It landed with a clink, like two champagne flutes heralding a toast.

Then he bent and sealed his mouth on hers.

The kiss was slow, languid. Diana tried to deepen it, but he held her carefully as he sipped on her mouth and massaged her neck with the lightest of touches.

She broke away for a long breath. "Let's suspend time, just for tonight." She wanted to forget necklaces and manipulating mothers and the distance between their fortunes.

"Can we do that? Forget everything else?" As she stroked a hand up his chest, she delighted in the delicious draw of his breath. "Tonight, nothing else exists. Our sole purpose is making each other feel good."

Ian clamped his hands over hers. "If you expect tenderness, you should know I can't be that way with you."

"You were in San Sebastian."

"That was—" He'd started to say, *a mistake*, but the way he caught himself gave her hope.

That, and the very tender way he was staring at her.

"I don't need you to be tender." She nipped at his lip to underscore her point. "Tenderness would undermine the entire premise of this being purely physical."

"Can you separate it so easily?" His hands explored the pockets of her skin exposed by the widening gap in the back of her dress. "I fear I won't be able to. That we'll do this, and we'll get caught up in a fantasy that we could have more together."

Lord, how his words exhilarated and wounded her. And what a tremendous relief that he suffered the same craving beneath his skin that she did. This present stolen moment together wouldn't fully assuage it. And her heart wrenched for the shared dream they could never turn into reality.

"We won't let it master us." She pulled the bottom of his shirt, and he lifted it off in a effortless movement. In the firelight, his skin was smooth and tanned. When her hands ran over his chest to trace the small Maltese cross inked over his heart, they both moaned.

His mouth took hers, and he urged her back on the bed. When he finally broke away, for a breath, he pinned her arms to the mattress. His dark eyes traced the length of her body with a sizzling look.

Everything south of her waist clenched and melted.

"Is this what you imagined, Diana?"

In truth, her fantasies had never quite taken this direction, and she chided her limited imagination because she loved the weight of his body on hers and the soft, commanding way he spoke.

"Is this what you want?" He panted.

"I want to touch you." She arched up and nibbled at his ear. "And I want my touch to bring you incalculable pleasure. I want to know what you taste like when you're completely undone by it."

She faintly thought speaking such obscenities out loud should mortify her, but it was exhilarating having no filter between them.

Arousing beyond measure.

With a rumbling growl, his lips came upon hers and finally delivered the pressure and heat she'd been chasing. Diana sighed in relief as she lost herself in his kiss.

Ian freed her hands from his hold so they could work together to rid her of the last of her clothes. He paused a long moment to observe her in her skin. The intensity of his attention made her overwhelmingly self-conscious.

She reached for him, but he caught both wrists in one hand. With the other, he glided a finger along her collarbone, then gently down across her breast. He traced her nipple with his nail, and an unhinged noise erupted from her throat.

It drew the brightest smile she'd ever seen him wear.

"For the last two days, I've been dreaming of this."

Slowly, Ian bent and took the peak of her breast in his mouth. The heat of his tongue coupled with the sharpness of his teeth brought her dangerously close to unraveling.

"Now I can see you, taste you, with nothing in between us," he murmured against her bare skin. "I want to savor it all when I make you come again."

The prospect made her cry out like a wanton, and he finally dropped his hold on her wrists. She plunged both hands into his hair and pulled it while he suckled her, stroked her body.

Fire crawled across her skin. She was in a beautiful agony as she hovered on a divine precipice.

"Shall I touch you again, the way I did before?" he taunted without letting up his tantalizing caress. "Perhaps I'll tease out your pleasure. Make it last all night."

"Don't you dare," she hissed.

"Impatient, are we?" His laugh rumbled against her torso. "Lucky for you, I'm an accommodating sort of devil."

He thrust two fingers inside her. She came instantly, explosively, with a roar that rattled the ceiling.

Her heart felt as if it would never cease racing, and she wasn't entirely sure she wanted it to.

As he held her through the aftershocks, Ian's breaths were as jagged as hers.

They stopped altogether when Diana rolled them over on the bed and palmed his erection.

"My...turn." She drew out the words slowly, a contrast to the frantic way she pulled at the buttons on his trousers and his underclothes.

When her hands came around his cock, they both gasped.

"Show me what you want," she whispered as she stroked him. "What you imagined."

He groaned deeply and moved to tear off his trousers.

Diana drank in the sight of his beautiful body. The wide breadth of his shoulders. His long, narrow trunk, corded with muscles, and the soft, dark hair on his chest pointing a path to his erect cock.

"Show me," she repeated, reaching for him.

His hand curled around hers to demonstrate the pressure and movement he liked, and when she shook him off and took up the rhythm on her own, he gave another primal groan.

When he threw his head back, she leaned down and took his shaft in her mouth.

"*Diana.*"

Her skin warmed all over and the ache between her legs returned as her tongue swirled around him and she took in his salty taste. His size was overwhelming, but she married the rhythm of her hand at his base with the movement of her tongue and her lips.

"Yes, *tesora mia*, exactly like that." He gasped. "Christ, you are so good. You are a dream."

The hoarseness in his voice made her clench harder as she drew him further into her mouth.

His entire body went rigid before he came, shouting her name.

And when Ian collapsed back on the pillow, boneless, and the terrible tension he carried in his brow and his shoulders had fled for parts unknown, Diana nearly wept from the beauty of his transformation.

He tucked her against his body, so her head lay on his shoulder.

"That was beyond my imagining," she whispered.

"That was beyond anything on heaven or earth," he confessed through labored breaths.

Diana laughed softly. "I enjoy getting what I want."

Ian propped up on his elbow and rasped, "Are you curious what I want, *tesora*?"

In San Sebastian, he'd also called her his treasure. She understood now why lovers gave each other pet names; when he said it, it made her skin heat and her body ache for him.

"Well, I thought you might have wanted the same thing I did," she hazarded. "You looked like you enjoyed it."

"Enjoy is an inadequate word." He crept over her to press soft kisses against her chin and teased his tongue along her throat and her chest. "Besides being accommodating, I'm also a greedy devil."

His breath coasted over her belly as his mouth traced her hip. "I want to know what you taste like too."

The brush of his lips at the cleft between her legs made her entire body quiver with desire.

"Will you let me?" he breathed.

"God, yes," she whimpered.

Gently, he pressed her legs apart to make room for him to nuzzle her. His warm breath and the featherlight kisses on her thighs were a sweet torment.

Forcefully, she grabbed a hold of his silky hair and pulled him between her legs.

He devoured her. The heat of his lips and the seductive stroking of his tongue as he took his fill of her was pure ecstasy.

Pressure built inside her. But as the glorious peak approached, he retreated with softer kisses and teasing caresses.

"Ian, please," she begged, clutching his hair.

"You're making me hard again, love."

"*Please*," she repeated, on something like a sob.

"Does that mean you like this?"

"Yes!" she wailed. "It's— I'm—"

"You want to come."

"Make me," she pleaded.

He finally slid his finger inside her, and stars burst across her vision.

When she returned to earth, she reached for the warm weight of his arms.

He nestled her against his chest as he murmured soft words in a smattering of languages.

Showing her all the tenderness that he swore he couldn't offer her.

CHAPTER NINETEEN

IN THE DARK HOUR before dawn, Ian finally found the willpower to rise from bed.

Diana slept sprawled across the mattress. She'd spent much of the night sprawled across him in similar fashion, which was one of the many reasons he'd remained awake.

He'd suspected they would be good together in bed, but nothing he'd imagined came close to the reality of being with her. One night would never be enough. Now that he had physical memories to match his fantasies, knowing what was possible—and not having it—would eat him alive.

He used the attached bathroom to wash and dress. His unruly hair and dark beard made his reflection in the mirror something sinister. He looked like someone who belonged roaming the docks.

"What time is it?" Diana's muffled voice called.

When Ian walked back into the bedroom, she had the sheet pulled tightly around her. He recognized that this was not some latent effort at modesty; it was an attempt to put distance between them.

"It's after seven," he replied calmly.

"Will you draw me a bath? I'd like to wash." Her eyes darted between him and the door, and he nodded slowly. Birdie or her sparrows were likely waiting outside.

Thankfully, the bathing room was fitted with running water, and Ian turned the cold tap to muffle the sound of their conversation.

Diana pulled the door to the bath shut behind her and leaned against it protectively. With the sheet draped around her, her chestnut hair tumbled over her shoulders, and a faint blush lingering on her cheeks, she looked like a goddess.

One he was eager to worship with his body again.

"I suspect Birdie's in the hallway," she murmured.

"And we have to assume she's working with Widow to lure you somewhere they can take the necklace without a fight."

Diana gave a reluctant nod. He hated the way she gripped the sheet closer to cover her breasts. The attempt was futile; he'd never forget what they looked like.

"I know we should talk about last night." Her throat bobbed on a swallow. "But if we do, I fear we'll never leave this room."

He paused a beat. "That can be arranged."

She bit her lip. "It was wonderful, Ian."

He felt his smile split his face. "It was."

The water rushed into the drain while they took a moment to revel in this accord before she said, "You promised you'd tell me what you know about the factions vying for the emeralds and what you intend to do about it."

It was the bargain they'd made, and yet, he hesitated. Once she knew the truth, the adventure he'd allowed himself to get carried away with would end.

"Ian?"

"Knowing will make you a target." He couldn't be polite about it, nor could he hold back a snarl. "Despite that, I also know that it's ultimately better for you to understand everything, because we both need to protect you from it."

"You keep trying to push me away from this. Have you considered that I'm already too entwined?"

"Yes." He scrubbed a hand down his face. "And if I tell you all this, I am asking you to agree to put that clever brain to work to sort out a way to sever you from it."

Before the glower she gave him could turn into another protest, he quickly said, "The necklace is the bounty for a dangerous competition. *Il Gioco*. It came about because three *famiglie*—I use the term loosely—have held historical claim to the emeralds over the last two hundred years.”

“One of them is Il Corno. Costa’s network.”

“The Sicilian *famiglia*,” he confirmed. “There is also the Manu Rosso, whose territory is in the South. And the Tarka.”

“They must be from Malta.”

He nodded. “It means shield.”

Diana extended her fingers over her heart, and he tipped his head to acknowledge her silent question that the shadowed lines behind the cross of his tattoo formed the symbol.

It stirred memories, promises he wasn’t ready to divulge to her yet, so he prattled on. “Legend says the battle for the gems used to be a trying series of physical tests, but the *famiglie* lost too many soldiers. Now, *Il Gioco* is played on one night, in one ruthless zero-sum game of cards. The winner receives the emeralds and everything the other players wager. Whoever wins holds the emeralds for life. And everything staked to them. The winner can sell the other assets—”

“But the emeralds can never be bought or sold,” she finished. “If only the three *famiglie* can play for the emeralds, how did your father win them?”

“He never told me all of the details, but it amounted to being in the wrong place at the wrong time and the Tarka deciding he would play for them.”

“Why didn’t they play when your father died?”

“There was a show of force from the newly unified Italian government to police criminal activity. It didn’t stick. But it allowed me a few years to seed rumors that the emeralds were stolen in the upheaval following my father’s death.”

“So when Jared tried to sell them—”

“He didn’t know what he’d set in motion. It was a secret my father insisted we keep from him for his protection.”

The water sputtered from the tap, and Diana reached forward to turn it off. “What did your father stake with the emeralds?”

A rap sounded at the door.

Eager to escape Diana's question and compose himself before confronting the potentially traitorous Stags, Ian crept out of the bathing room and withdrew his pistol. Diana darted back into the bedroom, seized her crumpled dress from the floor, and removed the knife hidden in the pocket.

The knock came again: two taps, a pause, and a third rap.

Diana met his eyes and nodded to confirm it was Birdie before she slipped the dress over her head. Ian opened the door a crack and found Birdie in the hallway with one hand tucked in the pocket of her coat. She took in Ian's rumpled suit, raised a brow, and sauntered into the room.

"Brought you a change of clothes, ma'am." Birdie tossed Diana a brown paper package. "Thought trousers and a cap would be the most versatile."

"Thank you." Diana accepted it with all of her society poise. "I won't sugarcoat what happened last night. Widow and I had a disagreement about the next phase of the operation. She has allowed me time to present her with an alternative."

"What's the plan then?"

The crew hand's tone was far too pleasant for Ian's liking. Birdie had to be itching at the discord between Diana and her handler.

"We should continue on the water," he said, following Diana's lead. "Costa will watch the trains."

"There's a tugboat with a course to Genoa," Birdie suggested smoothly. "Schedule says the boat casts off in two hours."

The woman wasn't even trying to conceal her eagerness to move them on that route. Ian choked down a growl.

"Make the arrangements," Diana said. "And you and your team should keep your heads down today," she added. "Going back to the townhouse is a risk."

"Aye."

It was such an obvious attempt at a trap; Ian marveled at how both of the women were keeping a straight face discussing it.

"And Birdie, if you have reservations about the direction of this operation, I can relieve you of your duty," Diana cautioned primly.

"That won't be necessary, ma'am." Birdie's tone was brusque and efficient. The epitome of an obedient operative. She was overplaying it by a mile, and Ian couldn't help stare at her pointedly until she backed her way out of the room.

The moment she left, Ian took up a post at the window overlooking the front entrance to the hotel, but the sparrows were smart enough to abscond using another route.

Diana withdrew to the bathing room to change. She reappeared a few moments later ensconced in woolen pants with braces, a flannel shirt, and boots.

He loved the way she walked in trousers. Her hips swayed freely; her strides were quick and smooth. He could watch the graceful fall of her steps all damn day.

As she attempted to pin her plaited hair against her head to tuck underneath the cap, she bemoaned the pins under her breath.

Ian walked behind her and caught her gaze in the mirror. He gestured to her hair. "Do you want help with that?"

She paused with her hands suspended over her head. "I didn't realize you were skilled in hairdressing."

"Don't tell me you forgot practicing on me?" he teased.

"Of course I remember." Her lips twitched. "You'd let your hair grow out all summer. You had so many more curls, I was green with envy and intent on ruining them with my experiments. I'm still shocked you agreed to it."

"Always a willing accomplice," he murmured as he reached for a pin. Handling her hair was staving off the howling need to caress her again, in more intimate places.

"Well, it's been close to twenty years since all of that. I guess you've found other means of practice?"

It was a carefully worded question about his past liaisons. He loved the urgency in her tone, the way her eyes wouldn't move from his while she waited for his response.

"Hardly any," he conceded. "I tried with two other models. Neither of them gave me a second chance to further my skills."

"How shortsighted of them," she murmured. Her blush deepened. "Of course, I have little perspective."

"No?"

"In the past, I've only ever seen to it myself."

He'd been the first to wring that pleasure from her, and his satisfaction in it shook him to his core.

As he placed the last pin, he couldn't resist grazing the bare nape of her neck with his finger.

She spun around to face him, and his attention centered on the blush rising over her cheeks.

"You never said what your father staked with the emeralds. You promised to tell me."

Denying it would be a waste of his breath. "The Tarka took the lion's share of the winnings, but Father had staked his dockside holdings in the game. They're still tied to the emeralds."

Diana lifted a hand to her mouth. In all the years he'd known her, he'd never observed her so visibly surprised.

"Jared knew nothing about it," he added. "As the current custodian of the gems, he may play for them if one of the *famiglie* choose him as their player. If he plays, he will undoubtedly lose."

"But you won't let him," she insisted. "Because losing the docks would mean more than losing Holt & Company."

Ian adored her quick mind, her ability to fill in the gaps left unsaid. And as badly as he wanted her for his partner in the many crimes he would commit vying to win *Il Gioco*, the idea that she'd be terrified or hurt because of him, in defense of him, was intolerable.

Slowly, he stepped away. "Her Majesty's government is monitoring *Il Gioco*."

"You're working with the Crown?" Diana huffed a short laugh.

"Sunderland convinced them I was their best defense."

Her mouth hinged open in a delicious O shape, then her brows descended. "Trusting Leo Ashton would be a colossal mistake."

Ian had no intention of revealing the bargain he'd made with the duke on her behalf; it would only make her want to settle the matter herself.

"Infiltrating *Il Gioco* will be complicated. Sunderland is in a position to help. This isn't negotiable."

A delicate snarl issued from her throat. "When Amelia finds out, she'll throttle me."

Ian didn't know the source of the strained history between Amelia and the duke, and he doubted Diana would divulge it if she knew. "If one of the *famiglie* wins the title to the docks, it will give them the foothold they need to take London. With that leverage, their crime syndicate could spread to all of Britain."

"But we're going to stop that from happening."

"*I* am going to try."

The cathedral bells chimed a quarter to the hour, drawing Diana's attention to the clock on the fireplace mantel. "We must go."

"Straight into the trap Birdie has laid for us?"

"There's still a chance she's not involved."

"If you believed that, you would have told her the truth about Widow," he countered.

Diana headed to the door. "I can reason with Widow—"

"No." Ian clasped her arm, but gently stayed her movement. "She is beyond rational thinking at this stage. There's too much at stake for her. Think of what she's already sacrificed. She ransomed innocent, abused women. She'll risk her own daughter if she has to."

"You know I want to stop her."

"Of course. But it's an impossible position for you. It would be for any child. You don't have the perspective you need. *Il Gioco* is in motion now. You need to let me take the lead."

"Let's get out of Monte Carlo first."

"This isn't up for negotiation," he repeated, irritated that he had to.

She wriggled free of his hold. "And you're delusional if you think what happened between us last night means you can order me around like some indentured servant."

There was no heat to her tone, but her assumption that he was like every other man who'd chased her skirts and her money stung.

"I'd never dream of taking that liberty," he volleyed back. "What happened between us has no bearing on the danger chasing us, and I'm the one who knows the territory. If you want to get out of this with your hide—and continue with your mission—you need to let me direct our next steps."

Diana tucked a lock of stray hair into her cap. "What is your counterproposal?"

"We miss the rendezvous with Birdie. Lie low here in Monte Carlo until I can signal for an extraction."

"Why should I trust the people *you're* working with any more than the Stags?"

"You shouldn't. I don't." Ian lifted a shoulder. "But I'm asking you to trust me."

Her expression softened. "I do, you know. And...it scares me how much I trust you."

She spoke the uneasy words that rested in his heart. And to assure her of it, he placed his hands on her shoulders and brushed his mouth against hers.

Diana studied him for an excruciating moment before sighing and bowing theatrically toward the door, gesturing for him to lead the way.

They departed by the rooftop exit Ian had reconnoitered the previous day and hopped across to the neighboring building, where they used the cover of a carriage queue to snake through the side lanes. As the morning waned, they hid among the canopied market stalls of the *centre-ville*. Ian sacrificed a few precious coins to pay a lad to retrieve ham and cheese tartines for them, along with two tin cups of cider.

Dark clouds hovered over the harbor, and eventually Diana said, "We're past the meet time. They'll be looking for us soon. Maybe we should risk the train?"

"If they're intent on trapping us, they'll have lookouts at the station. There's a church a quarter of a mile away where I can make a drop." It would take more time to ask a priest to wire Sunderland, but Birdie's sparrows were watching the telegraph office.

They traversed the Place d'Armes, ducked past the fountains, and walked along a tree-covered lane that led to the church. Ian directed Diana to the small door on the west side. "It leads to the crypt. We can wait there until the rector arrives for evening confession."

He held open the door and mimicked the bow she had given him earlier, which made her roll her eyes before she marched into the dark basement.

Diana's footsteps halted as she froze on the stone floor.

Ahead of them, a man stood in the flickering light of the altar candles, pointing a gun at them.

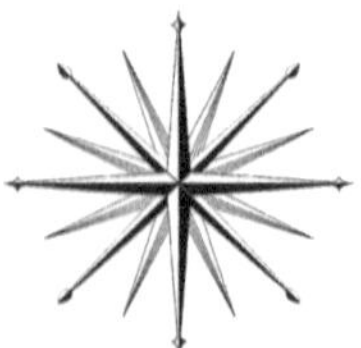

Chapter Twenty

If the brute had confronted them alone instead of accompanied by three more men brandishing guns, Diana knew that she and Ian could have flayed the bastard.

Since the night they'd fought together in Mayfair, she'd cultivated a deep appreciation of his physical prowess and defensive acumen. But now that she knew Ian's body intimately, she was desperate for him to unleash his strength and agility to throttle the thugs who held them.

Out of reflex, her fingers crept into her pockets.

"Hands up, Miss Rives," the assailant ordered in accented English as he turned the gun on her. "Wouldn't want you reaching for those pretty knives of yours."

Beside her, Ian remained ethereally still. Diana hoped he was bracing for an attack. Then she feared what would happen to him if he went off too quickly and she didn't have time to cover him.

The leader cocked the trigger of his gun. "I believe I asked you to *raise your hands.*"

Ian gave a feral hiss.

The armed men stepped closer.

The potential of it escalating to shots and seeing Ian's blood spilled on the stone floor made Diana quickly raise her hands. "I don't believe we've had the pleasure."

"You toffs never remember people like me." He flashed a manufactured smile. "Unless we give you cause."

Diana forced a laugh and willed her thoughts to stop whirling. They needed a diversion to facilitate their escape.

"You're a man of business; that much is obvious." She couldn't risk looking at Ian as she crept forward, or she'd reveal her efforts to befuddle their captors. "Let's negotiate."

"You're not understanding, *piccola*." The tough waved his gun around at her and his men. "There's no advantage for you to play."

"I respectfully disagree." Diana glanced at the man on their left. His hold on his pistol was shaky; he was the weakest link of the bunch and the best target to disarm. She prayed Ian noticed it too. "Everyone wants something. I'm prepared to provide you with a much more lucrative compensation than what your current employer is offering you."

"Who says I need a bribe to get my hands on you and those pretty emeralds?"

A howl erupted from behind her.

Diana threw her best right hook with her palm exposed and belted the leader in the nose. His disoriented state allowed her to wrench the pistol from him.

The fiend roared at his henchmen, but Ian had similarly disarmed the shaky one. With one boot on his neck, Ian pointed two pistols at the man who was still armed. The goon holding the gun at Ian pulled the trigger, but Ian ducked in time, and fired back to disarm the assailant by shooting the pistol out of his hand.

Diana kept her gun pointed toward the gang leader. Ian searched the basement for other accomplices before taking a post with his back to hers. The waves of heat coming off him made her heartbeat retreat to a less frantic pace.

"Are you hurt?"

They spoke in unison, and it sent a delicious thrill through the pit of Diana's stomach.

"I'm fine," she confirmed.

Ian uttered a low grunt to affirm the same before he swung around and aimed both guns at the leader. "Let's revisit our discussion."

"I don't think we will, *Signore* Holt."

A wiry man with graying hair appeared at the crypt altar. The same man who'd scrutinized them so closely during their visit to the Swan's Nest. Although short in stature, his posture held the same regal and lethal air as a lion king. Behind him stood six men, all armed to the teeth. Half of them wore *gendarme* uniforms.

The lion king flicked a hand, and the guards surrounded them before either Diana or Ian could move. They took the pistols. One of them quickly dispatched her of the knife in her pocket. The rough search of her person made Ian voice an incoherent, vicious protest, which earned him a silencing punch across the mouth.

Of all the moments for him to abandon his Herculean restraint. Diana silently pleaded for him not to do anything stupid on her behalf. She wished she could assuage him by telling him her other knife remained tucked inside the bindings wrapped around her breasts.

As she searched for some other escape route, her eyes clapped on Birdie, hiding behind the circle of men.

When they arrived in Monte Carlo, Diana had ordered the crew hands to keep tailing Ian, to keep up the appearance she remained distrustful of him. They'd obviously followed him as he'd reconnoitered the church.

The shame of her grave miscalculation heated Diana's cheeks. Embarrassment and fear morphed into hot anger, and the warning flash of Ian's dark eyes couldn't stop her from flaunting a deadly smile at the gray-haired man. "Have we met, *signore*?"

"Forgive me, *Signorina* Rives, I've forgotten my manners. You may call me Titus." His mouth twitched. "I did not expect I would need so much muscle to detain the two of you. That will teach me to follow the advice of your Widow."

Amelia had once accused Diana of single-mindedness for the White Stag mission. Until now, she'd never seen the danger in it. She'd wanted a cause to drive her, something to fill her up. A purpose. A calling.

It was easier to live solely focused on that mission. In the boundaries of the black-and-white orders, on Widow's black-and-white paper. She hadn't questioned a thing. Because her mother had conditioned her not to.

The woman who had manipulated and lied to Diana her entire life was in league with men who'd happily kill her over a set of emeralds.

"What exactly is your agreement with Widow, *capo*?" Ian's voice was cold, detached, a bastion of politeness. But his body remained coiled tight, poised to pounce the moment he had the advantage.

"Ah, you *can* show respect when you choose to. All that time in England must have made you forget what Don Alberti taught you." Titus shook his head. "That's why you didn't bring us *i gioielli*. But now that your memory has returned, Holt, I won't need to remind you about the rules. And you won't move while my *compagnos* relieve Miss Rives of the necklace."

With a flick of his hand, Titus directed two of the *gendarmes* to approach Diana.

Diana stifled the urge to twist the ties that bound her hands and reached for the only weapon she had available: her wiles.

She glanced at Titus from beneath her eyelashes and dropped the pitch of her voice to a husky tone. "I'm wondering, Mr. Titus, if you would appease my curiosity."

"We all know what curiosity does to cats, *signorina*."

"Indulge me, *signore*. What did Widow offer you in exchange for the necklace?"

Titus laughed and wagged a finger at her to mock her attempt to beguile him. "If Widow hasn't told you, *piccola*, I won't. But I'll give you a hint."

He signaled to a *gendarme*, who belted Ian in the stomach.

As Ian doubled over, guards seized him by each elbow, while two others gripped his neck in a headlock.

"There's no need for this, *signore*." Diana wrestled against her restraints. "Let us negotiate."

"This is not something we can haggle over. You have nothing left to concede. And no incentive that would persuade me to abandon my plans."

It took three of them to hold Ian down while they pried his jaw open. One of them poured a vial down his throat and smothered his nose and mouth, forcing him to swallow it.

"What are you doing?" Diana bellowed, because she'd never stop the ratbags by shrieking like some harpy. Rage made her limbs convulse, but she clung to it because it was far more useful than terror.

"This is business, *signorina*." Titus shrugged. "Widow insisted we keep you alive. I thought about taking you both as insurance for our agreement, but you're too unpredictable and I don't have money to waste on more men. These *gendarmes* are costing me a fortune." He laughed as if he spoke about a new pair of horses.

Ian's legs buckled, and he fell to the ground on his hands and knees.

Tears pricked at her eyes, and Diana didn't fight them. "We gave you the necklace. There's no need for this."

"Consider it an education," Titus quipped. "So neither of you forgets the rules again."

The men wrestled Ian to the ground and pulled at his shirt. Buttons scattered across the stone floor as the cloth parted and exposed his skin.

And the small splash of ink above his heart.

"Wait!" she roared loud enough to attract Titus's notice. "Ian wears the mark of the Tarka. Beneath his shirt."

The men paused.

Titus ripped Ian's shirt back and acknowledged the tattoo with a faint grunt. "So. Alberti marked you."

He shoved Ian's face into the ground and motioned to his men to lock their pistols before he turned to Diana. "Until *Il Gioco* concludes, I can't harm anyone bearing a mark of an heir. But the two of you have held up this competition long enough."

The men bound Diana's mouth with a gag while the burliest guard threw Ian over his shoulder. The rest kept their pistols aimed at them as they dragged them out of the church to a waiting wagon. Diana protested against her gag, but with the *gendarmes* standing guard, the few people they passed didn't give them a second look.

The cart stopped at the harbor, and the guards dragged them to a dilapidated pier, where a rickety rowboat was moored behind an ancient tug. They shackled Diana's bound hands to the rudder and hauled Ian's limp body onto the boat.

Titus nodded approvingly. "We'll let nature take its course. Find out if you're a strong as you think you are."

He raised his walking stick, and the horn of the tug blew. The sound pierced Diana's ears and she arched over Ian's body to protect him.

As the tugboat lurched away from the port, the horn blew again to drown out her screams.

A viselike pain strangled Ian's head.

Consciousness found him shortly afterward. The first thing he detected, along with the pounding at his skull, was that he was bobbing up and down on the water.

He pried his eyes open, found hard wood digging into his back, a dawn-lit sky above him, and the scent of salt and sulfur. He gripped the wooden hull, pulled himself up, and bent over the side of the boat to relieve the contents of his stomach.

A hand gently rubbed his back. "Ian?"

"I'm all right," he rasped. He wiped his mouth and kept his eyes screwed shut. "Need to work out whatever they gave me."

Diana pressed a cool hand to his forehead, and he couldn't resist sighing.

"They must have given you laudanum. Laced with something fast-acting," she murmured.

A sickly sweet taste lingered on his tongue. "I can't open my eyes or things will get ugly again. Please tell me they didn't harm you. My memory's too hazy."

"They didn't hurt me."

"No, they merely terrorized you and left you to die on open water."

"The only thing that frightened me was not knowing if you'd wake up."

Her voice was low, but there was still a scrape to it, and it made him wish he was well enough to hit something. Or preferably, someone.

His hand searched and found hers. "I'll be all right in an hour or two."

"We'll be back onshore by then. No, don't open your eyes." Diana brushed her soft hand against his brow. "A trawler took pity on us and he's towing us back to Menton."

"That's hardly a few miles from where we cast off."

"The tide was in our favor. And we would have drifted further if Titus's men weren't a complete gaggle of ninnyhammers. Turns out this little dinghy has an anchor. As soon as the tug pulled out of sight, I dropped it."

Ian contemplated risking the blow to his head and stomach to open his eyes and assure himself that she was well. And once he knew she was sound in mind and body, he would not spare her feelings. Or her pride—or his, for that matter—when he confronted her with the dangerous reality her lack of trust in him had landed them.

"That bungle was a rare mistake," he said. "Titus carries the walking stick of a *capo*. He's a high-ranking soldier with the Manu Rosso."

"And now he has the necklace." She huffed. "This is all my fault."

"We don't have to talk about it now." His head would shatter.

"They caught us because of the call I made to keep Birdie's tails on you," she insisted. "If I had trusted you—"

"It wouldn't have stopped them from following me."

"No, but we could have confided in each other and made a plan."

The regret in her voice took the sting out of his anger. He propped himself on his elbow and wrenched an eye open to a squint. Diana's pale face hovered over him; violet shadows clung beneath her eyes. But the tight brackets around her mouth released, and the way her mouth curved made it worth the effort it took to reach his thumb beneath her chin and stroke it. "We are going to have to come to an agreement, not just on what we do next, but how. I expect you to hear me out, and I will do the same. But one thing is certain; things cannot go on like this."

"You're right."

"Can you repeat that? I must be delusional from the hypnotic."

"I said you're right, you salty devil. Now lie down before I throw you over." She urged him back with a gentle hand. "We'll settle this when we're both well enough to argue."

At the Menton port, Ian disembarked without passing out. Diana found them a shabby but clean boarding house, where they secured a room using one of his silver cufflinks for payment. The amount was generous enough to include breakfast. Ian refused it—he couldn't think of food without his stomach rolling—and ordered hot water and a hip bath sent up to the room.

The combination of his aching head and the awkward stance needed to use the hip bath made him feel less than alluring, so he insisted on managing it without Diana's help.

As he stepped out from the screen with a towel wrapped around his waist, the way her gaze lingered on his bare skin warmed his bones more than the bath.

"There's still hot water left for you," he said hoarsely.

She pulled the cover back from the bed. "Get in or you'll catch a chill."

He hesitated. "I can sleep on the floor."

"Why?"

The sharp pitch of her voice made him fight off a smile, and the relief that she had no qualms about sharing a bed again made his knees weak. "I'd never allow you to sleep on the floor. And if we share a bed, I won't rest."

Her cheeks flushed in that way he loved as she crept closer. "Whatever you have in mind will be even better after a few hours of sleep."

His arm wrapped around her waist. "I'm suddenly feeling extremely alert."

She laughed against his chest and wound an arm around his neck. "Liar. You can barely stand. Get into bed. Don't make me raise my voice. Your head can't take it."

With a gentle shove, she slipped his hold and ducked around the screen for her own bath.

Ian fought to keep his eyes open as he double-checked the lock and the chair they'd placed beneath the door. Thankfully, the tiny room had no windows.

He missed his pistol sorely.

"Did you keep any cutlery from breakfast, or did the maid take it?" he asked as he staggered to the bed. "We could do with a weapon."

Her bare arm curled around the screen and hurled a knife onto the beaten wooden dresser.

Ian laughed out loud.

"There's a sound I haven't heard in ages."

"It's a rare moment when I get exactly what I ask for. Especially with you."

She hummed in agreement, and a comfortable silence fell between them, punctuated by the soft splash of water as she bathed. With the weapon by his side and the warmth of the quilt, tension seeped out of his body.

"I'm sorry I didn't stop them from taking your other knife," he said groggily. "I'll get it back for you."

"Thank you. I'll enjoy watching that."

The husky quality in her voice made his cock stiff, and he willed himself to hang onto consciousness. He turned his mind to the mire of things they needed to untangle, and half wondered why Diana didn't press him for more information on Titus. But thinking about the *famiglie* meant thinking about the decisions they needed to make, and he admitted he didn't have the strength to do what his strong sense of self-preservation dictated.

The shuffle of Diana's footsteps preceded the stroke of her warm hand on his forehead. "Get some rest, Ian. We're safe here for the moment."

He relented to sleep; he needed it to recover his strength for their protection. And so he could eventually cherish Diana's body again.

When the midday bells of the cathedral woke him several hours later, the ache and heaviness in his joints and limbs persisted, although his head had stopped throbbing. Carefully, he turned and found Diana lying next to him, her lush lips parted as she curled on her side, facing the wall.

He ached to draw her warm body against his and bury his face in her hair. While he wanted to taste and touch every inch of her, the act of sleeping entwined with each other was as irresistible as pleasuring her.

She said she trusted him. Enough to slumber a breath away. But would it ever go beyond that? It wasn't fair to demand something of her he couldn't give himself, and he could never give her his whole heart. Over the years, he'd learned to harden it to become the Devil of the Docklands. All to protect the precarious legacy his father had left him.

It had been a convenient way to rationalize why he hadn't fought for Diana. He'd convinced himself that he was following her lead, maintaining his distance so his past couldn't taint her. Because he'd believed she wanted a life he couldn't give her: marriage and a family.

How wrong he'd been. Since the day of her aborted wedding, she'd shown him example after example of why any woman of her position and fortune would never marry.

Ian had never entertained the idea of matrimony for himself. He'd known *Il Gioco* was waiting for him.

And Diana was the only person he could ever pledge his life to.

He couldn't allow what was unfolding between them to deepen. The only way for him to win *Il Gioco* and manage the aftermath was with a hardened heart.

If he had to tear his own out to save her, it would be worth the sacrifice.

CHAPTER TWENTY-ONE

Santa Maria del Fiore's cascade of bells assaulted Ian's tender head as he strode into the dining room in pursuit of as much coffee as he could drink without burning his esophagus.

Through a series of discreet carriages, cargo trains, and more godforsaken wagons, Sunderland had secured their safe passage to Italy. Two arduous days of travel delivered them to the city of Ian's birth and the townhouse the duke obtained as their base of operations.

"Come and have some breakfast, Ian."

Diana stood before the dining room buffet in a narrow patch of morning sunlight. She wore a walking suit of navy wool trimmed with cerulean silk, and he couldn't help staring purely to watch the way she moved.

"Stop frowning," she commanded as she sat down to her plate of preserved apricots, cured ham, and *cornetto* pastries. "It's too early for you to be cross with anyone."

"Can I be cross with Giotto for erecting that bloody bell tower?"

"Yes. That bastard deserves it for disturbing the peace of generations of innocent people."

When she arched her brow, Ian had to shove his hands in his pockets for fear of grabbing her and latching onto her pert mouth.

The servants bustled in with coffee thick as tar. Ian added hot milk to the cup and gulped it all in one go before pouring a second.

"I daresay sipping it would be more enjoyable," Diana murmured.

"That would imply you like the taste."

"I enjoy bitter things."

He wrenched his attention from buttering his *cornetto*, and the hint of color on her cheeks gave him hope that she'd missed having him in her bed last night. The servants had shown them to separate rooms. The aftereffects of the poison and his weariness from traveling sent him into a deep, dreamless sleep.

"Has Sunderland surfaced?" he asked.

"No, but he sent a note asking us to meet at a tailor shop." Her tone turned markedly cooler at the mention of the duke's involvement.

Ian knew enough about her and women that it was an invitation for an argument, but he wouldn't squander a breath or his energy provoking her. These were his last moments with her. Possibly forever. He wouldn't ruin them.

After squabbling over their walking route, he begrudgingly agreed to Diana's suggestion to take the longer path along the river, which was too exposed for someone to attack them and escape easily.

The sun came and went beneath the clouds, and a cool breeze stirred the ruffle of her cape as it brushed against him. She'd taken his arm, but kept a loose hold, in case she needed to move in defense. He wistfully longed for a day when they could walk arm in arm with each other without such a care.

Diana glanced over her shoulder casually to check for tails. "When was the last time you visited Florence?"

"Before my father died. After...I couldn't risk one of the *famiglie* spotting me." They would have demanded he turn over the emeralds.

"Are you at home here?"

"Not anymore." He pulled her closer to avoid a collision with some fool on one of those absurd pedal-bicycles. "Florence has changed. Or maybe I have. Whenever I'm here, I'm searching for something that no longer exists."

"That's how I feel when I'm in Bristol. Why I love to travel. It's like I'm searching for home too." In an unusually tentative voice, she asked, "Will you show me where you and your mother lived?"

He ached to take her there, despite knowing it would unravel him to experience the physical reminder of what he'd lost. Things Ian couldn't put into words lived there, and he wanted to show her. He wanted to spend time in a place with Diana wrapped in the familiar warmth of family.

But doing so would sever him in half. It would fool him into wanting something they could never have together.

Today, they needed to complete their plans to gain access to *Il Gioco*, and he'd have to manage some way to minimize Diana's part in it.

"We can't risk a visit," he said. "The *famiglie* know it. Someone will be watching."

She gave a small sigh. "I am disappointed. I was looking forward to stopping at the bakery for one of those *pastizzi*."

They found the tailor shop. It boasted a respectable inventory, although it was a far cry from Savile Row. Ian could imagine the deprecating digs Sunderland was compiling when he waved them into the back room of the shop. With the flick of his fingers, the staff scattered like birds after a gunshot.

Diana buried her prejudice beneath her elusive mask and bobbed a curtsy.

"No need for such formality with me, Miss Rives," Sunderland drawled. "I'm happy to have you fighting on our side of this. You're not a woman I'd want as an opponent."

He abruptly turned to Ian. "*Il Gioco* is set. Two days from today, somewhere here in fair Firenze. What a happy coincidence you led us here, Holt."

It was neutral territory. Ian suspected Il Corno and Manu Rosso wanted a rematch of the last game, which had also taken place in Florence. "Have the factions nominated their players?"

"Only one we've confirmed is Costa. The Manu Rosso are still arguing over who will have the seat."

"Do we know the actual game?" Diana asked.

"Baccarat, *chemin-de-fer*. There will be only one table and no banker, which gives no one a chance to influence the cards being dealt. Our player will have to play to win." Sunderland paused. "And there's also the small matter of securing your invitation."

Diana's wide eyes landed on Ian. "*You're* going to play for the Tarka?"

"If they'll let me."

"And if you lose…" She rattled her head, unable to say aloud the dread Ian had been living with for eight long years.

Win or lose, if he played for the Tarka, he'd be forever in the debt of the Maltese *famiglia*.

Ian reached over and tilted her chin up so her eyes would meet his. "I won't lose."

"Before any of that, you must convince the Tarka leaders you can win," Sunderland said matter-of-factly. "Your audition is tomorrow night, Holt. We'll be hosting a private reception for the *capobastone*."

The duke rapped at the door to the shop, and attendants scurried in. "Now, let's get you both something to wear."

To Diana's surprise, the Tarka criminals behaved like perfect gentlemen.

As she sat at the green felt-topped card table the servants had arranged in the town-home's salon, she admired the elegant gray wool of the *capobastone*'s frock coat. His son—the resemblance was too close for either of them to deny—wore a necktie with an intricate knot she envied and wanted to try herself. Both sipped their *bajtra* cordially, while they stared daggers at Ian.

Sunderland had assumed the role of the banker for the last hand of the horrible rehearsal. His affable manners hadn't fooled Diana into overlooking the way his stare prowled over everyone and everything. The duke had proved himself a deft player. He'd trounced the *capo*'s son easily and gave Ian a run on more than one hand. But she suspected Ian had let Sunderland win, to throw off suspicion from his talent for calculating which cards were in play.

"Final bets, *signori*," Sunderland called.

The game had dragged on for hours, and Diana fought against sighing with relief that it was ending.

They'd worked all day and most of the night, strategizing how to disrupt *Il Gioco*. Every time Diana had broached the subject of what would happen after the game, one of the men drew the conversation back to some technical element of the operation.

Tonight, Diana would ferret it out of Ian. No matter how difficult the conversation. From the moment he told her about *Il Gioco*, she'd known he would have found some way to play for the emeralds. But if he thought that after everything that had happened, she'd allow him to push her away, he was sorely mistaken.

As Beatrix had said, women like them needed to fight for their happiness.

The duke drummed his fingers on the table. "Call."

The players turned over their cards. When Ian revealed his winning hand, the *capo*'s mouth twitched, and his son mumbled something unintelligible.

Ian's blank expression didn't falter. If she hadn't been sitting right next to him, witness to the fact, she would never guess he'd won a victory.

"You play well, *Ingliz*," the capo remarked.

"*Grazzi, sinjur.*" Ian tipped his head to acknowledge the compliment. "You were challenging opponents."

The capo exchanged a brief nod with his son. "We will discuss the terms the Tarka will stake and send word to you tomorrow."

He rose from the table and as the majordomo helped him into his overcoat, the Tarka leader looked at Ian with a gleam in his eye. "You count cards better than your parents."

"My father," Ian corrected, a little too quickly.

The capo gave a gruff laugh and wagged a finger. "Your mother taught him how, but she was better. You have her talent. I look forward to seeing what else you can do with it."

It was a compliment wrapped around a subtle threat, and the possessive way the *capo* watched Ian before he took his leave made Diana fight off a shiver.

"That went well," Sunderland said cheerily.

Ian blew out a breath. "Do we know what they are planning to stake?"

"Contracts, most likely. Construction projects across Milan and Zurich. Our informant claims Il Corno is putting up railroads across Portugal and Italy. And Costa's three warehouses are his personal stake."

"Personal stake?" Diana echoed.

When neither man met her eyes, she stepped between them and whirled on the duke. He'd concede to her nonverbal admonishment quicker than Ian.

"There's a price of admission," Sunderland conceded as he pulled on his overcoat. "You two will need to decide what you're willing to bet. And I know you're going to row over it. So I'm moving camp to the Porta Rossa. Send word if you settle it before morning."

He left them standing in the townhouse foyer, with Ian's hands balled into fists and Diana's head spinning.

"How long have you known there was a personal stake?" she asked when she found her voice.

"I didn't intend to keep it from you."

"That means from the start then." She shook her head. "What is your plan?"

He hesitated. "A false contract. Exclusive shipping access between London and Istanbul. Sunderland has excellent forgers in his employ."

"When they find out it isn't real, they'll kill you for trying to dupe them." Her voice shook. She detested how weak it sounded.

Ian's was heartbreakingly calm as he replied, "That is a risk we'll have to take."

After everything they'd endured together, he'd stake his own life before asking her for the money.

Diana swallowed accusations about his inflated pride and outsized sense of duty. She wanted to shake him for thinking it would protect her when the only way she felt truly safe was with him.

"*Signorina?*" The majordomo approached. "Some parcels have arrived for you. And Cook is asking about tomorrow's menu?"

Diana slowly turned away, relieved for once to be attending to something domestic. Left alone with Ian, with her fury seething, she'd say or do something she would regret. "Please show me, *signore*."

After she finished with the staff, she resisted the urge to cool her temper by stepping into the back garden. Ian was somewhere upstairs, likely pacing and brooding over what he would stake in the game, and they needed to have it out between them.

A stillness had fallen over the house as she traversed the open hallways surrounding the atrium. When she didn't find Ian in his room, or hers, she doubled back to the drawing room.

Moonlight streamed through the open curtains. It splashed over the Persian carpet and rococo furniture, and across the large tapestry hung on the wall. Ian stood in front of it with a glass of whisky in one hand. He carried tension in the tight pull of his shoulders and his punishing grip on the glass. It was a stark contrast to the softness of his face and the languid way he'd looked at her when they'd shared a bed, and each other's pleasure, in Monte Carlo.

The possibility that she might never see him that way again choked her breath.

In an instant, her anger dissipated. She was tired of acting as a catalyst, constantly spurring him toward a fight.

She approached him and stopped to look at the tapestry. "If you're considering pilfering that to stake, I don't imagine any of the *famiglie* will accept it."

"Too many holes," he agreed.

He swiveled to face her and extended his arm to offer her the glass of whisky.

She accepted it and took a small sip to steel her nerves. And so that her lips could linger over the spot his had just occupied. "There's so much to sort out and my mind is a complete muddle. We will quarrel over what you're staking for this bloody game, but can it wait until morning?"

As a peace offering, she handed him back the glass.

Ian took it with a terse laugh. "I don't have the heart to argue tonight either." He tasted the whisky. "We will have our work cut out for us tomorrow, though."

Diana kept her voice steadier than her nerves. "Tomorrow, we must also agree on what happens after the game."

"I'll belong to the Tarka." Ian rubbed the spot on his chest where the tattoo branded him. "Do you understand now why I had to involve Sunderland? He can protect you afterward. The only way I can be sure you and those we care about are safe is if I disappear."

She came within a hair's distance of railing at him. She wanted him to feel as raw and enraged as she did about all of it.

But she didn't want their last night together before the game to be filled with rancor. "We'll find another way."

Ian heaved a sigh and finished the whisky.

"If he wasn't a villain intent on separating us forever, I'd like your *capo*," she murmured. "He behaved like a gentleman."

"Alberti was that way. He protected my mother for years before I was born." Emotion brought a flush to his cheeks. "And after."

"You learned your protective ways from him."

He nodded slowly. "My father was a wonderful man, but he had his flaws too. He made a lot of poor decisions and didn't know how to safeguard his family or his business."

Diana didn't voice her opinion that Ian had been left to deal with the fallout of his father's choices. "Despite it, you still love and respect his memory. I'm envious. It's difficult for me to remember the good parts of my childhood without remembering the pain of my mother leaving."

She hadn't recognized how much it weighed on her until it slipped out; she was unaccustomed to admitting weakness.

"Betraying a child that way should be criminal," Ian declared with an edge in his voice. "It would have been hard enough surviving that, but then she turned back up in your life and demanded your unfailing devotion. While withholding her affection and attention."

Diana flapped a hand to dismiss the notion, but Ian caught it nimbly and spooled her into his arms.

She inhaled deeply to savor the scent of his soap and him, and a whimper escaped her. She'd ached to linger in his embrace this way since they'd left Monaco.

Within the warm, safe circle of his arms, she finally acknowledged that the only thing truly dividing them was their own free will. She could either choose a path driven by fear and the need for certainty over everything—or she could release her death grip on control and open herself up to happiness.

The choice was hers. And Ian's.

As she melted against his chest, he murmured, "I can forgive my parents their mistakes, but I'll never get past the way your mother hurt and manipulated you. I understand why you wouldn't want a family."

"I never said I didn't want a family."

Slowly, Diana raised her head and met his gaze. "If you wanted, I'd have one with you."

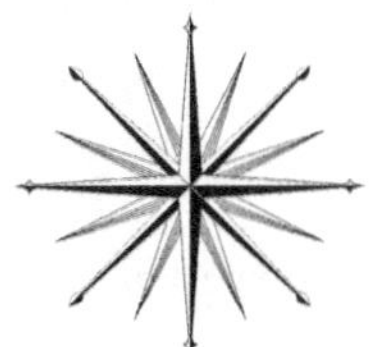

CHAPTER TWENTY-TWO

Ian wavered on his feet.

A strange tingling sensation pricked his fingers. In the back of his mind, he knew it was a symptom of someone who'd gone into shock.

He blinked at Diana.

She wanted something he'd dreamed of and never admitted to himself until that moment.

He tried to remember all the reasons he couldn't welcome her confession.

He failed.

And he couldn't stop himself from grinning like a hopeless fool.

No, not a hopeless one. That was the trouble.

His hopes were immeasurably high.

Diana maneuvered them to the nearby settee. She muttered something about fetching another whisky, but his arms clamped around her waist.

"Don't go."

"I shouldn't have said—"

"Yes, you should," he growled.

Her blush deepened, and her dimples surfaced. It was more satisfying than trouncing the *capo* at baccarat.

She rested her hand over his. "Do you remember when you came to visit us in Bristol, the summer after your mother died?"

"Of course. It was the first time I hadn't been miserable in months." His lips twitched. "You'd had a huge strop with your mother. She banned you from dessert for the entire week."

"A month in total." She winced. "Mama caught me eavesdropping on you and your father. I was listening in the servants' hallway while you were dressing for dinner. Your father asked you if you minded coming to Bristol with him."

An ache rose beneath Ian's ribs, and when he simply stared at her beautiful face, Diana wound her arms around him and tucked her head beneath his chin.

"You said visiting us felt like having a family," she said.

Against her hair, he murmured, "I meant being with you."

"I know."

He held her quietly until the hammering of his heart slowed. "You know now I'm pledged to dangerous people. It will be next to impossible to extricate myself. Anyone close to me is a fair target. And the idea of you or—" He didn't have the courage to say *children*. "If my choices and actions resulted in you getting hurt, it would destroy me."

Her arms tightened around him. "The possibility of anything happening to you is so unimaginable, I won't allow myself to think of it. That's why we're going to end this. We will cut the Tarka, and the other *famiglie* and *Il Gioco*, out of our lives."

She raised her head. "It's possible if you stake the *Ever Hart*."

When Sunderland had let it slip Ian would need a personal stake in the game, he'd known Diana would suggest it. It didn't make refusing her any easier. "And if I lose?"

"I have a big fortune, Ian."

"When the Tarka win, they'll think they'll have a claim to it, if you're with me."

"They can only take it from us if we let them." She caressed his cheek. "I'd risk everything if it meant taking back control of our lives. You've staked too much for me too many times."

He grasped for something to prop up his fragile psyche, because her words were undoing him. "It's my job to fix problems."

"While I adore how clever you are at it, it's what you *do*. The way you work so hard at it, for the people you protect, that's who you *are*, and why I've spent every minute since we met completely enamored with you."

"I've never been able to hide how much I want you. God knows I tried." He pressed a kiss into her hand. "Exiling myself to the shadows, becoming the Devil of the Docklands. It was a cover for the target on my back, an easier way to convince everyone—especially myself—that I could never be part of your world. Despite how much I desperately wanted to be with you."

"All I've ever wanted was you, Ian Holt. Not for a night. Or to win some contest." She drew him closer. "For forever."

His mouth met hers eagerly, and her fingers threaded through his hair. The gentle way she tugged at his scalp made him growl nonsensical things as his lips scraped against her neck. "You don't know what you're asking, Diana."

"I'm asking you to let me love you. All the ways I know how."

With a groan, his lips sought hers. She responded enthusiastically and deepened the kiss; they were both heated and moaning in the space of a minute.

He caught a gulping breath. He ransacked his brain for some argument that would shake sense into her, but he couldn't believe any of his own excuses.

There would be no more lies between them.

She brushed a thumb over his mouth. "The way you look at me. Can you forgive me for all of my scheming to lure you along, keep you close?"

"Diana, I don't recall a time when I wasn't completely in love with you. I'd live every excruciating moment again, if it meant I could finally be with you like this."

His mouth crashed against hers, and they exhaled against each other. Her hands hastily extricated him from his shirt, button by button.

When it fell to the ground, she gave a satisfied hum as her fingers explored his skin. They dove along his sternum and caressed his ribs, before arriving back to stroke the ink stamped over his heart. Her lips followed the path of her fingers. As she pressed hot kisses against his chest, everything south of his waist grew hard.

His fear that he would spend in his trousers again resurrected a modicum of his restraint.

"Wait." He clasped her face between both hands. "If we continue like this—"

"If we don't, I will die of wanting. And too many people are depending on us for you to allow that."

With a growl, he scooped her into his arms and marched down the cloistered hallway to her bedroom. He slammed the door shut with his foot and tumbled them both onto the bed. She murmured faint words of gratitude, which he cut off with a searing kiss, and refused to allow her to escape as he took his fill of her sweet mouth.

He drew out the kiss until she was so heated and breathless that when he finally broke away, her chest was heaving like bellows.

"Have a care, *tesora mia*," he rasped. "This won't be like before. What we're doing will change everything. I've wanted this for so long. Wanted you, for so long." He traced her ear with his lips and adored the way she shivered. "I've loved you so many ways from a distance. I'm terrified about the possibility of what it will be like when we're finally, truly together."

She stroked his neck and his shoulders. "It's going to be glorious."

In the faint light from the lamp, her cheeks were aflame and her chestnut curls cascaded back against the pillow. She was utterly exquisite.

The enormity of the moment was a palpable thing; he could not shake the fear that this joy would slip away from him.

"Ian." She reached for his hand and drew him to her. "If you're not ready for this. If you don't want to be with me tonight—"

He denied it with a penetrating kiss. "You don't think I've dreamed of this, night and day, since I learned about sex?"

Her fingers danced along the waistband of his trousers. "With me, specifically?"

"Don't tease."

"Don't pretend you don't like it." Her hands hovered over his buttons. "You do like it, don't you?"

The truth was, he loved it. She'd taunted him for so long. Now, he recognized it as a display of affection, and his heart grew wings.

"Is this your way of telling me what you like?" His mouth skimmed her neck. "Delayed gratification?"

Her hands continued their exploration of his skin. "I don't really know. You're the only person I've ever been with."

For a moment, her wide eyes made her look as innocent as she had when they'd played together as children.

But as she stared at him, and her gaze grew hot, she whispered, "I've never imagined doing this with anybody but you, Ian. You're the only man who's ever roused me." Her voice caught. "If you love me, don't make me wait another moment to show you what I've been dreaming about."

His composure cracked wide open, and his mouth descended on hers as he pulled her close. "Tell me what you want."

"Take off your clothes. I want to feel every inch of you against me."

"You first."

She wriggled off the bed and turned for him to help unfasten her dress. Together, they dispatched her of the evening gown, corset, and drawers, and Diana lifted her arms for him to pull off her linen shift.

Her skin glowed in the lamplight, a canvas of pink and gold. The sight made him breathless again.

"I will never tire of you looking at me like that," she whispered.

"How, *tesora mia*?"

"Like a sailor marooned on a desert isle who finally discovered a fresh spring."

"Let me take a sip."

He bent so his lips could take in the rosy peak of her breast, and when her knees buckled, he caught her and gentled her back onto the bed, between the sheets.

She moaned his name. Violence tinged her tone as she tugged at his trousers. "Off. Now."

"What happened to delayed gratification?"

There was a distinct sound of ripping, and when Ian glanced down, the top button of his trousers was missing, and Diana held her blade with a black thread dangling from it.

He clamped down on the weapon. "Your impatience is noted. It's a good thing I'm wildly aroused by your ability to improvise."

"Then stop talking and get to work."

He pried the knife out of her hand, tossed it onto the table, and quickly removed the rest of his clothes. His lips returned to her mouth as he drew his body over the length of her, so they were barely touching. "Is this what you imagined?"

"Better," she rasped, and curled her fingers around his stiff cock.

They both groaned at the contact. Her hold was featherlight, teasing.

He was going to perish from ecstasy and from frustration.

"I want to taste you again," she said.

When she moved, he nudged her back against the mattress. "That will end this far too quickly." They were sealing themselves to each other; he wanted to make the experience as spectacular as he could for her.

If they failed in their endeavors, this might be their only night together.

"I intend to savor you, love," he promised.

He nibbled his way down her body and dipped his tongue in her navel. The light, teasing kisses he pressed along her hip made her squirm.

"Be still," he warned as he licked up her thigh. "Or I'll have to start again from the top." When she complied willingly, he enjoyed that in this one instance, he exerted some control over her.

"Please," she moaned.

"There are those society manners," he murmured, before his mouth seized her core.

Her taste was intoxicating; his lust swelled as she cried out and rocked her hips. His erection was hard to the point of pain, but he didn't care. He was determined to prolong her pleasure.

Diana screamed his name as she climaxed, but he'd no intention of relenting until she was as addled with desire as he was. He tasted and nipped at her luscious cleft until she pushed him away.

"Now, Ian." She gasped.

He caressed her face and brushed aside the trickle of perspiration that trailed down her throat. As eager as he was to fulfill her command, he abhorred the idea of hurting her, even a little. "One word, and I'll stop."

"I know." She pressed a kiss into his hand. "Now hurry and deflower me. Don't wait another second."

Slowly, he entered her. Her tight, wet heat around the tip of his cock made his head reel but before he could give over to the craving to move, a faint gasp stopped him cold.

As he started to withdraw, Diana's warm hand clamped on his arse. "Don't stop, please. I'll be fine in a minute."

She raised her chin in stubborn defiance, as determined to conquer her pain as she was to overcome any challenge.

He shook off the searing way it stoked him and reminded himself of his vow to protect her. Even from himself.

He stroked her hipbone in a soothing caress. "Relax, love. Here." He kneaded her muscles gently. On her exhale, he felt her resistance give and he pushed in further.

"That's it. You're so tight, but your skin is soft," he rasped. "You feel incredible, Diana."

She moaned again, and then he was fully sheathed inside her.

"Oh, God," she breathed.

He nuzzled her neck, as she adjusted to him.

"Yes, oh, that's better," she murmured. "There's hardly any pain now."

He leaned down and kissed her, and she took possession of his mouth. Between jagged breaths, she declared, "I'm ready now."

Slowly, he stirred his hips, testing his control and her response. It took everything for him to rasp, "Good?"

"So good," she affirmed breathlessly. "More. Please, Ian, I can't stand it."

He wrapped her leg around his hip and picked up his rhythm. As his thrusts grew more intent, he held onto the edge of restraint. Every exercise, all the training he'd undertaken to master control of his body had been to prepare him for this moment of bliss.

Another night, he'd show her his devil side.

Tonight, he stood at the gates of heaven.

She cupped his face. "How could we deny ourselves this for so long?"

"Never again," he vowed.

Her hips drew him closer and she bucked against him with delicious friction. "Don't hold back. I know you're at the edge with me, darling."

He pumped in and out of her, and her hoarse cries endangered the thin hold he had over his control. "That's it, *bella tesora*. You're so close, but I'm a selfish devil." He slowed his pace. "I've wanted this so long, I want it to last forever."

A glimpse of that dream unfolded before him, and he grew heady with the image of staying in bed, never needing to leave her.

With a wanton groan, Diana scraped her nails down his back. "I don't think I can take much more of this."

"Then touch yourself," he commanded.

Her fingers grazed the place where they were joined, and his climax approached. He folded his hand on top of hers, to give her the pressure he knew she loved. She came with a shattering cry that gave him wild satisfaction.

He had scarcely enough time to withdraw and spend his own release between the sheets.

Diana reached for him. He folded her into his arms while they both regained their breath and buried his face against her hair to ground himself.

When she shifted, her sharp gasp made his chest ache.

"I'm sorry for the pain, love," he murmured.

"It's over now," she whispered. "And what came after was the best pleasure I've ever known."

He grunted in agreement; the words to describe what had transpired between them surpassed him. "Shall I draw you a bath?" Despite her assurances, she had to be sore. He'd taken care to withdraw, but they were both damp with perspiration and remnants of their bed sport.

"That would involve getting up, and I don't want this moment to end."

"It won't." He traced a hand down her arm to caress her silky skin. "This is just the beginning for us."

He believed it now. In a way he hadn't dared to before.

They rested quietly while Ian absently played with her hair, letting her russet-brown locks sift through his fingers like water.

Diana caressed the ink on his chest. "I remember the first time I saw this. It was that summer it was so hot, the one before they sent you away to school. I must have been only seven or eight. We escaped to the shore before anyone noticed we were gone. You'd taken off your shirt to jump in the waves and I gawked at the mark before my governess found us and dragged me back inside. Later, I asked Papa if you had a tattoo and he said, 'Of course not,' but I argued you did because all true pirates had tattoos."

"My staunch defender." He laughed. "When Alberti knew he didn't have long to live, he inked it himself. I was barely three years old."

"Good God. Did it hurt?"

"Like the devil. My mother was horrified when she found out. Alberti told her he wanted everyone to know they were both under his protection, even when he was gone. But I don't think she ever forgave him for it."

Diana continued stroking his chest lazily. Her voice was thick with drowsiness when she said, "Your father played *Il Gioco* to win your mother, didn't he?"

"No one has ever confirmed it. And it's barbaric to me that anyone would trade in human lives like they're commodities." He sighed. "From what I gather, my father was playing to free her. It all happened before they...formed an attachment."

When she scoffed, he chided her with a squeeze before amending, "A physical attachment."

"Everyone remembers how beautiful your mother was. But the only thing my mother could ever talk about was the way your father looked at her. As though she hung the stars and the moon and the sun altogether. They must have loved each other very much."

"They were happy," he agreed. It surprised him that he could admit this without pain. In fact, the idea warmed him. "I witnessed it every day of the short time we had together. I've never stopped wanting it back. Which makes me a fool."

"If you are, then everyone else is too."

"After all my time in the shadows...I'm not sure I fully understand how to live that kind of life."

He hoped she'd understand what he couldn't come out and say: he was terrified that if she committed her life to his, he would let her down.

"I disagree, darling. You've shown me the complete opposite."

Diana gently tugged his chin and sealed her mouth against his. He parted her lips easily and slipped his tongue inside, greedy for her taste again.

When she withdrew to place a tender kiss over his heart, she murmured, "The rest of the world doesn't matter. Wherever I'm with you, however we choose to live, I'm home."

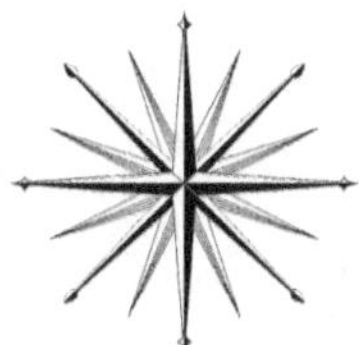

CHAPTER TWENTY-THREE

"You look delightfully...refreshed, Holt."

Sunderland sprawled in a chair in the townhouse dining room as he sipped coffee from a steaming cup.

"Wish I could say the same about you," Ian replied.

The duke's hair fell rakishly over his forehead and his necktie dangled around the open collar of his shirt, which was also stained with an unmistakable stamp of lip rouge.

"It's not what you think." Sunderland flashed him a wicked grin. "Actually, scratch that. What are you thinking?"

"How we survive tonight." As he downed his own cup of scalding coffee, Ian wished he'd stayed in bed with Diana. He'd only slipped out to run to the bakery so he could buy some *pastizzi* for her breakfast.

"Crotchety in the morning, aren't you?" Sunderland clicked his tongue against his teeth. "My evening involved little sleep, but I'm much more pleasant about it."

Ian didn't want to visualize what the duke's evening had involved. Or hear about it. "Everything ready at the Porto Rosso?"

"My team is in place at the hotel," Sunderland confirmed. "I take it you and Miss Rives agreed on stakes. Should you care to relay all the details of your negotiations, I'm an excellent listener."

He ignored the duke's taunt. "Diana has agreed to stake the *Ever Hart*."

"Her Majesty's government will not be amused if you lose a ship of that caliber."

"If I lose, there's more to worry about than upsetting half a dozen bureaucrats."

The trace of the smirk faded from the duke's face. "You're going to need a strategy if things get dodgy."

"The best option is to let the *polizia* capture me when they raid the game."

Sunderland scratched his chin. "Could take a few days to get you out of the clink."

"It's a last resort. And I'll only do it if you swear you can get Diana out of Florence when all hell breaks loose."

"That I can arrange." He leaned back in his chair. "My sources also received a report that a shipment of gunpowder went missing from Genoa three days ago. No one's talking about it because, allegedly, three women stole it."

Wearing oilskin coats and woolen caps and probably brandishing his pistol, Ian would wager. Since Birdie's betrayal, they'd been waiting for Widow's operatives to make some move.

"They wanted the necklace to trade for information about *Il Gioco* so they can eliminate some of the most powerful traffickers in Europe in one go," Ian surmised.

"They're getting reckless if they're planning to plant explosives at the hotel. Hundreds of innocent people could die."

Ian dreaded telling Diana. "Is the threat credible?"

"Hard to say, old man. Usually, the only way we confirm these things is after the fact."

When people and buildings lay in pieces.

"It's too much of a risk to have Diana at the game." His throat grew tight at the prospect.

"On the contrary. She's a deterrent against the Stags doing anything too rash," Sunderland argued. "Widow needs Diana's fortune to fund her operation. They won't let anything happen to her."

The duke swallowed a final swig of his coffee. "On the other hand, you, Holt, they'd have no qualms about killing."

That evening, while she put the final touches on her toilette, Diana renewed her appreciation for the power a beautiful dress could grant.

She'd come to love the men's clothes she'd worn during their travels. Free from the underpinnings of corsets and petticoats and bustles, she was more in tune with how her body moved. She didn't have to second-guess her posture, and that kind of liberty was intoxicating.

As she smoothed her hand down the fitted bodice of her red silk evening gown, she willed the nerves fluttering in her stomach to settle. To ensure no outsiders discovered they were holding a high-stakes illegal card game, a masquerade reception at the Porto Rosso would serve as a cover for *Il Gioco*. Diana's costume was conspicuous by her choice. The low-cut neckline and shimmering beaded silk set off a ruby pendant nestled in an array of diamonds forming a flower.

Beneath the robe-style gown, she donned a leather harness that the excellent staff of the townhome had purchased from a local acrobat troupe. Neither Sunderland nor Ian knew she'd taken this precaution, but after what had happened in Menton, Diana had taken redundancy planning upon herself.

She glided down the narrow staircase of the townhome and took distinct pleasure in the way Ian's gaze consumed her. The sight of him in his costume threatened her own composure. His tailor-made dress blacks paired with an obsidian shirt, tie, and a silk waistcoat that matched her ruby made him look like the devil himself.

The Porta Rossa was a short walk away. Despite the anxious energy pricking them both, they didn't rush. Diana's throat was too clogged with emotion to say anything. They were barreling to the end of the mad adventure she'd set them on, and she was terrified that by the end, neither of them would keep the promises they'd pledged to each other the night before.

When they reached the steps of the hotel, Ian pulled a black domino from his pocket, and she lifted her red silk and feathered mask from her reticule.

He insisted on helping her tie hers. As his deft fingers fastened the ribbons slowly, he bent toward her ear. "When this is over, I want to spend hours with you wearing nothing but this mask."

"Devil," she murmured. Her cheeks heated beneath the silk. "Now promise me you won't invent some excuse to prevent me from joining you tonight."

"It would be a waste of energy. You'd eventually wrangle a way in." His fingers caressed the sensitive skin on the back of her neck. "But you need to promise me you'll stick to the plan."

Diana didn't waste breath arguing that she'd depart from the plan the minute she sensed his life was in danger. She flashed him a seductive smile and ushered him into the foyer. Their invitation card secured them an escort through a series of stairways and back corridors until the faint murmur of voices and clinking glassware drew them through a gilded door.

Before them, a set of stairs led to a sunken reception room, where spectators circled the perimeter of a card table staged in the center of the parquet floor. Along the upper floor, more people mingled between pillars wrapped with gauzy fabric. Like Ian and Diana, they were all dressed in rich costumes.

"I didn't think there would be so many observers," she remarked as Ian led her around the game table.

"Recognize anyone Widow would employ?"

"Not yet." They could have been in the crowd somewhere, which made her stomach clench. "Your *capo* and his men are at the back, behind the table."

Ian drew her to a shadowed corner of the wall, where they had a clear view of the entrance. "Before this all starts, I need to tell you something."

"Is it how lovely I look in this dress?"

"You bewilder my senses in that dress," he rasped. "One of the many reasons I want you by my side tonight. But we are going to have to separate."

"Like hell—"

"Excuse me, I wasn't finished."

How he could be so sharp and so soft at the same time baffled the breath out of her.

Her chest, in fact, was smarting with a sharp, familiar pain. They'd pledged to be truthful with each other merely hours before, and Ian was already backsliding from it.

His attention flicked away from hers, and while she mentally composed the tirade she'd throw at him for not having the bollocks to look at her while he was shirking his promise, she registered what had captivated him.

A brown-haired woman circled the upper floor overlook. She wore an exact copy of Diana's red dress. And had her arm entwined with the Duke of Sunderland.

The two scoundrels had conspired to use the Stags's shell game to shut her out of *Il Gioco*.

"You always were a quick study; I'll give you that." Diana wriggled, but Ian held her arm in a viselike grip.

"Everyone is watching," he warned.

"Then I shouldn't have worn this dress."

"My love, you could wear rags and still gather every eye in this room."

The low pitch to his voice and the underlying warmth in his eyes beneath his mask abated her anger.

Momentarily.

"You and Sunderland hatched this scheme some time ago, if you secured additional players," she threw at him.

"It was the duke's idea, and he was right to insist on it. We're going to have to split up for the game. This is an added layer of security."

"And you didn't think to consult me in that discussion?" She huffed. "It makes me think you won't ever truly trust me. Like we'll never be on the same side."

She had a horrible, nagging sensation that if they didn't rectify it now, they'd continue trying to outplay each other forever.

"I'm always on your side, Diana," he said softly. He relaxed his hold on her arm and drew her hand to his mouth to press a searing kiss against her gloved palm. "And you're the person I trust more than anyone else in the world. Which is why I'll risk your anger and frustration if it means keeping you safe."

She locked her spine and raised herself to her full height. "Waiting until the last moment to tell me this is no different from the way my mother manipulated me."

His mouth parted on a jagged breath.

The accusation was an extraordinary defensive maneuver.

And Ian's sudden stillness told her he was at least partly impressed by it.

She held his stare until he finally muttered, "You're right. It was a despicable move."

He still expressed no regret about it. But she could not overlook the glances he kept sliding around the room to evaluate who was observing them.

Sunderland and her doppelgänger crossed the room. There was no time to argue and press her case to dissuade him. "I am only agreeing to this because you've backed me into a corner. But do not, for one second, believe it means I forgive you for it. We will have this out between us after the game. And you'll never dream of pulling this kind of stunt again."

"I welcome that challenge." Ian pressed another fervent kiss on her gloved hand.

He nodded to the potted ferns beside the bar, but as he steered her toward Sunderland, a hush fell over the room.

Diana turned to the entrance. A gaggle of men stood at the top of the stairs. Titus descended the steps first, trailed closely by Costa. As they sauntered to the table at the center of the room, that would decide her fate, the sight of their arrogant smiles made her flesh crawl.

She'd barely recovered her repose when Jared strode down the stairs after them.

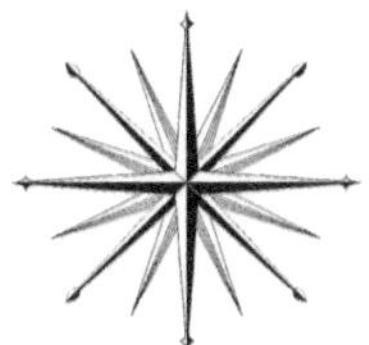

CHAPTER TWENTY-FOUR

"Don't react," Ian warned Diana.

He'd already considered and dismissed the idea of placing his body between her and the other players; he didn't want to remind his competitors of how easily they could get inside his head if they threatened her.

"Why is Jared here?" Her voice rose an octave. "*How* did he get here?"

"One of the *famiglie* must have tracked him down and threatened him. They brought him here to rattle me."

"But you won't let them," she insisted, her fists balled in her skirts.

Her belief in him—fresh on the heels of their argument—made him want to pry her hands open and kiss each one of her fingers and every inch of her exposed skin.

"Jared's going to want a word with me. Please, Diana. I need you to go with the duke."

As Sunderland approached, Diana gave a faint growl and said, "I will find you. Don't do anything unwise."

He only had the brush of her hand at his cheek before he and Sunderland swapped scarlet-dressed women like they were partners in a reel.

As the imposter threaded her gloved arm through his, Ian drew a deep breath and walked toward the spot at the bar where Jared stood. Ian could tell from his unfocused glare and the wobbly way his brother was holding his whisky glass that Jared was already foxed.

"Keep quiet and stand behind me," he ordered the Diana stand-in.

The woman made a low harumph noise in the back of her throat that was eerily Diana-like.

"I'd say it's lovely to see you," Jared slurred as he greeted them. "But we've never been the kind of family to exchange endearments."

"No, but I'm glad that you've recovered," Ian offered.

"Liar. You couldn't wait to escape with that traitorous bitch cowering behind—"

Ian's hand grasped his brother's thumb and forced it into a suspended angle. "One more insult and I snap this."

"Savage mongrel," Jared spat. "You belong with this lot of bloody lowlifes."

Ian kept his pressure on Jared's hand, his voice lethal and low. "Whatever it is you're planning to do here, forget it. The *famiglie* must know about Polly and Johnny. If you try to interfere, they'll come after your woman and your child."

"Why do you think I'm here?"

Slowly, Ian released his hand.

Jared shook it off and downed his whisky. "You think I chased after this? I didn't know about any of this madness until I tried to sell the emeralds. The old man never mentioned a word to me." He jutted a trembling finger at Ian. "But *you* knew."

"Why else do you think Father left me nothing in his will?" Ian's steady voice belied his roiling anger. "He wanted you and the business to be clear of it all. The emeralds were in my life long before you knew I existed. The necklace is my legacy to defend."

"Never met anyone who acted like they possessed a bigger set of bollocks than you." His brother jutted his chin toward where Titus sat at the table. "The night before you ran off with my blushing bride, that bastard drugged me and forced me to sign over the papers to the docks. He gave me a forged contract for Diana's properties as a consolation gift. Everything would have worked its way out if you hadn't interfered. But you did. So they dragged me here to make sure you play nicely."

Ian had spent his first years in England terrified of the hate in Jared's eyes whenever he looked at him or his mother. A strange tightness would form in his chest and migrate down into his stomach, and he often couldn't eat for days.

Jared still regarded him with that same loathing. They'd never shared a moment of brotherly camaraderie between them. Ian doubted they ever would.

But Jared had loved their father. And he wouldn't have let the business he built slip through his fingers so easily.

"Why are you here, Jared? What else did they offer you for the docks?"

After a beat, Jared said, "If you lose, I walk away with the money to clear my debts and take Polly and Johnny far away from this depravity."

Ian pitied how readily his brother believed the lie. "You truly think that will happen if Titus or Costa win?"

Shaking out his cuffs, Jared gave him a dismissive glance. "I won't bother wishing you luck."

"I won't need it," Ian drawled.

The players prowled around the oval-shaped table as they sized up the piles of chips and each other. Titus and Costa exchanged a cold nod, which made Ian slightly less anxious. It truly would be every player for themselves around the table.

Alberti had taught him how to play baccarat as soon as he'd learned to count. His mother and father had also played with him. Father had bristled whenever Ian remarked his mother was a better player. But he'd properly lost his sense of humor when Ian had almost been sent down from Harrow for organizing an underground card game.

The tongue-lashing hadn't stopped him from seeking illicit gaming hells to sharpen his skills. He rarely lost, and even more rarely, became caught up in the emotion of chasing a win.

A gong sounded from somewhere behind the bar, and the murmuring voices of the spectators dwindled. As Ian took his seat at the table, the Diana imposter melted back into the circle of onlookers behind him. He lounged back in his chair with a cocky slouch and surveyed the four corners of the room to locate his Diana. Eventually, he found her among the spectators next to the curtained pillars on the second floor. The sight of her on Sunderland's arm lessened Ian's disquiet fractionally.

He closed his eyes for a fleeting moment and imagined her eyes on him. He pictured her bow-shaped mouth wearing the soft smile that hid the depths of her passion and determination. If he failed to win tonight, and Sunderland didn't keep his promise to protect her, he vowed his ghost would haunt the duke until the end of his days.

"Good evening, *signoras e signori*. Tonight, *Il Gioco* is *chemin-de-fer*," the hotel manager announced. "We deal with six decks of cards." He showed six sealed boxes of cards to the players. "*Signori*, you have six rounds of play, allowing each punter to serve as banker twice. Punters may bet their hand against any of the other players. The hand with a total closest to nine wins the round. Whoever claims the most rounds claims the game."

A collective coo among the spectators underscored the seriousness of the rules.

"If the players are all assembled, let us begin," the manager continued. "The punter in possession of the emerald necklace may choose to serve as banker in the first or the last round."

Titus withdrew the necklace with a cocky smile and dropped it in the center of the table. "I choose to go first."

"Very good, *signore*. What do you set for the opening bank?"

"Twenty thousand pounds."

The crowd murmured at the staggering sum. Ian met the eyes of the Tarka *capo*, and he tilted his head to confirm Ian should match Titus's bet.

The hotel manager rapped on the felt-topped table and opened each sealed deck of cards with a silver penknife. Like the other men, Ian scrutinized the decks laid out in a row on the table. Three of the decks had the standard red printed design found in any shop in Italy. The rest boasted a black-and-white pattern of concentric starbursts surrounded by a block print of lines and dots that was as familiar to Ian as the ink tattooed on his chest.

Alberti had taught him to play cards with a deck exactly like the ones before him. The old man had shown him how to make a set with the knave, the king, and the queen. And then he'd instructed Ian in the hidden language of deciphering how to detect those character cards while the cards lay face down.

As Titus shuffled the decks together with a dramatic flourish and called for them to place their bets, hope gained a threshold in Ian's heart.

Tucked behind the velvet drapes on the balcony, Diana detested her relegation to the role of surveillance. Her assignment was to monitor for signs of the Stags, but it was a struggle to drag her eyes from Ian.

She was carefully assessing how she might subtly wriggle free of Sunderland's persistent hold on her arm when the duke murmured, "The decks are what we expected."

"Meaning no one tampered with them?"

"Still a possibility. But thankfully, the black cards on the table are a Florentine set printed by Domenico Alberti."

Diana pursed her lips together. Ian had failed to mention that the man who'd looked after him and his mother was also a legendary card designer. "Doesn't that put the Tarka at an unfair advantage?"

"Half of the Continent plays with Alberti decks. Ian isn't the only one who knows how to edge sort the face cards—tell them apart by the designs on the back, which are set marginally differently to the numbered cards," Sunderland explained. "It's more valuable for *chemin-de-fer*, since the face cards hold no value."

"Is that how you win, Your Grace? By cheating?"

"It's simply playing an advantage," Sunderland said tightly. "And I don't hold with cheating. Implies one lacks intellect. Or a spine."

"Lying is cheating the truth. And I know you're an expert liar." Diana laced her tone with sweetness so it wouldn't draw attention from the people standing by her.

"Pot and kettle," the duke lobbed back mildly. "And if you have some frustration with Holt you're working out on me—"

"While I don't appreciate the two of you conspiring behind my back, I was referring to your other past crimes."

He shook his head and widened his eyes in feigned confusion. "Whatever could that be?"

Amelia never said what had transpired at Lady Rosewood's ball during their debut season, when Diana had found Amelia quietly crying on a bench within the hedge maze. Just before she'd come upon her, Sunderland had fled past as if a pack of hounds had chased after him. He'd been Ashton then, the lowly third son of the duke.

"Only you and Amelia know what truly happened all those years ago," Diana said. "But nothing you can say would change my opinion of the impact you had."

Sunderland regarded her from behind his black domino mask for a long moment before giving a slow nod. "That's only fair."

The intensity of the duke's catlike eyes put her ill at ease, and she returned her attention to surveying the room. Her eyes clapped on her doppelgänger standing behind Ian. "Where did you recruit my twin?"

"I vetted her myself. She's sound."

There was something about the way the sleeves hung on her imposter that bothered Diana, but the woman was too far away to assess it thoroughly. "The same tailor made her dress?"

"Of course. I take wardrobe and those who represent my operations seriously." The duke's demeanor matched his tone; it didn't possess one ounce of self-deprecating humor.

Below them, the game proceeded. At the end of the first round, Ian lost twenty thousand of the Tarka's pounds to Titus. While Diana reassured herself it was part of their scheme, her insides quivered with nerves. To her surprise, Titus did not maintain the advantage of the banker for the second hand and passed it to Ian. When Ian called for bets, Costa raised the stakes of the round to one hundred thousand pounds.

"Posturing," Sunderland muttered. "Titus was smart to test how much cash the Il Corno are willing to burn through to win."

Costa won the hand and gave them all a cocky grin when he took over as banker for the third round.

"God, I hate this," Diana whispered. "Ian should have won that hand."

"That's not what we have planned," Sunderland reminded her. Ian couldn't trounce them too quickly. They needed to extend the play long enough for the *polizia* to arrive and break up the game.

Costa set the next round at two hundred and fifty thousand pounds. After a moment's contemplation, Titus agreed to the raise.

Ian glanced at his cards. "I move to raise to three hundred thousand."

Murmurs broke out across the room. Diana used all of her restraint not to flinch when Titus accepted Ian's offer; the rules of *chemin-de-fer* stipulated Ian would play both of their hands against Costa.

Costa sneered and flipped over his cards: a three of clubs, a four of hearts, and an ace, totaling eight.

Ian held a knave, a queen, and a nine of diamonds.

Applause broke out to cheer Ian's daring and rewarding play. When her imposter stroked a hand down Ian's arm, it took all of Diana's strength to keep from flying down the stairs.

A gong announced a short break. When Ian rose from the table and slipped to the edge of the room to converse with the Tarka *capo*, she saw her opening.

She'd only managed to turn before Sunderland caught her elbow in a firm hold. "Two identically dressed she-devils standing by one player will send tongues wagging," the duke warned.

"Then send her somewhere else," Diana hissed. Her eyes flicked to the woman in her dress, and she was unnerved to find her staring directly back at them.

"You'll distract him if you go down there," Sunderland threatened. "Let this play out."

Refreshment trays circulated downstairs, and a crush of observers jostled past them to descend from the upper landing. The duke steered them to a back corner away from the fray. Below, her stand-in held Diana's gaze.

Then she casually lifted her hand and tugged her ear.

An irrational urge to laugh overcame her. She came up with that signal, taught it to her crew.

And they dared to use it against her.

"The Stags are here." Her voice carried an unfortunate wobble. "Your vetted operative signaled someone."

Sunderland cursed colorfully as his hand clamped tightly around her arm. "Exit plan. Now."

"We're not leaving Ian."

"This is his play. You and I made him a promise." He started to tow her to the staircase. Diana reached for her knives.

Neither of them got far in their efforts. Scarlet silk swirled around them and two more women wearing her dress cornered them back against the railing.

A doppelgänger thrust the end of a pistol beneath Diana's ribs. Another imitator dressed in red held Sunderland in a similar position.

"Silence, *signorina*. Or you will cause a scene," the Stag warned.

Frantically, Diana searched the reception room below. Ian was still deep in conversation with the Tarka *capo* at the back of the room.

"How may we be of service, ladies?" the duke asked in a frigid tone, which aristocrats typically reserved for insulting someone's breeding.

"Walk to the stairs. There are shooters pointed at you, so don't try anything."

The gong chimed, warning the play would resume.

"You're making a mistake," Diana said. "This won't work the way you want it to. It will only incite more violence."

"Stop talking and start moving if you want to get out of here alive."

The woman who held her was taller and broader, an enforcer by training, and Diana knew she couldn't physically overpower her to escape.

But the harpy didn't know that.

"I don't wish to harm you," Diana warned. "If you let me go, I will tell the authorities you cooperated."

The enforcer reamed the end of the pistol into Diana's ribs. "I said, quiet. Now move."

"Everyone will notice."

"Doesn't matter."

Six more women wearing Diana's scarlet gown and mask filtered onto the second floor. Half a dozen others assumed seats in the crowd.

Throughout this interlude, the duke made no protest. He didn't reach for his pistol, either. Diana could only conclude he wanted the play to proceed as planned and his callous disregard for Ian's life infuriated her.

Her captor yanked Diana's arm. "Walk."

In the reception room below them, a hush fell over the crowd. The manager handed Ian the decks of cards.

"Hold, *signori*," Ian's voice boomed from below them. "There is a problem."

Diana's pulse skittered. It was too early for him to make this move. He must have seen the Stags's imposters and was advancing the derailment of the game. The foolish man thought he could stand alone against every enemy.

By now, he should have realized Diana would never allow him to.

"These cards have a cut on the corner." Ian flipped one over. "Here, the knave of spades. And the queen of hearts." He pointed to the edges. "Someone has interfered with them."

Six more crimson gowns moved along the perimeter of the room. Despite the drama unfolding at the table, people in the crowd were taking notice of the women. They whispered and pointed at them.

"I must be mistaken," Costa rumbled. "You didn't accuse us of cheating."

Diana reminded herself of all the years and all the training—both physical and mental—to deliver her to a place where she had the strength and the conviction to act on what she'd decided before walking into the hotel.

A future with Ian was worth any risk it would take to protect him.

She tore her eyes from him and evaluated the velvet curtains bordering the staircase.

As the enforcer dragged her past the column, her fingers seized on the braided curtain tie.

"That would be a mistake, *signorina*," hissed her captor. "You don't want to be here for what we have planned."

Below them, Ian stood up and fanned the cards along the table. In a gravel-laden voice, he said, "The deck is compromised. And I certainly didn't do it. One of you is attempting to swindle us all."

Roars erupted from the crowd, and accusations of "traitor" were uttered in four distinct languages.

Diana seized her captor's momentary distraction to bury her heel in the woman's shins, before she grabbed the corded curtain tie and jumped.

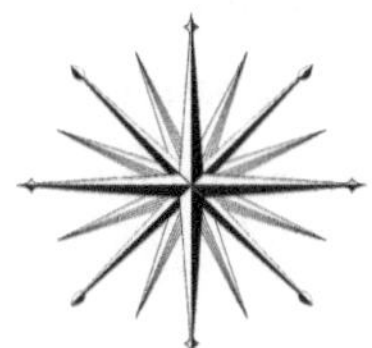

CHAPTER TWENTY-FIVE

WHEN THE SMALL ARMY of red-dressed Stags had appeared, Ian wanted to scale the stairs, throw Diana over his shoulder, and shoot his way out of the room.

Lacking the certainty they could escape that way, his only option was to escalate the timeline to disrupt the game and make himself the perceived target.

"You *maile ladro*," Costa growled before swerving around to face the room. "He is the cheat!"

It was an epic internal battle to resist running upstairs to Diana, but Ian would not surrender Costa's stare. With the precision of an expert archer aiming an arrow, he taunted, "Il Corno should have chosen a player who could prevail without resorting to amateur tricks. Someone who could win *Il Gioco* honorably."

A war cry broke out.

Titus and Costa signaled their guards.

Ian ducked the first blow aimed at his head and elbowed the next assailant in the kidneys. He crouched and crab-walked back away from the game table. He fended off another blow to his ribs before dispatching two frontal attackers with a right hook and a roundhouse kick. With the next breath, he searched the second floor, but there was no sign of Sunderland or Diana.

His fury carried him through the undulating mob. Halfway across the room, his progress halted when a guardsman knocked him to his knees and seized a strong choke-hold on his throat.

"Ian!"

Tears swam in his eyes as he searched the floor above.

Red velvet curtains descended in a crimson wave that made him think of raging bulls and battlefields. It landed on top of the abandoned game table.

The distracted guard eased his grip enough for Ian to stab his fingers in the scum's eyes.

The man clutched his face in agony. Ian darted away and clawed through the flood of people, shouting Diana's name.

At the table, the red mass of curtains parted and Diana surfaced, tied up in knots. As she frantically worked to untangle herself from corded curtain ties, the ominous shriek of a barn owl rose above the uproar.

Ian would detest the sound for the rest of his life, which he fought desperately to keep hold of, along with his sanity, as dozens of crimson-dressed women poured into the room.

"No!" He ducked a blow from another guard. "Hold on, Diana, I'm coming!"

The next screech that sounded brought him some modicum of relief. The familiar call of a police whistle pierced the air as a swarm of black uniforms overtook the room.

And then genuine panic descended.

Ian fought through the crowd and elbowed red dresses away. He'd been a bloody fool to believe their madcap plan would work. Everything he'd plotted and fought for was disintegrating.

He had no thought of the emeralds. Or the danger he'd face when any or all three of the *famiglie* caught up with him.

None of it mattered without Diana.

As he finally approached the game table, two Il Corno enforcers snared him by each shoulder. He writhed against their grip but one of them brandished a blade and shoved it against his throat.

The steel was cool. Sharp. One stray twist of his head would cut him.

He urged his body to go limp.

The goons laughed.

Then, successively, each gasped and fell.

A trickle of blood and a pearl-topped hairpin stuck out of their throats.

Ian whirled around and opened his arms to receive Diana as she leaped from the table.

"I'm sorry I'm late," she whispered.

"I'm sorry we're trapped."

He pulled her closer and drew an indulgent breath of her violet scent. There was only enough time for him to scrape his lips against her soft cheek before three police guards surrounded them, brandishing revolvers.

The small furrow of Diana's brow worried Ian more than his imminent capture; she was calculating the same potential outcomes of an escape attempt that ran through his mind.

Scenario one: Ian could surrender to the police officers, allowing the Stags to extract Diana from the hotel. There was a fifty percent chance he'd make it to a legitimate prison Sunderland could break him out of.

And an equal chance the Crown wasn't the only one lining the *polizia* pockets, and they'd kill Ian before he left the Porto Rosso.

Scenario two: He and Diana could take out the three policemen. There was a thirty percent chance of stray gunshots. And a greater chance the gun itself would go astray.

"Ian."

He glanced down at Diana. She'd lost her feathered mask in the tumble, and her hair hung in knots as it framed her face. Her expression was so open now, he could easily read her fear and affection.

It was the most beautiful thing he'd ever seen.

He brushed his lips against hers. "I'll find you."

She made an unintelligible protesting noise. He forced himself to shut it out as he slowly sank to his knees.

He never thought Diana would dart for the closest gun.

Gunshots echoed around them.

By the time he registered the noise, he found himself face down on the floor, a sharp boot buried in his neck and his hands bound in cuffs.

As he fought to get a glimpse of Diana, he could only see whirling waves of scarlet silk.

The throbbing pain in her arm woke Diana from a stupor.

She found herself on a narrow bed and struggled into a seated position. With one finger, she probed the screaming wound in her arm. Thankfully, there were no signs of a bullet lodged in it.

It took a concerted effort to stagger to her feet and examine her surroundings. The small room was a nun's cell, designed to avoid anything that would distract from reflection and prayer, including a window. The only adornment was an ebony crucifix hanging on the whitewashed wall. Unfortunately, not a viable weapon: the thing was fixed with metal screws and she would have struggled to rip it off the wall with two good arms.

She rattled her head to clear her fogged-in brain and recalled the chaos of *Il Gioco*. When Ian had bowed down on the ground before the police, it had sent her into a blind panic. She'd swiped the revolver from the unsuspecting policeman, but someone had knocked the gun out of her hand. There'd been a burning pain before a Stag enforcer smothered her mouth and nose with a cloth, and she'd blacked out.

A church clock tower somewhere nearby chimed five bells. She wished to hell she knew how long she'd been out, and if it was day or evening. Her dress was in tatters and the scent coming from her was far from fresh; she could have been lying there for days.

Two sets of footsteps sounded from the hallway outside. Diana sank down onto the bed and held her spine in a position so straight it would have made every single one of her governesses proud. She attempted to wrestle her hair into a plait, but the burning in her injured arm stopped her.

She shook out the rest of her knotted locks and dabbed at the sticky film of blood and dirt on her cheek, spreading it across her face. Then she tore at the unraveling neckline of her gown to expose her corset cover, and the remnants of the leather harness, which had shredded in her dive from the balcony.

When that door opened, they would find her utterly decomposed. A proper mess. Nothing her mother wanted in a daughter.

Diana suddenly felt as powerful as an Amazon warrior.

As Widow strode into the room with Birdie, it was impossible to tell if it was her dishevelment that stunned Widow, or if her mother's disapproving frown was related to the fact that her own daughter had tried to entrap her. Her mother's scrutiny made Diana want to laugh and also smash something to pieces. She ached for one caustic word. One sneer, to justify the vitriol she was ready to unleash.

"The *polizia* want you for questioning," Widow said without preamble.

"I'm not the only one." The ice in Diana's voice echoed her mother's tone. "Although you've outdone me, Mama. Authorities in three countries are eager to speak with you."

When Birdie placed a hand on her pistol, her mother shook her head once and gestured for Diana's former crew hand to step outside.

The absence of an audience didn't soften her mother's glare. "I'm disappointed."

Diana's laugh was sharp. "Good."

Widow struck her face before she could blink; it stung nearly as much as the bullet wound.

"Grow up, Diana. After all this time, you cannot still cling to some notion that you can have everything you want."

"I want to help people. To trust the only family I have left. But you've twisted the mission I dedicated my life to into something destructive and violent."

"Don't be such a naive fool. The only way to rid the earth of dangerous men is to do it in the language they speak. With brutality and bloodshed."

Her perfunctory rationalization of harm made Diana fight off a tremble.

"Family is an outdated notion." Widow dismissed it with a wave of her hand. "You should open your mind to a different structure, one of comrades. Soldiers in a battle against the chains that bind us."

"Chains like love?"

Her mother's lip curled. "If you want to talk about manipulation, look no further than my father and yours. Had I been born a man, I would have inherited my father's estate and made it flourish. *Your* father stole my fortune to build his."

"Did you care for him at all?"

It was not a question her mother had expected. Diana took some satisfaction in the time it took Widow to respond.

"Your father was the best of a set of terrible options. At least he wasn't a drunkard or a philanderer. His obsession was building an empire."

"You could have been a partner to him."

"Not to Harry Rives. He never trusted me. When you were born, I wept that you were a girl and would never be able to rise to his heights."

The idea of her mother being the first person in her life to put limitations on her because of her sex made Diana furious.

It also obliterated any regret she had about betraying her.

She mustered all her strength to keep her voice steady as she replied, "You miscalculated."

"It's true, I misjudged your father. But I was right about you." The assessing glitter in Widow's eyes would have been matronly pride on another woman, if it had an ounce of warmth to it. "I knew you would take to our cause, Diana. And I know that once removed from this scoundrel who's turned your head, you'll come to your senses."

Diana gritted her teeth around the throbbing pain in her arm and, as regally as she could manage, rose from the bed. "That's why you wanted me to steal the emeralds. Anyone could have taken them, but you deliberately wanted me to hurt Ian."

"They traded his mother like chattel for that necklace. Did he tell you that? She always looked so superior when she donned them at a party, while everyone whispered that John Holt had won her in a card game. Pathetic." Widow sniffed. "Ian is part of their sordid world and you'll never extricate him from it. If I hadn't acted, he would have tried to possess you too."

"That's not how it is between us."

"Dear girl," her mother drawled insipidly as she shook her head, "there is no man alive who could care about anything you offer beyond your fortune or your face. If Ian did, he would not have let you go so easily."

Diana was tempted to volley back Ian promised to find her—and he never broke a vow—but she had a terrible fear her mother would laugh out loud and make her ashamed of her conviction.

As she recalled the last days in Florence leading up to *Il Gioco*, and the last moments with Ian before he'd fallen to the ground before her, Diana's faith in him, as in herself, was unshaken.

Her loss of regard for her mother, however, was irrevocable.

"How can you claim to lead a mission to save lives and be so bloodthirsty?" Diana asked.

"Aren't you being a tad hypocritical? You've left quite a body count over the years."

"I only ever did it to defend others and myself," she said thickly around the tears building in her throat. "It's terrible that those men died at my hand. And it's why I want to end this violence."

"Calm yourself. You sound hysterical."

And how her mama hated hysterics.

Diana heaved a sob and shouted, "You forfeited Ian's life to Titus and the Manu Rosso in exchange for a *necklace*!"

"It wasn't his life I was negotiating for; it was yours." Widow's mouth puckered. "Whoever found you and the jewels first would have killed Ian. Costa threatened to make you his mistress by force. His plan was to murder his current wife, marry you, and commandeer your fortune."

Diana didn't want to believe her, despite having met the man and knowing what he was capable of. "We could have found another way. Ian and I were working on an alternative."

"That doesn't matter now," her mother said coldly. "We have the means to destroy the filth who steal women. And we will not be merciful."

"No matter what they've done or threatened, I can never support the scale of violence you're suggesting. Innocent people will be hurt, or worse."

"It's necessary, Diana," her mother chided, as if she was reminding her to brush her teeth before bed. "In order for us to create the world we want, we must burn the old one to the ground."

Widow knocked on the door to summon Birdie and another Stag enforcer. "Since the idiots you were associating with have sent too many factions searching for us, we'll be traveling in separate convoys. Don't do anything foolish."

Her mother didn't bother with any other words of farewell or care. And as the cold weight of her mother's rejection settled on her, Diana finally allowed her thirteen-year-old self to weep openly for what she had lost.

Hot tears soaked her face, but she welcomed the relief and the release that came along with watching Widow walk away. She didn't care if she ever saw her again.

When Birdie and the other woman approached to bind her arms, Diana's sobs grew louder as they wrenched her sore arm.

"You know, Birdie." She hiccupped a breath. "The thought occurred to me that since you betrayed me so easily, your loyalties might be of the constantly flexible type. What would it take to sway them back in my favor? A ship of your own?"

Birdie covered her unease at Diana's crying with a cocky smile. It reminded Diana of the way dockside cats looked when they'd caught a fish. "Shouldn't make promises you can't keep, pet."

"What did Widow promise you for your betrayal?"

"Already owe her my life for pulling me out of the workhouse. I would have died in that hellhole, had it not been for her." Birdie's voice dropped low. "You never asked where I came from, *ma'am*. Thought at first it was to keep things professional-like, out of respect for the fact I worked hard, and we shared a mission. Realized later that you didn't care at all."

"Do you think I'd allow anyone to man one of my ships?" Diana countered, her breath steadying. "Of course I knew where you and every one of my crew came from. And I did respect that and you. Show me I was right, Birdie. Let me go. Leave this behind and come with me. If you stay, Widow will ruin you."

Birdie shook her head. "She said you'd say that."

They bound her mouth with a cloth, and Birdie flashed her teeth. "No need for us to carry you, is there? You'll follow nicely, won't you?"

If one of them attempted it, Diana calculated a sixty percent chance she could relieve one of them of a knife or pistol, but it would be messy and awkward. A short-term gain for a potentially longer-term loss if the struggle resulted in another injury. It was better to cooperate until her odds of escape improved.

In the convent's back garden, a wagon waited for them. Two large barrels took up half of the back. Compared to a hired carriage, the cart would blend in more easily on the rural roads.

Diana was mildly chagrined to find a team of two decent-looking horses leading the cart; Birdie was in a hurry to move them and keep up with Widow's coach and four, which had departed ahead of them.

The enforcer seized her by her sore arm and maneuvered her into the back of the cart. They tossed a foul-smelling horse blanket over her and packed in some sacks of grain for good measure to weigh down the blanket. Her bound hands, sore arm, and blindfold wouldn't make it an easy escape.

But it wasn't the hardest one Diana had trained for either.

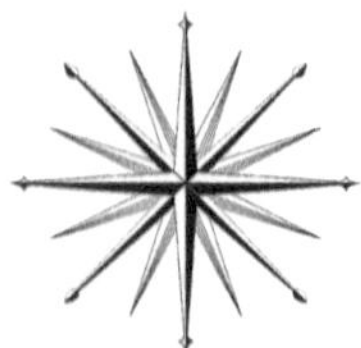

Chapter Twenty-Six

The *polizia* held Ian for two days before Sunderland's bribe secured his release.

At the gates of the prison, a messenger met him with a telegram and an envelope containing the local currency equivalent of fifty pounds Hepburn had wired. It was the remainder of Ian's cash savings. He'd have to make it last until he found Diana.

It was easier to circumnavigate the Ponte Vecchio by foot. In less than an hour, he slipped the *famiglie* tails and eventually found his way to a dingy *pensione* in Gavinana.

The proprietor's eyes lingered on his bruised cheek and cut lip for a moment before he confirmed they had a room for him. A maid delivered cans of hot water and a paper-wrapped parcel and fled quickly.

When he'd locked the door and placed a chair beneath the knob for good measure, he exhaled. Pain laced through his ribs. Over the course of his stay in jail, the other inmates had attempted to teach him the pecking order through a series of introductory assaults to his person. He finally tore his shirt off and exposed the ink on his chest, and they retreated quickly; no one had touched him afterward.

His relief at finding shelter was short-lived. The note Sunderland left with the parcel informed him the duke was still searching for Diana.

The only thing that lessened Ian's panic was focusing on the incremental tasks that would lead him to her. He forced himself to bathe, change clothes, and appease his howling stomach by swallowing a bowl of *osso bucco* before he ventured out to San Niccolo.

In the dim alley across from the tailor shop where they'd met Sunderland days before, Ian watched the tailor close up for the evening. Before the man had finished drawing the picture window blinds, he darted across the street and slipped inside the shop.

When the tailor turned, he acknowledged Ian's presence with a small shriek. He was graciously accommodating with information, thanks to Ian's loaded pistol, and quickly confirmed the address of where he'd delivered the dresses designed to match Diana's scarlet gown. Ian left him tressed and tied for Sunderland to handle while he headed back across the river.

Typically, he would have waited until full dark to scout the crumbling building tucked among the rising iron and glass of San Lorenzo's Mercato Centrale. But his patience had long abandoned him. And without knowing where Diana was, every step he took made him feel rudderless.

He ventured into the tavern across the small lane and ordered *antipasti* and a bottle of chianti. He drank half a glass of it and sent the rest with his compliments to the barmaid who paid particular attention to his movements.

When the market had shuttered and the streets emptied, he returned to the address the tailor had provided and broke into the warehouse. He managed enough restraint to leave the door on its hinges and stalked the perimeter of the empty room. In the fading daylight, he tried to quiet his pounding heart by reminding himself that he'd known he'd find the place deserted, and he couldn't behave like this at every turn, hoping Diana was there. If he did, he'd destroy himself before he found her.

The Stags had performed an exemplary job clearing the site. They'd left nothing behind. No stray biscuit tin or candle stub.

Ian propped himself against the exposed brick wall, sat down on the wooden floor, and unfolded the map Sunderland had sent. When it grew dark, he withdrew a candle and the tin of matchsticks he'd lifted from the tavern and continued studying the map until he heard the scuffle he'd been waiting for.

The door rattled open, and footsteps approached.

He kept his eyes on the map and only lifted his head at the cock of a trigger.

"You don't need that," he told his would-be assailant. "I won't hurt you."

The barmaid from the tavern scoffed. "Don't believe you. You're a desperate man. Desperate men do desperate things."

Ian didn't contradict her. He had a knife in his boot and another inside his pocket. And he could easily overwhelm her if he needed to. "Where is Diana?"

The woman shook her head dismissively. "You need to leave Florence."

"And you're going to let me?" He stood slowly, using the wall for support, as he eyed the gun in the woman's hand. "You broke White Stag protocol coming here."

"You know nothing about us."

"I know that a well-trained operative would never approach an opponent alone." He took a step forward. "Where's your second?"

Ian whistled the low cry of a barn owl, and when there was no corresponding reply, the barmaid clenched and unclenched her jaw.

"Widow sent you out here alone because you're dispensable." He inched closer. "She doesn't care if you return."

The woman wrapped a second hand around her gun. "That's what I signed on for."

"No, it isn't. You committed to a mission to help the helpless. You didn't agree to this."

"I—"

Her voice cut out as she swayed, then sank to her knees. She futilely tried to maintain a hold on the gun, but it skittered across the floor, where Ian picked it up.

"I'd have thought that all those Stag spies would have discovered the British navy's experiments with nerve tonic," he said. "It's undetectable when mixed with a fine chianti."

The Stag sputtered an inaudible gasp.

"In three minutes, you won't be able to sense anything below your neck," Ian continued. "In four minutes, you'll stop breathing altogether. Don't worry, it will be peaceful."

"You bastard," she spat out.

"Technically, yes. I am. But I prefer to be called a devil." With a flash of his teeth, he added, "In two minutes, an associate of mine will arrive with the antidote. If you value your life, you'll tell me where Diana is."

"I don't know." The woman wheezed. "They keep our crews separate for a reason."

"Where did they take her after *Il Gioco*?"

"Here."

"How would they travel to meet Widow?"

"It's different each time. But they're sticking to land this time."

"Why?"

"More options." Her words slurred. "Easier to divert or stop."

Ian crouched down. "And why would they need to do that?"

"In case anyone was hurt."

"Was anyone hurt?" he asked with a calmness that belied the rage stewing inside him.

"Don't know. Diana went with the first team out. Second team was on cleanup."

"And they left you here for me. Alone."

"It was fifty-fifty you'd make it out of the prison alive." She coughed, and her eyes bulged. "Please, you said—"

"I made no promises," he whispered. "And you've given me nothing."

He was acting with intentional malice; he held no remorse about what he would do to protect Diana.

The Stag's eyes squeezed shut. "They won't go far. They won't risk the trains or ships until they know what's happened to you, and they won't know until I miss my signal drop."

"Where?" Ian growled.

"Lucca," she choked out before her eyes rolled back and consciousness left her.

Ian's relief was so acute he hardly registered the approach of clipped footsteps across the floorboards.

His eyes flicked to the shadow who'd joined him. "You took long enough."

"I'm bang on time." Sunderland squinted at the woman. "Is she dead?"

"Unconscious from a tincture of cannabis and valerian root. In ten minutes, she'll come around without so much as a headache. " Ian brushed his hands as he rose. "She said the rendezvous point was Lucca."

"I have a carriage waiting at the mews. On loan, of course. We'll be in Tuscany in a few hours. Did she say anything about the gunpowder?"

Ian shook his head as he herded Sunderland out the door. He didn't care what weaponry the Stags possessed.

He'd battle an armada to find Diana.

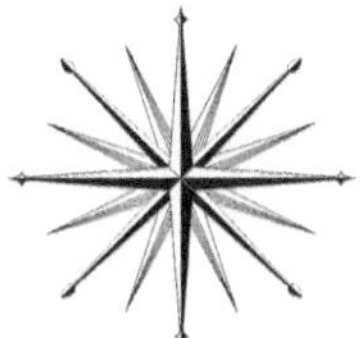

CHAPTER TWENTY-SEVEN

As the wagon pulled onto the road, Diana tested the ropes binding her wrists together. They were snug. The enforcer had never worked lines on a ship, or she would have known that tying a knot that tight ultimately weakens the rope. It only took some friction with the jagged boards of the cart at the pressure point of the loop to loosen the knot.

When Birdie forced the horses into a canter, the wagon swerved. Diana used the motion to cover her movements as she tucked her legs up to her chin, pulled her feet into her stomach, and wiggled her bound hands to the front.

If her sore shoulder hadn't been screaming so loudly, the smack on her thigh would have made her yelp.

"Settle down or next time, I'll use my knife," the enforcer threatened.

"Widow said no rough handling," Birdie countered in a bored tone. "We can subdue her, but only if she comes at us, and you won't do that, pet, will you?"

Her captors settled back into their seats. They didn't talk, which Diana resented, both for the lack of information she could have overheard and the fact that conversation would distract them from her subtle movements beneath the blanket to remove the gag and blindfold, and finally, the ropes. The mounting pain in her arm was making it increasingly difficult to focus.

When a crack of thunder sounded in the distance, the horses whinnied and jostled. Birdie and the enforcer argued with each other about how to keep the beasts under control.

Two louder rumbles heralded the approach of the storm.

On the third roll of thunder, the horses reared.

Diana prayed Ian would keep his vow to find her, and she leaped from the wagon.

As a torrent of rain belted against the tiled roof of the Lucca *pensione*, Ian recited every obscenity he knew.

"Your education at the docks has given you a spectacular vocabulary, Holt," Sunderland drawled. "And don't stare at me like you'll rip my throat out. My favors don't extend to staving off rainstorms. Consider it a sign from the divine that you need to get at least a few hours of sleep."

They'd spent the day tearing apart the town and the surrounding villages but found no trace of Diana. Ian's mood darkened with every dead end.

"I want to go back to the vineyard," he insisted.

"Not at this hour, in this weather," the duke replied.

"That farm is on the only road in and out of town. Someone knows something."

"If they do, they've been incentivized to keep it quiet."

And Ian had no funds to coax the return of their memories.

"Bribery can be ineffective for soliciting reliable information," Sunderland added. "People will invent anything to make a bob."

"Then perhaps we can consider other tactics."

The duke gave an audible exhale. "I'm not known for my kindness, Holt. So I have no qualms in telling you that you're an absolute disaster. Your hair and that scowl are wild enough—not sure we can do anything about that in the short term. But for God's sake, those whiskers need a trim."

A knock sounded at the door, before a maid brought in cans of hot water and towels.

Ian crossed his arms and stared accusingly at Sunderland.

The duke remained unruffled. "You might be able to survive on consuming nothing but whisky, coffee, and the fear of innocent townspeople. But I'm a man who requires proper feeding, which I shall partake of downstairs. If you want to regain the strength to find your lady love and terrify more pastoral Italians, I suggest you join me. But do not dream of sitting at a table with me until you attend to"—Sunderland flapped a hand from Ian's head to his shoes—"this catastrophe."

He punctuated his statement with a slam of the door.

Ian eyed the cans of hot water suspiciously.

The minute he bathed and shaved, he'd feel marginally better than his current state. He couldn't bear the idea of any sort of comfort while Diana was missing. The possibility that she'd suffered hurt or pain in captivity kept his anger on a constant simmer.

But the thing that stole his appetite was the unrelenting anxiety that he'd never find her again. That Widow and the Stags would convince her to stay hidden from him.

A strangled laugh escaped his throat at the possibility that any of them believed they could keep her from him.

And since he was a man who brokered compromises, he agreed to one himself by waiting for the water to cool before he bathed. He couldn't summon the strength to shave, but he trimmed back his beard to a less bedraggled state.

It preserved some of his piratical air and he enjoyed how much it piqued Sunderland when he strolled into the dining room.

He barely tasted the wine, or the *antipasti* of dressed bitter greens and pickled vegetables, but he forced himself to partake of everything.

"We need to clear out tonight," Sunderland said. "There's no trail left to pick up here, so we're down to deductive reasoning. The Stags operate better in city settings; they can hide more easily under the cover of local gangs, and they have better escape routes by the river and ports."

"Which they know we know," Ian argued. "Birdie was adept at moving us by rail. The question is, what direction?"

"There's another complication we haven't addressed. Diana could have escaped."

Ian allowed himself the indulgence of contemplating it. "If so, she'd try for the coast, where she can get on a ship."

"There's something that's been bothering me about all of this," the duke said between bites of *porchetta* dressed in mushrooms, fennel, and potatoes.

"Only one thing?"

"Diana's extraction from *Il Gioco* and the gunpowder theft that was easily reported. It's too messy for the Stags."

"Widow wants the emeralds," Ian said. "She's fixated on them in a way that's—"

"Obsessive?"

"Unhinged."

"She took an enormous risk that didn't pay off. Now everything she built is unraveling. Maybe she's looking for something to cling to," Sunderland mused. "Once we find Diana, we will have to resume *Il Gioco*. I convinced the players to agree to a brief respite given the scrutiny of the authorities, but they will want to settle the game."

"Every member of every *famiglia* can come at me full throttle. Nothing happens until we find Diana."

When the duke gave him a mock salute, Ian was so wired and so weary he laughed. It drew a rare, genuine smile from Sunderland.

He was beginning to not hate the bastard. "What is your true interest in all of this, Your Grace? And don't prattle off something trite about queen and country."

"Perhaps I was promised a reward that would rebuild my coffers."

"Even the queen couldn't afford that."

"True," the duke agreed. "I have a personal interest in securing the ruination of particular members within Il Corno. There is one among their ranks who owes me more than a favor. They owe me a life. And I'm willing to trade more than favors to secure my retribution."

"It would be gargantuanly stupid to make a direct move against them."

"Indeed. A blatant attack is not my style, as you know. But mark me, if it takes the rest of my life, I will take them apart, brick by brick. Until they weep with despair and pain over their ruination."

Sunderland's voice was coldly calculating in a way that would terrify most sensible people. But the duke's vow moved Ian. A man only made a declaration like that when spurred on by deeper, unnamed emotions. "When we find Diana and settle *Il Gioco*, I'll do whatever is in my power to help you."

"And I'll collect on that favor."

A harried-looking waiter rushed over and handed the duke a telegram. Sunderland read it in silence, while Ian gripped his table knife forcefully as he visualized impaling it in the flesh of Diana's captors. When the duke finally looked up from the note, his eyes flicked to the knife. "What are you planning with that little needle, Holt?"

"If I wanted to damage you, I wouldn't need a knife. What do your spies say about Diana?"

"Nothing." The duke folded the note into his pocket. "I'm a *voyeur* by profession, as you know, and one thing I keep a keen eye on is Amelia Hunter."

"Sunderland, I really don't like any part of that sentence. Whatever it is you're plotting, Amelia Hunter can't be a part of it. Diana will have my bollocks for breakfast."

"I assure you, I mean her no harm."

"Did something happen with the *Ever Hart* on the way back to London?"

"No idea. Miss Hunter never boarded it. She stayed behind in La Rochelle but is now traveling to her *palazzo* in Rome. And before you ask, I can verify it's true." He gave a sardonic grin. "I used to own it."

Ian stared at him. "She's taken everything you owned, hasn't she? Cleaned you out completely. What the hell did you do to her?"

The duke rose from the table. "If Miss Hunter is on the move, she's following a protocol she set with Diana. She'll know where the Stags might take her."

"We should take the train." Ian jumped to his feet. "There may be a sleeper from Florence—"

"No need," Sunderland interrupted. "Amelia stopped at a villa on the coast. If we leave now, we can get there by first light."

Diana tore into the cover of the trees bordering the road and cursed her aching arm for slowing her pace. When heavy raindrops fell, and the sky grew dark, her breathing eased fractionally. The path would be muddy for her, but it would also slow the wagon.

If she could make it back to the vineyard they'd passed on the way, she could slip into one of the vineyard's storage cantinas and wait out the storm. Despite the chilly rain soaking through her sopping dress, her skin was on fire. Her legs quivered, and she tried valiantly to lock down all of her muscles. This was not a moment she could afford to be weak.

In all of their scheming over *Il Gioco*, she'd never discussed meeting Ian outside of Florence. It was more than an oversight; some part of her had wanted it to be unnecessary because it meant resorting to her fail-safe plan to meet Amelia, which they'd only established in the event of an extreme emergency. She abhorred the idea of admitting such a defeat.

She fought her hold on consciousness with the fierceness of a cavalry commander. The rain slowed to a faint drizzle, but that positive development evaporated at the sound of a carriage barreling down the road.

It was too dark to distinguish fine details, but Diana saw it was a handsome black landau pulled by a team of four horses. Far too similar to Widow's coach.

The sky flashed above her, and she froze as the carriage sped toward her. When lightning crashed again, and the coach drew closer, panic flooded through her.

Out of habit, she reached for her blades and remembered too late that she'd lost them. Ian had promised he'd have a new set made for her.

She refused to let anything separate them again. Not Birdie. Or her mother. Or the agony in her arm.

As the carriage approached, she fled from the road into the vines.

"Stop the coach!" Ian rapped on the roof of the carriage so fiercely, he knew he was endangering its integrity.

"Keep calm, Holt, it's only a bit of lightning—"

"Now!" He pounded again, cursing the driver and the horses and all of their future offspring for taking so long to bring them to a halt.

The thing was still moving when he sprang out. He only made it a few steps before Sunderland arrested his sprint with a powerful pull on his arm.

"I saw Diana." Ian peered at the surrounding vineyard. "On the road, in the lightning. She's still in the dress. The red one."

Sunderland turned his head to the fields, then back to Ian. He didn't ask him if he was sure. He didn't call Ian a madman either.

Instead, he bellowed for the coachman's lamp. "Which way did she go?"

Ian spun around in circles. His eyes strained to find anything in the murky night.

He paused, gathered his breath, and sent every atom of energy in his body to his voice so it would rise above the rain and the wind.

"Diana! I'm here!" He searched for some sign that the figure he'd seen on the road hadn't been a dream, or a nightmare. "If you can hear my voice, make a noise!"

Sunderland swiveled. He held the lamp aloft as they both examined the black shadows of the night.

"Please, Diana," Ian begged. His throat was raw from shouting. "I never should have insisted we separate. You should have been by my side the entire time. I can't do any of this without you. Tell me where you are, *tesora*!"

From the eastern field, a faint screech of a barn owl sounded.

Ian seized the lamp and tore off, shouting Diana's name and alternating with the whistle cry of the Stags. "Where are you, love? I'm coming for you."

The whistle sounded again, fainter, but Ian followed it through the tangle of vines.

And finally found Diana lying on the ground.

He fell to his knees. His fingers caressed her jaw, detected her pulse and found it weak, but steadily beating. "Diana, we're here now. Open your eyes for me, *tesora*, please. Say something so I know how you are."

Sunderland brought the lamp closer so Ian could examine her. Blood caked around her left arm, and when he tried to roll up the sleeve, the matted fabric caught.

She uttered a small moan.

Ian wanted to worship the sound. And murder it.

Slowly, her eyes fluttered open. "Ian? I was coming to find you."

"Good, because I was lost without you," he murmured.

"Birdie and Widow are close," she rasped. "Can't risk a doctor."

"I know." He'd argue with her after she was safe inside the coach.

"San Genaro," she murmured as he gathered her into his arms. "Take me to San Genaro. Doctor there. Safe."

Sunderland guided their way back to the road and helped Ian hand her into the carriage. "We should listen to her."

"I always listen to her," Ian snapped.

The duke shook his head as he sat back across from him in the carriage. "San Genaro. That's where we were heading. The name of the villa where Miss Hunter is staying is San Genaro."

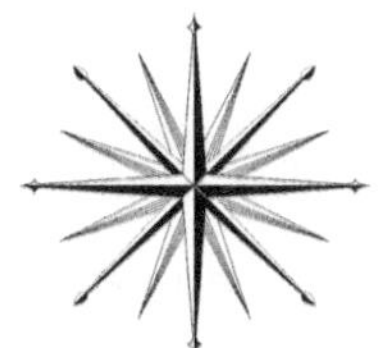

CHAPTER TWENTY-EIGHT

THE DRIVE TOOK THREE of the most agonizing hours of Ian's life.

They stopped briefly at the first town they came upon and paid the tavern owner a small ransom for hot water, soap, grappa, and bandages. In a private dining room, Ian ripped the sleeve off her gown so he could wash and dress her wound. When he poured the alcohol to disinfect it, Diana sobbed and called him the filthiest of obscenities.

On the road, she moved in and out of consciousness as she lay in his arms. The storm and the muddied roads stalled their progress. Finally, the carriage stopped at the bottom of a small cliff. Ian and Sunderland peered through the drizzling rain at the villa perched on top.

And the hundreds of stairs leading up to it.

Sunderland rubbed his jaw. "We should make a litter and carry her together."

Ian shook his head. "Go ahead of us and make damn sure there's a doctor waiting."

It took him a quarter of an hour to scale the steps carrying Diana. By the time he reached the stone drive leading to the house, he was gasping, sweating, and at the end of his reserve.

The majordomo waiting by the door gaped at him in mild horror before beckoning him inside. "This way, *signore*."

The servant led him through an atrium, filled with jasmine and lemon trees, to the open stairway, where Amelia stood.

"Thank God," she rasped as she clasped a hand to her chest.

Ian took the stairs two at a time. "Where's the doctor?"

255

A man in a rumpled suit emerged from a room off the hallway. He raised his eyebrows as Ian barreled toward him. "I imagine you're *Signore* Holt?"

"Out of my way," Ian growled.

"Ian, wait," Amelia cautioned. "This is the doctor."

"It's all right." The doctor waved them into a nearby bedroom and gestured to the bed. "Please put Miss Rives there, and then you may wait in the hallway. Miss Hunter may stay while I examine her, if you prefer."

Ian wanted to protest. Loudly. Leaving Diana with a stranger was akin to cutting off an appendage, but Amelia tilted her head beseechingly and cajoled him into complying.

Outside in the hallway, Sunderland offered him a towel and a whisky. "All will be well now."

Ian accepted the linen and pushed the glass away. He needed to stay alert. There was still an enemy to be vanquished to keep Diana safe. One he felt powerless against.

When his pacing had worn a hole in the terracotta floor, the doctor and Amelia finally emerged.

"The good news is that the only wound Miss Rives suffered was from the bullet that punctured her upper arm," the doctor said. "While the bullet went through, the wound was open a long time, which caused it to fester. The infection spread to her blood."

Ian grabbed the man by the shirt and growled, "What are you doing about it?"

"That's quite enough!" Amelia cried.

In truth, it was more of a bellow. It caught Ian by surprise—he'd never heard the shy woman raise her voice more than a few decibels.

Even Sunderland parted his lips in mild awe.

Ian released the doctor and mumbled an apology.

"Forgiven, *signore*." The doctor's lips quirked. "I've been married for twenty-two years. I'd behave the same way if my wife were so ill."

"What can I do for her?" Ian asked. He needed a task, some mission to put himself to use.

The doctor cleared his throat. "I don't want to give her more laudanum. Her pulse is already slow. The bigger danger is the fever. We must get it down. And the fastest way to do it will be unconventional."

"No one here gives a toss about convention," Ian said. "As long as it's within the bounds of the law, and it won't harm her further, do whatever it takes."

"A cold bath then. With seawater," the doctor said briskly. "I'll need the servants to draw buckets of it and ready a tub. Only a small amount of hot water to temper the rest."

"I'll arrange it." Amelia rushed down the hall.

Sunderland didn't bother to offer an excuse or commentary as he stalked behind her.

The servants worked quickly. In his manic state, Ian wondered if they were magicians who manifested the barrels of seawater out of thin air and delivered them to the bathing room.

Diana was groggy as Amelia and the maid undressed her. When they went to move her to the bathing room, Ian's composure snapped.

"Without her consent, no one else is touching her but me," he snarled.

He removed his shirt—he wasn't sure how active the bathing process was going to be—and gathered Diana into his arms.

"Ian?" Her lips were hot as they pressed against his throat. "I was dreaming of you. We were together, with nothing separating us."

"That sounds like my dreams, love."

"Do you know how I've longed for your skin against mine?" She grazed a hand over his bare chest. "Why must I be so ill when this is finally happening?"

"It's unfair," he agreed, his voice hoarse. He couldn't swallow her suffering.

"Where are we going?"

"Sea bathing, love. We brought the ocean to you. It's going to be brisk. It will steal your breath, and I know how you love to be breathless with me. Are you ready?"

"Don't go," she pleaded.

"I'll be right here."

As gently as he could, he placed her in the tub.

Diana shuddered and cried out. She clung to him by digging her nails into his chest, and he was glad he'd had the forethought to preserve his only shirt.

"It's too much," she sobbed.

"It's only a short while," he soothed. "I'm right here, *tesora mia*. Hold my hand while I tell you one of my father's stories about the selkies."

Her clasp on his hand grew limp as sobs racked her body. He'd considered himself a man of a certain strength, but the entire endeavor made him feel a helplessness that was worse than any weakness he could imagine.

By the time Amelia knocked on the door to deliver warmed towels and a fresh nightgown for Diana, he was sure he'd spent years in hell.

"Would you like some help getting her dressed?" Amelia asked, adding, "I know you don't need it—"

"Yes," he said with a grateful nod. "I would appreciate that. Thank you."

When he drew Diana out of the bath, her shudders subsided.

"Her skin feels cooler," Amelia said with a tight smile.

They settled Diana back into bed. The doctor returned and measured her temperature with a glass thermometer.

He turned to Ian with a cautious smile. "Better."

Ian staggered to the chair beside the fireplace, and quietly went to pieces.

Diana knew the fever was an insidious enemy.

She was grateful she couldn't remain conscious. Whenever she woke, they plunged her in the frigid sea bath. Afterward, she could only stop shuddering when Ian's strong arms gathered her tightly to him. She feared the infection had spread to her brain because she felt like she was flying as she searched for his heartbeat, and the warmth of his skin.

In her more lucid moments, she noted the tight lines that bracketed his mouth and forehead and hated that she'd caused him such distress.

Eventually, the persistent ache in her head subsided, and a heavy sleep came over her. When she woke again, she felt like an empty shell, but the horrible heat that had haunted her for days had fled.

Alone in the bed, she struggled to sit up.

"Diana." Ian was by her side in an instant, his hand pressed to her forehead. "The fever broke."

His relieved smile was brighter than the sunlight peeking through the curtains.

She wanted to return it, but her weakness made her, of all absurd things, suddenly shy.

"How do you feel?" he murmured.

"Grateful." She managed a wan smile. "And thirsty."

He poured her a small glass of water. "Sip slowly. I'll get the doctor."

"Wait." She reached for his hand. "Stay with me a minute."

Dark circles hung beneath his eyes but the relief in his expression made her swallow back tears.

"You found me," she whispered. "When I needed you most."

"I never doubted I would."

"And no one hurt you? Everything that happened after the game is such a blur."

He shook his head. "We can talk about it when you've had some rest."

"You're going to lecture me about going for the gun. I paid a high price for it." She sighed. "And Widow still escaped."

Ian drew a breath. "No, Di. She didn't."

He reached for the nightstand and handed her a cutout from the local newspaper. "On our way to San Genaro, we passed a fire on the road. We didn't stop to ask what had happened; I was too concerned about getting you to a doctor."

He smoothed his hand over her hair and pressed a kiss into her temple. "Sunderland's team made inquiries. They think a lightning strike hit something in the cart that caused a fire and forced a collision with the carriage. Three women and the coach driver died. One of them was wearing Birdie's coat and hat."

Diana laid back against the pillows and blinked. "One of the other women was my mother."

She waited for sorrow and pain. The gaping, hollow feeling that engulfed her was a surprise.

As was the relief that chased it.

"There were two barrels in their wagon. It could have been gunpowder. They died because..." Her voice cut out.

Ian drew her closer. "I'm sorry, *tesora*. For all of their sins, they did not deserve a painful death."

"It doesn't feel real. Or fair." Tears finally broke loose and cascaded down her cheeks. "I thought I was finished with Widow."

"She was your mother, and Birdie was part of your crew. You shared a mission that was the center of your life for years." He stroked a hand down her arm. "It would be impossible to let all of that go in an instant. And you can choose to mourn them—or not—however you want."

As more of her tears fell, he gently wiped them away with a clean handkerchief. In her entire life, she'd never felt more privileged than she did now, for having someone hold her through the quagmire of her grief.

She sat up abruptly. "Poor Amy is dealing with all of this on her own."

"Amelia is handling things brilliantly," he assured her. "You can talk with her when you're feeling better. And I should let you rest too."

He made to move, but she clung to his hand. "Wait. Please. Now that we're here, there are things I must tell you."

"We have time. I'm not going anywhere. Neither are you, until you're well again," he added with a small growl.

"The emeralds—"

"That necklace means nothing to me. Not compared with losing you." His voice shook uncharacteristically. "If my father's legacy burns, if the Crown tries me for treason for letting maritime resources fall into criminal hands, so be it. It will be a small price to pay to keep you safe."

Her eyes pricked with tears again and the gentle way he brushed them aside with his thumb made her heart soar higher. "I was going to say that the necklace is in the hidden pocket of my dress."

When his jaw dangled open, she summoned her strength to sit up and press a kiss against it. "But it makes me happy beyond reason to know you'd light the world on fire to save me."

He issued a low moan and kissed her with enough heat to make her wonder if the fever had returned.

Tenderly, he tucked her head to rest between the crook of his neck and his shoulder. "I vow to you, I will keep us safe from the *famiglie*. We will end *Il Gioco*."

"Indeed we will." She breathed in his familiar scent and sighed. "Let me tell you my plan."

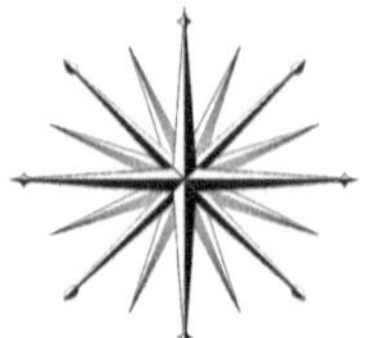

Chapter Twenty-Nine

Ian stood on the banks of the Arno River and evaluated the spires of the church of Santa Maria della Spina. He ruminated over the disproportionate number of churches where he ended up doing the devil's work.

"Quite a spot you've chosen," Sunderland murmured from beside him. "They remade this entire building a few years ago. River flooding was compromising it, so the city of Pisa dismantled the thing. Put it back together in a higher spot."

"It brings a certain poetry to what we're doing." Ian's lips curved.

"I doubt anyone will appreciate it."

"They're all assembled?"

"Including the men of the cloth. Let's hope they don't shoot first and ask questions later."

"They won't." The scheme was Diana's idea, and Ian had absolute faith in it.

He disliked executing her plan without her, but she was still recovering from the fever. The neanderthal in him was relieved; he never wanted her to breathe the same air as Costa or Titus ever again.

When he and Sunderland entered the church vestibule, two priests approached them with a woven basket and gestured for their guns. They graciously placed them inside, per the terms all parties had agreed to, and proceeded into the church.

Titus and Costa stood in front of the altar, flanking the bishop of Pisa.

"Dragging me to a church on the arse end of nowhere won't stop me from killing you," Costa greeted them.

"True," Ian conceded. His eyes flicked to the bishop's paling face. "But murdering me won't help you win the emeralds."

"You're here representing the Tarka?" Titus asked in a calmer voice.

"In this matter only." The Tarka *capo* was halfway back to Malta and had gladly accepted a generous incentive to agree to their plan. He'd confessed to Ian they were looking into new lines of business, which Ian hoped meant severing their ties to the trafficking trade.

"How do we know you have the necklace?" Costa asked.

Ian flicked the gems from his hand with a smooth motion. He supplied a jeweler's loupe in his other hand and offered it first to Titus, then to Costa.

"We cannot play here." Costa gestured wildly to their surroundings.

The bishop confirmed it with a stern nod.

"I'm not here to play, I'm here to negotiate," Ian said.

Titus barked a laugh. "That's not how this works."

"Why?"

Costa grumbled beneath his breath about Ian's stupidity. Titus expounded that Ian possessed bigger *coglioni* than a bull, before the bishop chided them all for their language.

"*Signori*, let me make things crystal clear," Ian said. "The rules of *Il Gioco* pass down from *famiglia* to *famiglia*. There are no contracts. No binding regulation."

"It's tradition," Titus declared. "That is how *we* do business."

"Yes. *You* make the rules," Ian said. "The game has already changed a great deal in its history. There's nothing that stipulates we must enforce the current rules."

"*Idiota!*" Costa jeered. "It's an insult. If people bend and break rules, they have no authority. *We* have no authority."

Ian nodded slowly, as if Costa had convinced him that change was impossible.

Instead of inevitable.

"You want to play for more than the emeralds, and the assets staked to them," Ian said.

"We play to win," Titus confirmed.

"I have a proposition, then." Ian walked to a small linen-covered table and handed the crystal decanters for wine and water to the bishop before spreading the emerald necklace across the table. "No one truly knows what this necklace looks like. It's never been painted or photographed."

"I recognized it," Costa retorted. "Anyone who was at the last *Il Gioco* would."

Titus snorted. "You were too drunk to remember your own name. I was sitting directly behind the players and barely got a glimpse."

Ian withdrew another coil of glittering jewels from his pocket and placed it above the emerald necklace. "Then it would be difficult to determine which one of these was the *Il Gioco* prize."

He handed the loupe to Titus and Costa so they could examine it.

Both men required a second look. And a third.

Eventually, Titus said, "This new necklace. The stones are twice the size."

"It belonged to the same Mughal emperor who built the Taj Mahal. Which makes it worth…" Ian turned to Sunderland. "Five times as much as the other necklace?"

"Seven," the duke corrected him.

The sudden quiet that fell over the church made Ian purse his lips together to prevent himself from smiling.

Costa tossed a hand. "Even if the gems are worth more, it is not an equal swap. The first necklace is tied to bounty beyond the gems."

"True." Ian turned to Sunderland, who handed him a small ledger. "This is the list of assets my father recorded, the year he won *Il Gioco*. The Tarka still possess most of them and will transfer them to the new necklace."

He placed a scrap of paper on top of the ledger. "This is what remains of my father's stake in the docks and its current market worth."

On top of that, Ian placed a smaller card. "This is a bank account with that same amount of money. It will also transfer with the new necklace."

Titus's eyes narrowed. "That's a lot of capital to raise quickly. You must have mortgaged everything."

Without Diana's investment, Ian would have. "The money is there. The bishop has verified it."

"*Mae de deus*," Costa spat. "None of this matters. The emeralds cannot be bought or sold."

"But they can be traded," Ian said. "No one needs to know."

"Everyone is expecting us to play *Il Gioco*—"

"So we play," Titus interrupted. "With the new necklace. And the money."

The Manu Rosso *capo* paused. "And without Holt."

Titus turned back to Costa. "He's impossible to beat without cheating. Less trouble for all of us if he surrenders his claim."

Costa reached for the bank slip. His lip curled as he raised his eyes to meet Ian's. "I never want you near my business or my family ever again."

"Likewise," Ian agreed.

The rain clouds hovering over the Tyrrhenian Sea were so beautiful, it made Diana wish she knew how to paint.

Through the view of the French doors in San Genaro's dining room, she detected whitecaps on the waves. The storm would arrive within the hour. She tried not to interpret it as an omen of the day to come.

"There you are."

Ian padded into the room in his stocking feet. He'd bathed and dressed but had foregone a necktie. A splash of his ink peeked through his open collar.

He'd returned from the showdown with Costa and Titus in the middle of the night, and after kissing Diana and telling her the plot she'd hatched had succeeded, he'd collapsed onto the bed in a fatigued stupor. And slept for the better part of the day.

Diana bid him a good afternoon. The brush of his lips silenced her for several moments while their mouths and tongues became reacquainted. He kissed her as if they'd been apart for years, instead of days.

"You look so much better," he murmured.

"I *am* better. And your color is much improved."

"Who knew sleep could be so restorative."

She laughed and gave him a playful shove. "It's almost time for luncheon, but I'll ring for coffee and *coronetto*."

"No need, I've already had both." He lifted her up from the chair, sat down in it and pulled her into his lap. "I thought I might convince you to return to bed."

"Maybe later."

He stroked a hand down her back. "What has your clever brain been fixating on that's made your shoulders so tight?" His hand brushed against her forehead. "Are you feeling poorly?"

Truthfully, her stomach was in knots. "I have something I need to tell you. And I'm worried it's going to upset you. It *will* upset you, and I hate it."

To her immense horror, tears pricked her eyes.

"Oh, love." He dabbed them away with his handkerchief. "It can't be that horrible."

"I don't know what's wrong with me." She gave a shaky laugh. "All I do these days is wobble."

"You're making up for all those years of perfect composure." His hand massaged her neck, and at the utter of her soft moan, he whispered in her ear, "I prefer you undone."

"Remember precisely how much, with what I'm about to tell you."

He nipped her earlobe. "*Tesora mia*, I came dangerously close to losing you. I'm still not convinced you're out of the woods yet, and that terrifies me more than any secret you could be keeping."

She drew a breath. "Do you like the villa?"

He blinked at the abrupt turn in the conversation. "This is the first I've seen of it, beyond our suite."

"I want to give you a tour."

He stroked a finger down her cheek. "I'd rather stay here."

"Stop indulging me."

"Actually, I'm indulging myself right now."

"Ask me why."

He sighed. "Why do you want me to tour the villa?"

"Because it's yours," she whispered. "You own San Genaro, Ian."

His mouth slackened, and his eyes quickly darted away from her to study the breathtaking view of the ocean and the damask curtains framing the French doors. Then his stare slowly moved to the polished walnut table, and the blue and white porcelain bowl topped with apples.

For an impossibly long moment, Diana waited, holding on for dear life to all of her hopes and dreams.

Eventually, his gaze returned to hers, and in an even voice, he demanded, "Tell me."

"Your parents spent time here. I didn't know until we arrived, and I recognized that." She gestured to a candlestick table bearing a silver vase filled with fresh flowers.

Ian brushed his hand over his mouth. "That's the view from my mother's painting." The single piece of art that hung in his London home.

Diana nodded. "When your father was dying, he wanted to buy San Genaro for you. But he didn't have the funds. And he couldn't break the trust that was set up to convey the business to Jared."

"I know."

"Yes, of course." She swallowed. "Your father had a small sum of money he'd put aside. Barely a third of what the owner wanted for San Genaro. He gave the money to my father and asked him to invest it for you. So that it would grow to a sum large enough for you to buy the house."

"And neither of you thought to tell me I had an inheritance?" His voice rose in justifiable outrage.

"I threatened to when I found out." It was the worst row she'd ever had with her father. They'd gone weeks without speaking. "Papa said that there were explicit legal instructions created to penalize you from withdrawing the sum from the investment before maturity. It could have made the money your father left you worthless."

She'd consulted three solicitors and none of them could find a way out of it.

"After Father died, I asked Amelia for help, and she made the money grow faster. When there was finally enough for San Genaro's owner to consider an offer, it took months to settle things. The sale only went through the day I left London."

Ian gave a strangled laugh. "What would have happened if I had stayed in London?"

"If you hadn't followed me on this wild chase, I left instructions to deliver the deed to you. But you did follow me. And I kept saying to myself that I'd tell you once I knew you were safe from my mother. And, well, everyone else."

She blew out a breath. "And then, for a short while, I deliberately didn't tell you. Because I thought if you knew, you would leave. And that was wrong of me."

"It was," he said softly. "I had a right to know."

"You did," she agreed, with as much strength in her voice as she could muster. "Of all the secrets I've had to keep, this was the second worst one."

"The first being your mother."

"No, Ian. There was another reason my father did all of those things for yours," she countered gently.

"Eight years ago, I sat by your father's bedside. And he read me that letter my mother had sent to manipulate all of us. But the charade that my father insisted we play out for my protection, and the ploy my mother made me seize on for her own machinations...it was all made under the false presumption that everyone believed. Including you."

She cupped his face between her hands and felt the pulse in his neck beat out a tattoo that marched in time with her own thumping heartbeat. "The promise was never about Jared. It was always about you."

He stared at her with such heartbreaking longing, she was sure he'd misunderstood her.

"Did you hear me?" Her voice escalated in mild panic as she searched his face. "The pledge I made was to marry *you*, Ian. I made that vow willingly. Not because you needed looking after, although you do. Your father wanted me to make that promise because he saw that we were besotted with each other before either of us could admit it. He thought that together, we would be unstoppable."

Ian's eyes glistened. "He was right."

Relief and warmth and a joy unequal to anything Diana had ever known radiated through her. "You believe me?"

"God, yes."

His mouth descended on hers, and her body folded into his, like a key fitting into a lock.

"Together, we *are* unstoppable," he echoed.

Chapter Thirty

THE ENGLISH CHANNEL, JANUARY 1878

"We can still turn the ship around," Ian murmured against Diana's bare back.

Her skin was warm and damp from his mouth and perspiration from their exertion over the evening. He was torn between stoking her for another round and letting her rest to conserve her energy for the days ahead.

"Not bloody likely," Diana slurred. "Too much cargo on this steamer."

In the months following the debacle in Florence, the Stags network as Widow had built it had dissolved. But Diana, Amelia, and a few trusted partners were still working to move women to safety.

"And I have no authority on this vessel," she added. "The Wildes own this ship, not me."

"That wouldn't stop us."

Her low laugh made his cock stir.

"We can't put off our return to London any longer," she insisted. "Beatrix and Henry need us."

It was the only reason Ian had agreed to abandon San Genaro, where they'd spent a blissful sabbatical away from the world. The first few weeks, they'd only left the villa to walk the shoreline and fish for sea bream. The rest of the time they ate, drank, and made love on every flat surface in the villa.

But reality had crept in. Correspondence found them. First, in the form of Jared's notice of resignation and his expatriation to America, with Polly and Johnny. Later,

Amelia and Sunderland each needed their counsel on the fallout from *Il Gioco* and the dissolution of the Stags. Then they were inundated with inquiries about the running of the various enterprises bearing their names. When Hepburn had finally sent word about Henry and Beatrix, they couldn't ignore the summons.

"I hated leaving the villa," Ian complained.

"You hide it so well."

He gave her a playful smack on her bare bottom and the muffled moan she emitted made him hard again. "I still think we could have managed it all from San Genaro."

"But then it would lose its magic," she argued. "It's our haven. I don't want business to invade it."

They'd intentionally avoided deciding anything about the future of Holt & Company and Rives Shipping until they reached London. In the waning moments Ian had with Diana before the rest of the world crowded in on them, he had no intention of wasting thought or energy on it.

"We'll go back." Her voice drifted off, and she was asleep before she could hear the promise he whispered as he gathered her close to him.

"As soon as we can, *tesora*."

He remained awake as he cherished the weight of her body against his. Their last round together had been heated, and reckless; he'd been so swept up, he'd come inside her before pulling out. Diana hadn't appeared troubled by it, but he was.

In their seaside paradise, they'd neglected to renew their discussions on marriage. When they'd stopped in Paris to usher in the new year, he'd slipped away and bought her a ring, but it hadn't seemed like the right time to give it to her. He didn't want to contrive their engagement because they needed to cover some scandal when they returned to London.

Diana deserved more than that.

They both did.

A sharp rapping at the door jolted him awake.

His pistol was in his hand before his feet hit the floor, and when he realized Diana was gone, he cocked the trigger.

"Sir?" a muffled voice called. "May I come in?"

Ian yanked the door open. "Hepburn?"

"Morning, sir." As his former valet strode into the room, Hepburn's eyes flicked to the pistol before Ian locked it.

"Where's Diana?" Ian demanded.

"Lovely to see you again as well, sir."

"How did you get here? What bloody time is it? And what the hell is going on?"

Hepburn snapped open a valise and pulled out a razor and brush. "To answer your questions in order, sir. Miss Rives is on the promenade deck, expecting you. I boarded when the ship ported at Calais. It's half-past seven in the morning, two hours before we're due into Southampton."

The valet cleared his throat. "And I think I'll let Miss Rives answer your last question."

In a daze, Ian allowed Hepburn to oversee his toilet, which involved a loud protest over the state of his former employer's hair as he trimmed it, the best shave Ian had received in months, and a full report on how Henry had fared during Hepburn's brief tenure with his friend.

"If I may be frank, sir," he said. "Mr. Eden doesn't need me half as much as you do."

Ian fought a smile while the valet helped him into a gray morning coat. "I missed you too, old man."

Hepburn made a harumph in the back of his throat and held the door open. "Your lady awaits."

As Ian tore down the corridor, he ignored the pleas to mind his hair.

When he emerged on deck, the sun rising over the English Channel momentarily blinded him. It was a miracle it had appeared at all in the dead of winter. His eyesight adjusted, and he scanned the open deck. A small cluster of people huddled in two groups, forming a makeshift aisle.

Diana stood at the end, shining brighter than the winter sun.

She wore a simple ivory gown with little embellishment beyond a lace overlay. A fur capelet and muff protected her from the frigid air. No veil would have survived the wind on deck.

Instead, she wore a tiara of emeralds.

As she caught sight of him, her face broke into a smile that no artist could capture. The one that could have launched a thousand ships and broken a thousand hearts.

It had healed his own.

Ian staggered across the deck. Before he could reach for Diana, Hepburn interceded and forced his arms into an overcoat of fine black cashmere.

Finally, he curled his arm around Diana's waist and gathered her close.

Her smile glittered as she raised her beautiful brow. "Did you know that a ship's captain has the authority to preside over marriages?"

"I did," he confirmed as he caressed her face.

"Then, Ian Genaro Holt. My scheming friend. My love. Will you promise to spend forever with me, in an official and legal capacity, as my wedded husband?"

Ian slipped the emerald and diamond ring around her finger as his mouth descended on hers. He warmed her cold lips with the heat of his kiss.

"I do."

Author's Note

Here is the section, my dear reader, where you can find some history nerd references and further reading about the events and settings that inspired this story.

The exhibition of the *S.S. Great Britain* in Bristol Harbor gave me a slew of primary sources and the physical grounding to help me recreate the maritime world of the Victorian era. If you're in the area, stop by for a visit.

This book was written in English, but you'll notice words and phrases throughout in French, Spanish, Italian, and Maltese. It's becoming less standard practice to italicize foreign words, but after trying both options and consulting with my editors, I opted to use italics for ease of reading.

Both *Keeping the Countess*, and *Runaway Rogue*, feature the Skinner's Lane Lads street gang, which, while fictional, is based on the well-documented history of London crime throughout the nineteenth and twentieth centuries. For further reading on this, I recommend *London's Criminal Underworlds, c. 1720 - c. 1930: A Social and Cultural History* by Heather Shore.

In the nineteenth century, Great Britain fought two wars with China's Qing Dynasty over opium and trade. The Convention of Peking treaty which ended the second war in 1860 enabled the free flow of opium in the U.K. until the Pharmacy Act of 1868 regulated its sale and distribution (along with fourteen other poisons) to qualified pharmacists. If you're curious about the effects of illicit markets on social and political economy, you may be interested in an article by John Collins, "Empire, war, decolonization and the birth of the illicit opium trade in Burma, 1800—1961" which you can find published in, James and Morrison, John and Winter, Aaron and Silke, Andrew, (eds.) *Historical Perspectives on Organised Crime and Terrorism*.

Runaway Rogue addresses the impacts and prevalence of human trafficking, which we define as the illegal trade of human beings and / or the recruitment, control, and use of people for their bodies and for their labor. If you would like to learn more about how to stop this cycle of enslavement, or file a report, please visit www.a21.org for resources and contact information.

ACKNOWLEDGEMENTS

This book exists because of readers like you who have championed *Keeping the Countess* and the *Damsels in Disguise* series. I'm immensely grateful to you for reading, reviewing, and recommending these books.

I would also like to thank:

My family (who I forgot to mention in the first book, yikes!) especially my mother, who encouraged my love of reading moody Victorian literature.

My critique partners and emotional support pumpkins, Maggie Eliot, Evie Jacobs, Maureen Ewing, and Caragh Leon, who didn't let me give up on this book even when I wanted to.

Kate Happ, for reading the earliest trash heap draft and giving me the tough love I needed to find Ian and Diana's story. Chapter Three is entirely yours, friend.

Rachel Shipp, for helping me see the forest for the trees in this plot.

Faith Williams and The Atwater Group for their eagle-eyed editing.

My spouse, for all of the roads, rivers, seas, and mountains we've travelled together.

This book is dedicated to Sarah MacLean and Jen Prokop, who I consider to be the fairy godmothers of romance. Listening to the *Fated Mates* podcast made me a romance reader and a romance writer, and irrevocably changed my life for the better. Thank you for all that you do.

ABOUT THE AUTHOR

Lille Moore is the author of *Damsels in Disguise*, a steamy Victorian romance series featuring cunning, courageous heroines, passionate heroes, and copious amounts of intrigue, seduction, and scandal.

Lille grew up by the coast in Massachusetts, in a town with the prettiest main street and most vicious geese in America. Her public diplomacy and strategic communications career took her across five continents and six of the Seven Seas and spurred a lifelong love affair with uncovering new worlds through storytelling.

When she's not chasing stories, Lille enjoys a well-brewed cup of tea, dancing like nobody's watching (hopefully), and binging *Miss Scarlet*. She lives with her spouse in Texas.

Sign up for Lille's newsletter to get an exclusive FREE novella at:
www.lillemoore.com
Connect with Lille online at Instagram, Facebook, Threads, and Pinterest:
@lillemoorebooks

Keeping the Countess Sneak Peek

WANT MORE DAMSELS IN DISGUISE?

Here's your sneak peak of ***KEEPING THE COUNTESS,*** the first full-length novel in the *DAMSELS IN DISGUISE* series.

After twenty years of searching, Reverend Jonah Sinclair finally has a lead on his father's killer. But his quest for justice is threatened when he becomes entangled with a countess hiding a dangerous secret. Will he overcome his forbidden desires to unravel the mystery that connects them, or will he sacrifice everything for the woman who has captured his heart?

CHAPTER ONE

Somewhere in Cumbria, 1878

It had not occurred to Reverend Jonah Sinclair that traveling in the dark on a rain-soaked country road might lead him to his death.

Rather an oversight on his part. His formative years in Southwark's alleyways had cultivated a healthy fear of the dangers that could greet him in the shadows. And presently, he was far from the relative safety of the known unknowns of South London.

Eleven hours of travel—nine by train, two by stifling coach, all amidst a downpour—had landed him in a place deserted by human civilization.

Somewhere in the rain and the dark and mists surrounding him was the Earl of Rochford's estate, and his assignment for the next month. It had been no small feat to position himself for it. His hopes and expectations of what lay ahead were unfairly high.

First, he had to find the bloody place. An endeavor that would have been simple if the aristocrats who had engaged his services had remembered to send their carriage.

With his temper flaring, he trudged his way up the hill from the coaching stop to the lone public house in the village, identifiable by a withering wooden sign bearing the name *The Saltcoat*. As he strode inside, he avoided thinking about the damage the mud was inflicting upon his best suit.

Mustering the swagger that had helped him survive a host of awkward circumstances, Jonah walked past the sparse collection of patrons cataloguing his every movement and approached the narrow wooden bar.

"Good evening," he began.

No one acknowledged the sound of his voice.

His simmering ire prevented him from softening his accent and his posture. "Would any of you be kind enough to point me in the direction of Ravenglass Hall?"

The men standing by him, along with the barman and barmaid, all turned away in an eerily synchronous movement. As cold dismissals went, it was one of the frostiest he could recollect. But he'd grown accustomed to setbacks and fending for himself. Twenty years ago, he'd been robbed of everything he loved. Two things had powered his survival: the determination to right the injustices served upon his family, and a healthy anger.

Harnessing the second in service of the first, Jonah marched out of the tavern, his vexation blinding him to any semblance of the direction where he headed. It did not take long to realize he was absolutely stranded, alone in a country wilderness.

In the disorienting shadows of the soaking evening, a seed of regret at his impulsivity sprouted. As he contemplated swallowing his pride and turning back to the tavern, a preternatural cry sounded on the moor.

The ground shook, heralding a beast rising out of the fog.

Jonah wouldn't have dared called the creature a horse; that was far too earthly a comparison. It sped toward him as if it had escaped straight from the ninth circle of hell.

Unholy thoughts clouded his brain. Unholier curses tumbled from his lips. He was pleased to discover the passage of time and years of service in Her Majesty's Church had not scrubbed them from his memory.

The shriek of the wind rose over the roar of approaching hooves. This was the exact reason Jonah avoided Gothic novels like vermin; he preferred interacting with the supernatural in the controlled boundaries of the King James Bible.

Through the sheets of rain, he spotted a slight figure mounted on top of the enormous steed. Was the rider attempting to bring the monster under control? Or did he urge it on, hoping he might flatten a weary traveler to the ground?

A shrill cry sounded from the rider. Was it a warning? An apology? A prayer?

"MOVE OUT OF THE BLEEDING WAY, YOU DAFT FOOL!"

With a screeching whinny, the beast reared up before him, a black wall of menacing horseflesh. As lightning flashed around them, Jonah braced his arms over his head and curled himself into a protective crouch, precisely as the hell-beast tossed its rider from the saddle.

A moment of raw stillness followed.

The rain relented, revealing where the rider lay motionless on the path.

Jonah staggered across the short distance toward the body. With a deep breath and a short prayer, he kneeled down to examine the fallen man.

The crash of two thick skulls meeting each other upended his balance. He slipped on the drenched ground, falling on top of the rider, who protested wildly by snarling in a manner more feral than a quayside cat. The body entwined with his was as scrappy and slim as one. He had to be a young lad.

"Get off of me!"

"I'm trying!" Jonah protested as they tussled in the mud. Muck worked its way beneath the collar he'd starched himself, to make a good impression for the toffs who'd forgotten him. The potential embarrassment he'd face if he ever arrived at his destination burned energy into his limbs.

An instinct he thought he'd long retired kicked in and he rolled, quickly pinning the rider's shoulders by pressing his own weight into the lad's chest.

And therein, he discovered a very distinct set of curves that most decidedly did not belong to a young man.

The body beneath him hissed.

Jonah scrambled away and staggered to his feet. With his last remaining ounce of sense, he extended his hand to the rider.

The *woman* he'd just groped in the darkness.

"My humblest apologies. Are you hurt?"

Ignoring his attempt at civility, she rose without touching him and hastily pulled her drenched scarf closer to her face. In the darkness, he couldn't distinguish any of her features, only a dark spark somewhere in the vicinity of her eyes. An alluring scent of citrus permeated the space between them.

"You are lucky to be alive, you absolute lob."

Her voice was gruff and a little breathless, but the insult didn't sting him. He'd been called much worse.

"My sincere apologies. As you may have deciphered, I'm spectacularly lost," Jonah confessed, hoping the rider might appreciate such honesty.

Her corresponding silence implied she did not.

With a swish of a cape, she swirled past him and gathered the horse's reins. At the soothing brush of its master's hand, the stallion quieted.

Jonah debated offering to help her mount, but by the time he untied his tongue, she was already swinging up into the saddle. Once seated, she paused as if she was evaluating him. Intensely. Impossible to tell in the dim light, but he sensed, rather than saw, she was quietly fuming.

He had a somewhat unhinged notion to ask her to take him with her wherever she was headed, so that neither of them would have to face the night alone.

"I regret any...inconvenience I may have caused you," he said roughly. "If you'd be kind enough to help me get my bearings, I will trouble you no longer."

A lifetime passed before she replied, "Where do you wish to go?"

"Ravenglass Hall. Do you know it?"

"Yes."

"There was supposed to be a carriage to meet the coach," he explained. "But it seems there was a misunderstanding with the directions I received from the estate steward."

"What business have you with him?"

Cheeky of her to be so demanding of his private matters when she clearly had her own secrets to hide. He could not judge her for it. There were too many reasons why a woman might be dressed in such clothes and traveling in such haste by herself on a miserable night.

She was not the mystery he needed to solve. His own mission would fail if he remained stranded in the dark, in the middle of nowhere, lost and sopping and, now that he thought of it, starving.

"I'm Reverend Jonah Sinclair. The Bishop of London has sent me to tutor the Earl of Rochford's ward."

He couldn't determine if the snort came from the horse or its rider, or if it was merely the gusts rising again as the rain pounded.

A hazy limb extended toward the village. "Return to the Saltcoat and follow the post road east for another mile."

Glancing at the direction she pointed toward, he loosened a sigh of relief before turning back to thank her.

But she'd already vanished into the darkened lane.